# The erotic beauty of man and horse . . .

Alex and the mare moved through the meadow as if they were one. He rode leaning forward, his hair streaming behind him, his powerful thighs clasping the mare's back.

He drew up beside her and swept her body with those smoldering, brooding eyes and wordlessly extended his hand to her. And as if in a trance, Chelsey found herself seated in front of him.

They raced like the wind across the meadow. It was wonderful, thrilling and wildly arousing.

Alex's solid heat wrapped around her. His breath grazed her cheek. His large, hot hands cupped her breasts.

Chaos erupted inside her as he stroked her breasts, and she ached for his touch. As he pulled her back tightly against him, she felt his hardness against her buttocks.

The passion pounding in her temples could no longer be denied. Regrets be damned. She wanted him....

Dear Reader,

You're about to meet one of the most mysterious, magical men!

Alexandre Duport is many things, but none of them is ordinary, as Chelsey Mallon—and you—are about to find out.

And neither is any of the four heroes in American Romance's new MORE THAN MEN series. Whether their extraordinary powers enable them to grant you three wishes, communicate with dolphins or live forever, their greatest power is that of seduction.

So turn the page—and be seduced by Alexandre Duport.

It's an experience you'll never forget!

Regards,

Debra Matteucci
Senior Editor & Editorial Coordinator

# MARGARET ST. GEORGE

## A WISH...
## AND A KISS

*Harlequin Books*

TORONTO • NEW YORK • LONDON
AMSTERDAM • PARIS • SYDNEY • HAMBURG
STOCKHOLM • ATHENS • TOKYO • MILAN
MADRID • WARSAW • BUDAPEST • AUCKLAND

Published September 1993

ISBN 0-373-16501-3

A WISH...AND A KISS

# Chapter One

"I have come to do your bidding, mistress."

"Great," Chelsey said, looking up from the long wooden table with a distracted smile. She had been so absorbed in cleaning a tarnished silver cup lamp she hadn't heard anyone enter the workroom. "I'm Dr. Chelsey Mallon, assistant dean of archaeology. But I guess the personnel office must have told you who I was and where to find me."

The rag with which she tried to clean her hands only deposited more grime on them. Chelsey made a face and shrugged.

"Guess we'll save a handshake for later." She examined the only applicant who had shown up for what had to be the worst summer job on campus—helping her inventory a huge building crammed with forty years' worth of archaeological artifacts, most of which had been forgotten by whichever professor had collected them.

The one and only applicant was about her age, Chelsey guessed, thirtyish, which wasn't surprising with so many older students returning to college. He wore the same uniform as younger students: running shoes, faded jeans and a gray sweatshirt with the sleeves cut off. Straight dark hair fell to his shoulders, longer than was fashionable, but it softened the angles of his roughly hewn face.

The first thing Chelsey noticed, though, was how great-looking he was. In fact, "great-looking" didn't do him justice. This man was drop-dead handsome. At least he was if you were the type of woman who was attracted to a brooding, smoldering, keep-your-distance type of guy.

Chelsey gazed into his face, concentrating, and tried to recall if she had ever observed eyes of that particular, almost translucent, shade of blue green, or eyes as deeply fringed with curling black lashes.

When she realized she was staring, she cleared her throat with a self-conscious sound, then ran her hands down the thighs of her work jeans, leaving black streaks across the faded denim.

"Okay, here's the program," she said. He stood before her, muscled arms crossed over his chest, studying her with an unblinking expression that contained the faintest hint of hostility. She didn't blame him. The job she was about to offer expected too much and paid too little.

"There's no way we're going to finish inventorying this building before the fall semester begins. We'll accomplish a miracle if we complete one floor." She glanced around the cavernous workroom, at the rows and racks of shelves and drawers receding into the afternoon shadows. The task ahead was daunting. There were half a dozen workrooms as large as this one, plus a rabbit warren of storage rooms stuffed to the rafters with boxes and cartons containing heaven only knew what. And the university had agreed to give her only one assistant.

"Most of this stuff has been here so long that no one remembers what it is. The good news is we might uncover a surprise or two, maybe a treasure. Archaeologically speaking, of course."

He didn't say a word; he just watched her and listened. In fact, Chelsey didn't even notice him blink. His intense blue-green eyes bored into her as if he had heard the rumors about her and believed every slanderous word. The only movement he made was the small motion of rubbing a fold of his sweatshirt between his thumb and forefinger.

"For instance," she continued, irritated that lately she felt driven to fill any conversational silence, "you see this little cup lamp? This is the only example I've ever seen made out of silver. I discovered it almost by accident inside an unlabeled drawer over there on..."

Chelsey recognized boredom when she saw it. The man standing before her was utterly indifferent to the unusual silver cup lamp.

"Never mind," she said finally, tucking a strand of ginger-colored hair into the blue bandanna she wore against the dust that seemed as much a part of Wickem Hall as the wooden floors and tiers of shelving. "The hours are long and the pay is lousy. But the job is yours if you want it."

"I am yours to command, oh learned mistress." Bending at the waist, he leaned into a bow. Actually it was more of a salaam as he touched his fingertips to waist, chest and forehead, ending with a flourish.

It was a cute bit, the stuff about being here to do her bidding, being hers to command, except the routine didn't quite work. Cutesy didn't suit him. He was more gothic.

"I assume that means you accept the job," Chelsey said after a minute. "So, what's your name?"

"I am your genie, Mistress Mallon. You may address me however you prefer." His second deep bow was the tiniest bit mocking, with a touch of irony in the motions, but he performed the salaam with grace and finesse.

Still, Chelsey decided he was just too ruggedly masculine to pull off this kind of silliness. Certainly she wasn't the right type to play along and keep the joke going. When men turned cute on her, Chelsey turned tail. She found herself tongue-tied, annoyed and desperate to escape.

"Seriously," she said in a level voice, "what's your name?"

"You wish to know my Christian name?"

*Oh, brother.* Maybe this I'm-your-genie/I'm-yours-to-command routine had coeds eating out of his palm, but Chelsey was rapidly finding it tiresome. Not for the first time, she decided there must be a cosmic rule that stated really good-looking guys had to be jerks.

"I'm afraid I don't have much patience for games," she said sharply, not bothering to disguise her irritation. "Unless there's some reason for keeping your name secret...."

There was something about really good-looking men with perfect bodies that brought out the worst in her. She turned brisk and irritable, impatient and critical.

"My name is not a secret." His voice startled her, but it fit the rest of him—attractive, deeply pitched and taut with annoyance. "No one has asked my name in a very long time."

"Probably not since you left the campus personnel office about an hour ago, right?"

"Not in two centuries."

Chelsey shook her head and rolled her eyes. "Look, a dozen experts couldn't finish this inventory if they had a year to do it. You and I have this summer, that's all. The point I hope I'm making is that we don't have time to waste on foolishness."

She gave him her famous do-I-make-myself-clear look, polite but dripping ice.

"Alexandre Duport." The name emerged grudgingly, as if Chelsey had dragged forth a deep, dark secret.

"That wasn't too painful, was it?" Carefully, she packed the pottery cup lamps back into the drawer she had cleaned and freshly labeled. "Do I detect a faint accent?"

Her instinct was to guess France, but his accent wasn't quite French. Close, but...

She closed her eyes to focus on the nuances of his pronunciation, and when she opened them again, she found him standing directly in front of her worktable, studying her with those intense blue-green eyes. For a moment Chelsey held his gaze, unaccountably feeling her heartbeat accelerate. She wondered if Alexandre Duport knew how damned sexy he was when he wasn't acting cutesy. What was she thinking? Of course he knew.

"Never mind the accent," Chelsey said when it became obvious that her new assistant balked at personal questions. Next to him, Marcel Marceau was a chatterbox. But that was okay. She wasn't looking for a personal relationship. All she wanted was an assistant.

She capped the jar of silver polish and returned it to the supply box before she wrapped the little silver cup lamp in chamois cloth. The artifact, now polished to a gleaming finish, had blown her away with its beauty. It seemed a shame to place such an amazing find in a drawer with pottery lamps where it might remain forgotten for another forty years.

"You may leave the lamp here or take it with you. It is no longer important," Alexandre Duport said. Leaning forward, he ran his palm across the worktable as if admiring the smooth touch of old wood.

"I beg your pardon?" Chelsey's voice turned shrill and suspicious. Was he suggesting that she steal the cup lamp?

"The lamp belongs to all and to none. It will vanish after your third wish."

"After my— Oh, I get it. We're back to the genie thing." Alexandre must have noticed her polishing the silver cup lamp when he entered the workroom and that's where the genie business originated. "The lamp is university property—it stays here," she said sharply, placing the chamois cloth in the drawer with the other cup lamps.

She looked behind her for her purse, stalling a little. Then came the moment of truth, the moment that in some way altered and defined all her relationships with men, even a relationship as tenuous as this one was and would remain.

"Alex—may I call you Alex?—would you do me a favor and bring me my cane? I believe I left it over there, near the south door."

Bending, Chelsey reached for her briefcase, not waiting to observe the startled look she knew would cross his face. By now the sequence of reactions was well-known to her.

First he would look surprised. He might even murmur, "I hadn't realized..." Then he would feel a little embarrassed. After he saw her walk with the cane, he'd feel compelled to make some remark, some acknowledgment that he wasn't ignoring her circumstance. Maybe he would comment on the cane itself, ask what wood it was made from or something inane like that. Or maybe he would flatter her, try to persuade her that she looked chic carrying a walking stick.

"Your cane, Mistress Mallon."

This time it was Chelsey who was startled. She hadn't heard him walk across the wooden floor, didn't think enough time had passed in any case. But he stood beside her with her cane in his hand.

"Thank you." Briefly she met his gaze, brought up short when she realized he didn't display a flicker of curiosity. Which only made her want to explain.

"I had polio as a child," she said in a casual voice as she adjusted her purse strap over her shoulder. "One leg is about two inches shorter than the other. I wear special shoes, so usually it's not a problem." After collecting her notebook, she walked toward the door. Because she knew he was watching, she felt acutely self-conscious. "Unless I'm especially tired, I don't really need the cane." After waving Alex through the door, she flipped off the lights and stepped into the hallway. "But on days like today—when I've climbed up and down a dozen flights of stairs—it's nice to have it." Her calf muscles were on fire and aching.

"I know."

She stopped and looked at him, abruptly aware of how tall he was. Chelsey was five foot nine in her stocking feet, but Alex Duport stood a full head taller than she. "You know?"

"I know everything about you."

"Is that right?" She stared at him. "Whom did you speak to in personnel? And exactly what did he tell you?" Then he knew about last summer and the rumors, she thought. A rush of paranoia brought a bitter taste to her mouth, and she closed her eyes and swallowed.

When she opened her eyes again, she gasped and her muscles jumped.

It was the damnedest thing. They were standing in front of Wickem Hall—but Chelsey had no memory of walking down two flights of stairs, crossing the tiled lobby or exiting the building. She dropped her briefcase and threw out a hand to steady herself, grabbing Alex's arm and looking around with wide, startled eyes.

Nothing else seemed out of the ordinary. From where she stood at the side entrance, Chelsey could see groups of summer-session students strolling along the walkways between buildings or sitting on the grass, chatting together or reading. No one glanced in their direction.

Alex lifted his face to the late-afternoon sun. "The warmth of sunshine," he murmured softly. "The scent of grass and leaves and summer air. No feat of memory or imagination can reproduce this, these scents or—" He noticed her stricken expression and frowned. "Are you well, mistress?"

Immediately Chelsey snatched her hand away from the hard muscles rising on his warm bare arm. "This is really weird. I don't remember... This is so..."

Never in her life had Chelsey Mallon experienced a blackout, and it was hard to accept that she had done so now. But the memory of walking through Wickem Hall and exiting the door was simply...not there. It was as if she had closed the workroom door, turned around and was instantly outside, standing on the flagstone floor of the west terrace.

"Did I lock the building?" she wondered, staring back at the door and striving to remember. She had no memory of that, either.

"If you wish the building locked, mistress, then it is locked."

"Look, knock off that genie crap and stop calling me mistress." Instantly she felt mean-spirited for taking out her confusion on him. She drew a deep breath. "I'm sorry," she said in a softer voice. "I've had some problems and...well, I've got a lot on my mind. I'm in no mood for games. The genie thing was cute in the beginning, but you're overdoing it. I've tried to tell you nicely, now I'm telling you bluntly. Stop acting like a genie, okay?"

The humorless smile twisting his lips contained an edge of bitterness that Chelsey didn't attempt to understand. "Believe me, Mistress Mallon, if I could, I would."

"Just do it," Chelsey said between her teeth. "And don't call me Mistress Mallon. Mistress Mallon sounds like something you'd name a dominatrix or whatever they call those women who dress up in leather and chains and slap men around. Call me doctor or professor or call me Chelsey if you like. But no more mistress, okay?" She leaned on her cane for a moment, steadying herself then descended the terrace steps onto the walkway that led across campus. "Bye. See you Monday morning at eight o'clock sharp," she called over her shoulder.

She hadn't taken three steps before Alex Duport appeared beside her. "Would you like me to carry your briefcase?"

His dark hair was sleek and shiny in the afternoon sunlight. It swung across his shoulders when he looked down at her. Now that Chelsey saw him in bright light instead of the dusty gloom of the workroom, she noticed his jeans fit like a glove and the gray sleeveless sweatshirt molded his heavy chest and upper-arm muscles. More than one coed watched him pass with a predatory gleam in her eye.

"Thank you, but I doubt we're going in the same direction."

His dark eyebrows slashed together in a frown. "I don't know how to interpret much of what you say. It's annoying."

Chelsey stopped dead to level an incredulous stare. "Excuse me? *I'm* annoying?"

"It should be obvious that I must go where you go. I must remain within the sound of your voice. I have no choice—that is the rule."

"What the hell are you talking about?"

"You summoned me, oh confusing mistress." The words were mild enough, but his blue-green eyes glittered like winter ice. "But you spoke for a time as if you wished me to *choose* to serve you. You made it plain—at least, I think you made it plain—that you wish the contents of Wickem Hall inventoried, but you suggest the task cannot be accomplished. Very confusing. You pry into my past but seem furious that I know of yours.''

"All I did was ask your name, for heaven's sake!"

He raked his fingers through his hair, then spread his hands in frustration. "Finally you walk away with a word of farewell as if our business is concluded and seem surprised when I follow after you. Yet you have not stated your wishes, nor have I yet presented the coins!''

A few students cast curious glances in their direction as they squared off and faced each other on the sidewalk, both speaking in voices pitched louder than normal. Chelsey realized they were in fact creating a small, angry scene. Ordinarily, she would have crawled over lava rather than embroil herself in a public confrontation. But this situation was far from ordinary.

As she listened to the sincerity beneath his tone, a dawning suspicion gripped Chelsey's thoughts. She deliberately placed her hand on Alex's arm and patted him in what she hoped was a calming gesture. She drew a breath and gazed into his eyes. Did one just come right out and inquire if a person was seeing a therapist?

Actually, there was no doubt in her mind that Alex Duport was seriously disturbed. The only surprise was that she hadn't identified the problem earlier. She was grateful he believed he was a genie instead of Charles Manson or Jeffrey Dahmer. Better to serve someone than carve them into fish food.

"I'm sorry I didn't understand sooner," she said, patting his arm. From the corner of her eye she searched the quad for a campus policeman. "Alex, what is your doctor's name?"

He glared down at her. "What?"

"Maybe you think of him as the genie master. The head genie." She gave him a bright, encouraging smile. "The genie master will want to know if you served anyone today. Don't you think we should phone him and tell him how well you did?"

Alex pulled back from her, staring at her as though it was Chelsey who was deranged. Chelsey attempted a different approach. "Do you know your address? I think you should go home now, Alex. Don't you? I'm sure someone is getting very worried about how long you've been gone."

"You think I'm insane." Incredulity thickened his voice "You don't believe I am who I say I am. You think I'm crazy."

"Not at all." Where the hell were the campus police? She didn't really believe Alex was dangerous, but when it came right down to it, she didn't know diddly about him. It seemed prudent to humor him. Chelsey patted his arm and arranged a reassuring smile on her lips. "Of course I believe you're a genie. I was just testing to see if *you* believed it."

He lifted her hand off his arm and moved backward a step before he spread his arms in a frustrated gesture. "What do I have to do to prove to you that I'm a genie?"

A couple of frat boys walked around them, swinging tennis racquets at their sides. They grinned and gave Alex a thumbs-up. "Hey, baby, we can vouch for him. The guy's definitely a genie. He can show you some magic that you won't believe. Right, dude?" They fell against each other, laughing.

"Fun-ny," Chelsey muttered, glaring at them.

If Alex noticed the frat boys or heard their comments, he gave no sign. He continued to glare at Chelsey. "I appeared before your eyes when you summoned me by rubbing the silver lamp. Your cane materialized in my hand when you requested it. To spare your leg I moved you from the workroom outside to the terrace in the blink of an eye. Your inventory is finished." Knots rose along his jawline when he clenched his teeth. "What else must I do to convince you, oh stubborn mistress?"

Chelsey froze. Her mind raced backward.

She had indeed rubbed the little silver cup lamp—had, in fact, been concentrating so hard on polishing it to a high gloss that Alex could very well have materialized in front of her without her being aware—

She couldn't believe she was actually thinking this!

But she recalled noting at the time that she had not heard him walk to the door to get her cane. And he'd handed it to her almost instantly.

Then there was the craziness of turning around from the door of the workroom and discovering she was standing on the flagstone terrace in front of Wickem Hall.

"No, I don't believe this," she whispered, staring up at him with eyes the size of drachmas. She tried to swallow but her throat was too dry. "I'm an educated woman. I hold a doctorate. I've traveled. I've studied history. I don't believe in genies."

"You will."

Chelsey's thoughts felt like physical objects, bouncing off the inside of her skull. "Uh, Alex. You said—at least, I thought you said—that the inventory was finished." It couldn't be. That wasn't possible. Not even remotely. Not in a million years. She was allowing her imagination to run away with her, allowing a couple of peculiar unexplained incidents to bend her mind. "Uh, what did you mean by that?"

He nodded impatiently toward Wickem Hall behind her. "Every item in every room is described in detail as to its location and the known history of the item."

Chelsey turned toward the building and leaned on her cane. "Wickem Hall has five stories and two basement levels."

"Each item is cross-referenced as to date of expedition, site of expedition, leader of the expedition, type of artifact and the known age of the artifact. Is that sufficient?"

Chelsey turned her head and looked him squarely in the eyes. "What you're claiming is absolutely impossible," she stated in a low, firm voice. "To accomplish what you just described would require a team of at least two dozen people working ten hours a day every day for at least three years. I'm not convinced it could be done even then." They held each other's gaze as students hurried around them on the sidewalk, heading for dorm lines or local eateries. "Where are the inventory lists?"

"Twenty-eight notebooks are lying on your worktable."

There was a simple way to conquer the crazy thoughts buzzing around her head: she turned on her heel and started walking back toward Wickem Hall. Part of her mind reared back in astonishment that she actually meant to waste her time verifying Alex's ridiculous claim.

"You wait here," she called to him. She didn't want to find herself alone in an empty building with a muscle-bound stranger who had just been proven a certifiable nut case.

"I must remain within the sound of your voice. That is the rule."

"Really? And just who makes the genie rules?" Chelsey asked, turning back to him. "I'd really like to know the head genie's name, Alex."

She gasped and sucked in a hard deep breath.

They were no longer on the sidewalk beyond the Wickem Hall terrace. They were inside Chelsey's workroom on the third floor.

And the neon lights above her long worktable shone down on twenty-eight neatly stacked and labeled notebooks.

Chelsey stared at the notebooks and listened to her heart slam against her rib cage. When she thought she could speak, she lifted a bone-white face to Alex. "I don't believe this," she said in a husky whisper. "We're inside Wickem Hall, aren't we? I thought so. You teleported us here. Or whatever it is you call bipping people around in time and space. But you did this, didn't you? You used some kind of magic to bring us here."

The suggestion of a smile hovered at the corners of his lips. He managed not to look smug, but Chelsey could see it was a struggle.

"My God! I'm not dreaming this...?"

"No, mistress."

Dust tickled her nose. The wooden floor was solid beneath her feet. She knew this room as well as she knew her name. This experience was real. "And those are the notebooks you told me about. The inventory. Right? You inventoried and cross-referenced every item on five floors and the two basement levels." Reaching a shaking hand, she opened one of the notebooks. It was everything Alex had claimed. In fact, he had neglected to mention the illustrations. Which were breathtaking. "And you did this in about, oh, sixty seconds, maybe."

"Yes, mistress."

"I see," Chelsey murmured, feeling her eyes start to cross. The inventory that couldn't be done was finished. In fabulous detail. A genie had done it.

"Nice job," she whispered.

Then she fainted dead away, falling backward across a damask-covered chaise lounge that hadn't been there a split second before.

# Chapter Two

Alex transported the chaise lounge and Chelsey Mallon to her rented house on Pleasant Avenue. The house was small and modestly furnished, but that would change. She would spend her first wish to accumulate great wealth; they all did. A month from now Chelsey Mallon would be living in a palatial mansion staffed by a half-dozen servants.

He sipped a glass of wine and glanced at her. Unconscious, she didn't look as stubborn or feisty, not as self-absorbed with her own selfish world. At this moment she looked innocent and childlike. He could almost believe this mistress would be different.

But he had fallen into that trap before. By now he knew better than to expect anything but the worst from human nature. Like all the others, Chelsey Mallon would be greedy, selfish, ambitious. She would wish for wealth, power, maybe revenge.

It didn't matter anymore. He no longer took much interest in his masters or mistresses, didn't care if they sensed his indifference or contempt. He deeply resented pandering to the worst in human nature, but his resentment was seldom noticed. His masters were too absorbed in gloating over their newfound riches.

Rolling the wine on his tongue and inhaling the fragrance of a lilac he had plucked from the bush outside the door, he examined the items on the mantelpiece while he waited for her to regain consciousness.

Prominently featured was a family photograph taken a week before the avalanche that killed her parents. The photograph was flanked by pottery shards that were mementos of her first archaeological dig. The items interested him only to the extent that he wondered if Chelsey Mallon understood how fortunate she was to be surrounded by reality and fresh memories, by life with all its varying textures and richness. Nothing he could give her would equal what she already had.

When the energy changed in the room, he knew she was awake. Turning, he watched as she swung her feet off the chaise lounge and stumbled to her own faded plaid sofa, staring at the chaise as if it might attack her. As the chaise had served its purpose, he dispensed with it. The small room was crowded enough.

She screamed and collapsed backward on the sofa. "Don't *do* that!"

"Don't do what?" he asked, frowning. She was the most contrary mistress he had encountered in over two centuries.

"That silent magic stuff! If you're going to do magic tricks, at least give me some warning. Clap your hands or point a finger or wink or say 'shazam.' But do or say something so I'll have a second to prepare myself!"

"As you wish, mistress." Holding his wineglass to one side, he performed a deep, showy salaam. As always, he resented the gesture of servitude demanded by his role. "May I serve you a glass of malmsey?" She still looked white and shaken.

In times past, no one had fainted at his appearance or made him prove his identity. Previous masters and mistresses had accepted him at once and proceeded immediately to the wishes. On the other hand, the aggravation of dealing with Chelsey Mallon's disbelief was balanced by the extra time in the reality plane.

Chelsey flattened her shaking palms on the thighs of her jeans and frowned. "You look real," she said slowly. "Are you real? Or am I imagining you?" A distracted look appeared in her eyes, and Alex wasn't certain if she was addressing him or talking to herself. "I can see the hair on your arms. I can see muscles shifting when you move. I can see you breathe. Can I really be imagining all that?"

"I assure you that I am real." It irritated him to deal with this type of nonsense. In the brief time allotted him, he'd rather taste and touch and experience all he could.

"I believe I'll accept your offer of a glass of wine," Chelsey whispered. "What did you say you were drinking?"

"Malmsey. It's a sweet white wine from Greece." He glanced at the coffee table in front of her. A glass of wine appeared.

She gasped and a tremor raced through her body. "Shazam, remember?" She gave her head a violent shake. "I'm seeing this, but I still can't accept it."

He made the wine disappear. "Shazam," he said flatly. The chilled glass reappeared. Perhaps that would be enough proof. Part of him longed to prolong his time in the reality plane but another part of him, disillusioned with humanity, simply wanted to complete his business and be gone.

"Thank you," she said in a tight voice, tasting the wine. When she placed it on the coffee table, the glass was full again. A sigh dropped her shoulders. "I guess you know I have a thousand questions," she said after a minute.

Her comment surprised him. He turned away from stroking a begonia leaf between his fingers to look at her directly. After today he doubted that she would ever again wear work jeans, an old shirt and a dusty bandanna. He noticed that her left leg was trembling slightly.

"You summoned me by polishing the silver lamp. I am here to grant you three wishes. Once your wishes are granted, I will leave you," he said impatiently. "Does that answer your questions?"

"Look, I'm sorry if my skepticism irritates you," she said. "You're probably accustomed to materializing out of thin air and offering people their dreams on a platter, but this is the first time something this fantastic has happened to me. Until this minute I've always assumed genies were flights of the imagination or inventions concocted to spice up children's stories. Not in my wildest, most whimsical dreams did I for one minute imagine that genies actually existed. I apologize if that offends you, but that's why I'm having trouble accepting you. I see the magic, but I'm having great difficulty believing."

"You will believe after your first wish is granted," he said, not interested in the conversation.

He moved around her small living room, running his palm over chair backs and tabletops, breaking the leaves of her houseplants and holding them to his nose, lifting and stroking the books scattered around in piles. He knew better than to believe he could store the sensations in his fingertips, but he always tried. While his new mistress had been unconscious, he had opened the windows and the French doors leading to a small patio. The mingled scents of lilac, honeysuckle and summer grass permeated the room, the fragrance so real and heady he felt almost intoxicated by it.

"So. What happens next?" Chelsey asked, interrupting his examination of an arrowhead. He closed his fist around the flint wedge, wanting to sample the sharp edges. Pain was a sensation he had not experienced for longer than he could remember.

"On the table before you are three gold coins." He opened his hand to examine the red marks left by the arrowhead. The flint edges hadn't cut his palm, but he had felt the possibility.

The three gold coins glowed against the glass tabletop, about the size of silver dollars. Chelsey lifted one and centered it in her trembling palm. No date was stamped on the coin; it betrayed no hint of its origin. The only marking was an impression of a scimitar.

"Each time you make a wish, you must surrender one of the coins," he explained. Alex had presented this speech more times than he cared to recall. It was necessary but uninteresting. "The rule is, I cannot grant your wishes unless they benefit you directly."

Chelsey didn't feel faint anymore but she still wasn't functioning on all burners. Despite the accumulating evidence, her mind balked at the thought that she was talking to a genie. "I never imagined a genie would look like you."

This wasn't surprising as she had never tried to imagine a genie at all. If she had, she felt reasonably certain that she would not have imagined a genie dressed in sexy tight jeans, a cutoff sweatshirt and Nikes. "Wouldn't it be easier to convince people that you are who you claim you are if you looked more like genies are supposed to look?"

A grimace tugged her lips. Those were probably the dumbest two statements she had ever uttered. She rolled her eyes and reached for the wineglass, wishing she hadn't said anything.

"How do you imagine genies are supposed to look?"

She laughed and spread her hands. "I guess you should be big and blue and sound like Robin Williams."

"I beg your pardon," he asked, staring at her.

"I don't know. Something exotic, I guess." Her only experience with genies came from old reruns of "I Dream of Jeannie," and Disney stories of Aladdin and the magic lamp.

"Would you find something like this more convincing?"

In the span of a heartbeat he stood before her clad in the damnedest outfit Chelsey had seen. Red silk pantaloons ballooned above green slippers with long, upward-curving toes. His golden chest was bare, exposing a thatch of dark hair and swelling muscles. Gold bracelets enclosed his wrists and heavy upper arms. Gold links circled his neck, and he wore a jeweled hoop in one ear. A red-and-green silk turban hid his hair. He crossed his arms over his chest and glared at her, obviously irritated.

"Is this what you expected?"

Chelsey drew a quick involuntary breath and held it. Alex Duport was the most flawless, most exciting male specimen she was ever likely to observe.

He was magnificent. Perfectly proportioned, a sensual exhibit of muscle and sinew. Smooth golden skin. Taut, hard flesh. He was truly a beautiful, thrilling and consummate man.

His shoulders were broad, squared and rippling with muscles. His torso narrowed in a classic wedge shape to a hard flat belly framed by washboard ridges. Through the red silk pantaloons, she glimpsed heavy tapered thighs and well-shaped calves. The sight of his male perfection made her feel funny inside, as if someone were pouring warm honey through her body.

"Okay, you've made your point," she said finally, wrenching her gaze away from the arrow of dark hair pointing down his chest toward the red pantaloons. "I was wrong. If you'd popped up looking like that I would have called the men in white coats to haul you away."

She sensed the outlandish costume was intended to make her feel foolish, and it did. Also, seeing him half-naked was oddly arousing, which embarrassed her. "Let's go back to the jeans and sweatshirt."

"As you wish, mistress." Instantly he returned to his original choice.

Chelsey twitched. "Shazam, remember? Or clap your hands. Something." Creating that costume fantasy had been unnecessary and had displayed an element of contempt. What struck Chelsey as curious was her impression that Alex's contempt was directed at himself as much as at her.

"I have an idea that you're not too wild about being a genie," she commented. He gave her a steady look that revealed nothing. "And I'm getting the impression that you don't like me very much."

God, where had that come from? Embarrassment flamed on her cheeks. Why should she care if he liked her or not? For all she knew, they weren't even part of the same species. Certainly this was not going to be a long-term association.

Alex chose not to address either of her statements. Keeping his features expressionless, he replied carefully, "If my demeanor offends you, mistress, I apologize. You have only to state what annoys you and I shall cease that action immediately."

The words were conciliatory, but the tone was off. His tone suggested he had nothing for which to apologize and he did so solely to appease her and thus get on with the job at hand.

Chelsey folded her arms over her chest and scowled. "You're a genie with a bad attitude, do you know that?"

Alex's gaze narrowed into slits of blue-green and his mouth tightened. For a moment Chelsey thought he would respond to her own rude comment, but he didn't. "If you are prepared to make your first wish..." Staring at her, he inclined his dark head toward the gold coins.

"You want me to get on with it, right?" Chelsey said, glancing down at the coins. She still couldn't believe this was actually happening. "I'll make my wishes and then you can return to wherever you came from and I'll stagger off and have a nice little nervous breakdown." She glanced up at him. "That was a joke. Don't you ever smile?"

He ignored her question. "Your first wish..." Lifting his wineglass, he took a sip and held it on his tongue.

"Okay," Chelsey said, directing her attention away from him and toward the gold coins glowing on the coffee table. After drawing a deep breath, she touched a fingertip to one of the coins and pushed it forward. Despite the evidence she had already seen, she didn't wholly believe that Alex Duport could truly grant her three wishes. Such an incredible event was just too fantastic, too good to be true.

But she couldn't help thinking: What if it was true?

"Okay. I'm ready." She closed her eyes, flexed her arms, then drew another deep breath. "I wish for a cure for AIDS." She thought a moment, then opened her eyes and pushed forward the second coin. "I wish for lasting world peace." The coins felt unusually warm and smooth beneath her fingertips. "And I wish for an end to world hunger."

Alex stepped forward to stand in front of the coffee table. He crossed his arms over his chest and scowled down
at the coins, then raised his eyes to Chelsey.

"There," she said, dusting her hands briskly. "We're
finished. So. Aren't you supposed to take the coins and
disappear?"

This thought caused her an unexpected pang of regret.
Alex Duport was surly and cool, enigmatic and distant. But
he was a genie, and there were dozens of questions she
would have liked to ask him. He was also the best-looking
man Chelsey had ever spent time with, and she found herself strongly attracted to him. She wanted to know what lay
behind that brooding exterior.

"I thought I explained the rules." His scowl deepened.
"Each wish must benefit you directly."

"You can't grant any of my wishes?" Maybe this whole
genie thing was a hoax, Chelsey thought. Then she remembered Alex saying so before—the wishes had to benefit *her*. "Wait a minute," she said, working it out. "This
rule means the wishes must be entirely selfish. No wonder
you don't seem to hold a high opinion of human nature."

A shrug moved the sweatshirt across his shoulders.
"They usually are."

"Mine weren't," Chelsey reminded him.

His eyes widened slightly in surprise. "I don't recall a
master or mistress who spent their wishes on anything noble or selfless as you tried to do. Usually it isn't necessary
to mention the wishes must directly benefit the wisher. That
is the master's first inclination."

Chelsey tilted her head. "How many times have you
granted someone three wishes?"

"Why do you ask such questions?" Annoyance drew his
brow.

"I'm a curious person. Is there some rule that prevents you from talking about yourself?"

"Not that I know of." Again he looked surprised. He fixed his eyes on her. "Most masters or mistresses are far more interested in the wishes than in he who grants them." After a brief hesitation during which he watched her with an expression of curiosity, he added, "I have had hundreds, maybe thousands, of masters and mistresses."

Chelsey considered. "And all those thousands of wishes satisfied selfish desires." She leaned back against the sofa cushions and focused a long look on this incredible man. "Tell me something. Are you human or are genies a different species? Were you born a genie? And how old are you? You speak of centuries like I might speak of years."

He stiffened, and the surly attitude she disliked returned along with his scowl. "What difference do those things make? What is your first wish, mistress?"

"I'd like to know something about the man who is going to make all my selfish dreams come true." Chelsey wasn't sure if she was trying to lighten a tense moment or if she was delaying her first wish. She held her wineglass up to the flare of sunset glowing in the window. The undrainable glass fascinated her.

"Indulge me for a minute," she said. "I'm trying to figure this out. You've done a lot of razzle-dazzle in the last couple of hours, performed several feats that are magical to me. What I don't understand is how completing the Wickem Hall inventory differs from the wishes attached to the coins."

Alex leaned back against the mantelpiece and turned his head toward the scent of lilacs drifting through the open French doors. "The wishes attached to the coins originate with you," he explained, rocking back on the heels of his

Nikes. "Any other magic originates with me. Do you understand?"

"No." She watched him search for the patience to answer a question he didn't consider relevant.

"My obligation is to serve you, mistress. If serving you best means cushioning your faint with a chaise, I may choose to do so. I may choose to offer wine or food. I may choose to complete your inventory."

"Or you may choose not to do those things?"

"Yes," he said slowly. "In which case you would have found it necessary to expend a coin to complete your inventory."

Chelsey felt absurdly pleased. He could have let her crash to the floor when she fainted but he had chosen not to. "I'm grateful to have the inventory finished, but I wouldn't have used a coin to wish for it. In fact, that inventory is going to cause a problem. How on earth am I going to explain to the university that I've already finished a project they expect will take three to five years to complete?"

Alex was more interested in her porcelain candy bowl than in Chelsey's problems. He sampled a lemon drop, then ran his fingertips over the smooth surface of the candy bowl with a poorly concealed expression of pleasure.

Chelsey lifted a puzzled eyebrow. "I've never met anyone as touchy-feely as you. What's that all about?"

"It's been sixty years since I was last summoned. And my time here is limited," Alex said softly, stroking his thumb over the smooth contours of the bowl. "One forgets the rich scents and tastes, the different textures..." His hair moved across his shoulders as his head snapped up. Back came the frown, as if he were angered at revealing part of himself. "Your wishes, mistress, what will they be?" He replaced the porcelain bowl on the table beside Chelsey's favorite chair, then moved to stand before her, a look of purpose stiffening his expression. "Do you wish for wealth? For revenge? Power? Love?"

Chelsey imagined that his intense blue-green eyes bored into her brain and examined her darkest desires. "Can you read my mind?" she inquired uneasily.

"No." Unless she imagined it, a ghost of a smile touched his firm lips. So he wasn't entirely humorless, after all. "You will have to state your wishes aloud."

"Okay." Chelsey licked her lips and twisted her hands together in her lap. "This is it." She contemplated the sunset glow captured by the gold coins while myriad possibilities sped through her mind.

She could wish for fame. And fortune. She could wish for her own fully funded expedition to search for Ebrum, a city lost in the far mists of antiquity. For years she had fantasized that she would be the archaeologist to finally unearth Ebrum; she could make that fantasy a reality simply by wishing it. Or she could wish for the return of the marble busts. For the restoration of her professional reputation. She could wish for a dream laboratory with state-of-the-art dating equipment. Or maybe a home of her own with a working fireplace and no stairs to climb. Maybe she could wish for someone to love who would love her back....

The choices overwhelmed her. "You know, this isn't as easy as I thought it would be," she said, glancing up at Alex. A puzzled frown deepened the lines framing his mouth. "Did your other masters experience any difficulty deciding what to wish for?"

"Never." His frown deepened.

She thought for a moment. "Look, is there a time limit on this? I mean, do I have to make my three wishes now, right this minute?"

"You don't know what you want to wish for?" He looked incredulous.

"If you really are who you claim to be—and I think I'm beginning to believe that you are—and if you really and truly are going to grant me three wishes, then I don't want to rush into this and make a hasty decision." She leaned forward, speaking earnestly, thinking as she spoke. "I guess it isn't necessary to tell you that this is a once in a lifetime opportunity. I don't want to make a wrong choice that I'll regret for the rest of my life. So, would it be acceptable to you if I thought this over for a couple of days?"

"A couple of days?" he repeated. His eyebrows soared like dark wings.

After a moment the incredulity fled his features, replaced by an expression of dawning joy. Clearly Alex's surprise was so great that he didn't realize how mobile and transparent his expression had become. The hostile, almost gothic resentment vanished, transforming his face. Chelsey had thought he was handsome before; now, with eagerness leaping in his eyes and with his body suddenly taut and vibrantly alive, the brooding suggestion of mockery gone, he simply took her breath away. An unconscious sigh flowed past her lips.

"By all means, mistress, take as much time as you like!" For the first time, his concern for her well-being seemed genuine.

"I take it the idea pleases you," Chelsey said dryly, stating the obvious. The startling change in him made her smile.

"More than you could possibly know." Now he stopped pacing and relaxed into the chair facing her. When he looked at her, his face was softer somehow, the tense lines eased. Chelsey suspected she might actually see him smile before this was over. The transformation pleased her enormously.

"The coins! They're gone." Had she forfeited her wishes?

Hastening to reassure her, Alex lifted a hand that was surprisingly elegant considering the rest of him was so large and ruggedly masculine. "You have only to say 'I wish,' and a coin will appear in your palm."

Another first occurred. Alex gazed at her with a flicker of puzzled interest, as if he were seeing her for the first time. For a long moment their eyes held, then, when Chelsey felt her heartbeat accelerating, she cleared her throat and glanced at the grandfather clock standing near the dining room door.

She started. "Damn, I forgot. Betty will be here any minute. We planned to grab a pizza, then see a screening of *Robin Hood: Prince of Thieves.*" Chelsey looked down at herself in dismay. "I have to shower and change and I don't have time for any of it. And how am I going to explain *you?*"

Alex actually smiled, a stunning smile that revealed white, white teeth. And sent Chelsey into a state of momentary paralysis. "Shazam."

Instantly the paralysis broke. A light, tingly feeling rose on her skin as if she had just stepped out of a shower. The faint scent of her favorite soap surrounded her. Chelsey raised a tentative hand to her hair and found it curled and clean to the touch, arranged in the wild, curly style she had worn in the photograph on the mantelpiece. When she looked down, she was wearing a black silk cocktail dress, dark nylons and sequined high-heeled pumps.

The nerve-racking part was that she hadn't felt a thing. But she reacted violently to the aftermath. Her heart flew around inside her chest, knocking painfully against her ribs. She felt her pulse slamming against her wrists, throat and temples. When she could speak, she swallowed hard and gave him a wobbly smile.

"Thanks. I'm grateful for the assistance, but the evening isn't this formal. And I never wear skirts," she added in a level voice, meeting his eyes. Skirts made her feel self-conscious of her leg. "If you're going to dress me, I'd prefer my white slacks and the red cotton sweater, if you wouldn't mind. And my own white shoes." Which were constructed to compensate for one leg being shorter than the other.

"Shazam."

She closed her eyes and gritted her teeth, but she didn't feel anything this time, either. When she opened one eye and looked down, she saw that she was dressed as she had requested. Falling backward on the sofa, Chelsey passed a hand over her face, then tried again to drain the undrainable wineglass.

"I'm beginning to wonder how I could ever have doubted you." She gave him a critical look. "You might consider an upgrade for yourself while we're dressing for the evening."

Actually she wasn't concerned about Alex's clothing. She was wondering if there had been a split second, a microinstant that only genies could glimpse, when she had been naked as he was dressing and undressing her. The possibility made her feel annoyingly warm and tingly.

He didn't say "Shazam" this time, but she was expecting an altered appearance when she looked up again. Now he was wearing khaki slacks and a shirt that almost matched the remarkable color of his eyes. Tasseled loafers completed his outfit. "More appropriate?" he asked. To Chelsey's astonishment, an unmistakable suggestion of humor twinkled in his eyes. "I've never been skilled in the sartorial arts."

She would have assured him that he looked fine, but the doorbell rang and she felt a stab of panic. Jumping to her feet, Chelsey glanced toward the front door, then looked back at Alex. "Look, we'll say you're a colleague, okay? We met...in...in college. Right! Your accent... Okay, we'll say you're from France. You are from France, aren't you? Originally?"

God only knew when originally had been. And maybe he wasn't French at all. Maybe genies spoke some kind of genie language which gave them an accent that sounded vaguely like archaic French.

"Whatever you wish, mistress."

She stopped with her hand on the doorknob and hissed back at him, "For God's sake, don't call me mistress! Call me Chelsey. And listen—no magic! None. That's key, Alex. No magic in front of other people."

Before she pulled the door open, she paused and drew a deep breath, then squared her shoulders. How was she going to get through this evening without Betty noticing something weird? She could wrest a promise from Alex but she wasn't confident he would comply. Or that he could even if he wanted to. Magic seemed automatic to him, an habitual response that required no special thought or effort.

"Hi, come in," she said, opening the door. "You look great tonight, but you always look great. Do you like my new hairstyle?" Which was about four inches longer than it had been mere minutes ago. "I used to wear it this way. Hey, there's someone I want you to meet." Babbling, ignoring Betty's surprised expression, she prodded her into the living room. "I should have called and canceled but I didn't think of it until too late. You see, an old and dear friend of mine is in town for a few days and—" She stopped, made herself breathe, then waved a hand. "This is Alex Duport. From France. We met at Cornell. He's, uh, a professor back east. Alex, this is my best friend, Betty Windell. She's a computer whiz who specializes in setting up programs for businesses small and large. What she does is so complicated that no one but her understands it. All I can say is that she's the best there is at whatever it is she does."

Betty, a vivacious brunette with large, intelligent dark eyes, stared at Chelsey with a quizzical look that managed to ask, "What's the matter with you tonight, and why have you been hiding this hunk for so long?" She turned to Alex and extended her hand.

"You've known Alex since college?" she asked, gazing into his eyes with frank interest.

Chelsey hoped Alex had provided her with a good genie deodorant after her genie shower; this was going to be a nervous-perspiration night. She drew a deep breath, then waved her fingers in a dismissive gesture.

"I've mentioned Alex before, dozens of times. You've just forgotten. I'm sure I told you about running into Alex last summer in Istanbul." One of the problems with lying lay in knowing when to stop. A person could lie themselves right into a pit as Chelsey was doing now. She cast Alex an imploring look that begged him to intercede and make her stop prattling.

"I'm afraid I don't know much about computers," he said smoothly, offering Betty the glass of wine that appeared in his hand. Chelsey leaned against the wall and closed her eyes. "But I'm fascinated by the idea of them."

Betty touched her chic hairdo and gave him a flirtatious smile. She tasted the wine. "Umm. This is good. Don't tell me you write papers and keep notes in longhand."

Before Betty could notice the level in her wineglass did not recede, Chelsey pasted a bright smile on her lips and spoke in an overly loud voice. "Look, maybe we should take a rain check for tonight," she hinted, giving Betty a long, penetrating look. "It seems like a lifetime since I've seen Alex...." She and Betty had been friends for enough years that Betty should have picked up the obvious message. Betty chose to ignore it.

"Nonsense. We're all here, we all have to eat. We might as well go," Betty said, cutting a smile toward Alex. "Are you a Kevin Costner fan?" Turning, she linked arms with Alex and started toward the door. "Frankly, I'm glad you're visiting Chelsey," she said in a conspiratorial tone. "Maybe you're just the tonic she needs. Certainly she could use some cheering up. If you were in Istanbul last summer, then you know how hard it's been for her since. All her friends are worried about her."

Chelsey rolled her eyes and cast Betty a look of exasperated affection. The friends Betty referred to had dwindled to a precious few. But Betty had loyally stuck by her, dismissing the rumors and the professional and personal slurs as outrageous and beneath notice. If there was anyone in the world in whom she might have confided about Alex, it was Betty.

But Chelsey couldn't bring herself to do it. Even a friend as steadfast and nonjudgmental as Betty would find it hard to believe that she had found a genie.

"WHATEVER HAPPENED in Istanbul must have happened after I left," Alex said evenly, studying Chelsey across the restaurant table. "I'd like to hear about it."

"What? My mind was drifting."

Chelsey was having trouble adjusting to the difference in Alex. From the moment she had requested a delay before making her wishes, Alex Duport had become a different person. The angry lines around his mouth and between his

eyes had eased. Although he continued to touch everything around him, and he ate prodigious amounts of pizza,
he almost seemed relaxed. Clearly he was enjoying himself, and he had actually smiled several times during dinner.

Betty looked stricken. "Did I put my foot in my mouth?
I assumed Alex knew about last summer."

Fascinated and appalled, Chelsey watched Betty take a
slice of pizza from the tray. Immediately the empty slot
filled and the pizza was whole again. The regenerating pizza
was making Chelsey's nerves stand on end.

"I thought you knew everything about me," she said in
a distracted tone.

"I know the basics. What happened in Istanbul last
summer?"

Chelsey gave herself a mental shake, dragging her gaze
away from the pitcher of Coors that remained full no matter how many glasses were poured from it. Alex was
watching her closely, waiting for an answer.

Raising her arm, she pushed back the sleeve of her red
sweater and made a show of consulting her watch. "We'd
better go or we'll miss the start of the film."

"The film will begin when you wish it to begin, mistress."

Betty looked at the slice of pizza in her hand, then at the
tray. "You know...something really weird is happening
with the pizza. And the beer, too. I could swear that—"

Chelsey jumped to her feet. "Time to go," she said,
pulling Betty out of her chair.

Biting her lip, she glanced at Alex's smile and experienced a sinking feeling that things were only going to get
worse.

# Chapter Three

While Alex settled the bill, Betty dragged Chelsey outside the door of the restaurant. "You're having an affair! Why didn't you tell me? I thought you were still seeing Howard Webber."

"I am still seeing Howard," Chelsey said, irritated. She might have guessed something like this would happen. "I'm not having an affair with Alex."

"Oh, come on. He referred to you as his mistress right in front of me." One of Betty's eyebrows soared in a skeptical arch. "I know what I heard."

Thrusting her hands deep in her pants pockets, Chelsey leaned toward the restaurant window and glared at Alex inside. "I wish I could explain this, but I can't."

Inside the restaurant, Alex instantly stiffened and turned sharply to face her. He started toward the door as a warm, round object appeared in Chelsey's hand. One of the gold coins. Good God, she had said "I wish." Frantically, she shook her head and waved Alex back. The coin vanished from her palm.

Feeling her legs shaking, Chelsey leaned against the outside wall of the restaurant and held her breath for a moment. She began to see how easy it would be to blow this opportunity. Now the coin system made sense. It permitted a brief interval to correct an error or allow for second thoughts.

"Are you all right?" Betty asked, concerned.

"I am *not* Alex's mistress!" Betty's insistence was painting erotic mental pictures that made Chelsey feel fluttery inside, sort of overheated, tense and nervous.

"Methinks the lady doth protest too much." Betty studied her with a thoughtful expression. "The only reason I can think of to explain why you want to keep this affair a secret is that Alex is married."

"Believe me, that isn't the reason. There is no affair."

"Well, is he? Married?"

Chelsey threw out her hands. "I don't know, okay? I haven't asked him."

"You're having an affair with an old friend and you haven't bothered to ask if he's gotten married since you saw him last?" Betty looked appalled. "Listen, Chelsey, you have the right to know! My opinion of Howard Webber is no secret. You know I think he's small, petty and a pompous ass. And no one in their right mind would choose Howard over a gorgeous hunk like Alex. But at least Howard isn't married!"

Chelsey tried to calm herself by taking a long, deep breath and holding it for a count of five. "Look, this is simply a misunderstanding that's getting out of hand. It doesn't matter whether Alex is married, because I am not—repeat, *not*—having a fling with him!" The only good thing about this conversation was that Betty had been diverted from thinking about the regenerating pizza and beer pitcher.

A flash of anger and hurt jumped in Betty's dark eyes. "I'm not blind. I saw how the two of you looked at each other over dinner! Look, if you don't think you can trust me with your secret...well, okay. It's none of my business, anyway."

Chelsey groaned. She took Betty's hands in hers and spoke in an anxious voice. "It isn't like that. You know I trust you absolutely! It's just... It's just that..."

Betty's eyes widened. "I just figured it out! You suspect he's married, but you're not sure so you're keeping the relationship a secret. Chelsey Mallon! You're *afraid* to ask him, aren't you? You're afraid of the answer!"

Suddenly Chelsey felt weak. If Alex had been real and she had been having an affair with him... Well, maybe Betty's claim came too close to the truth.

"I left my cane in the car," she muttered, looking for an escape.

"Well, *I'm* not afraid to ask him!" Betty said firmly. A grimly protective expression tightened her mouth. Shoulders squared, eyes suspicious, she stepped up to Alex as he pushed through the restaurant door. "Are you married or not? And don't lie—we can check it out!"

"I beg your pardon?" Alex's eyebrows lifted, and he shot a questioning look toward Chelsey.

Chelsey sighed and threw out her hands. "This is your fault. I asked you not to call me mistress."

"Quit stalling. Do you have a wife?" Betty demanded. It didn't matter to her that people were moving around the island they created in the restaurant doorway. She sensed a friend in danger, and that possibility was enough to send her on the warpath.

Alex fixed his eyes on her flushed face, judging the extent of her indignation. "I had a wife," he said finally. "It was a very long time ago."

"Then you're divorced?" Betty wasn't letting the subject drop until all ambiguities were cleared.

"My wife is dead." No hint of emotion altered Alex's tone. He stated the fact in a flat, even voice.

Betty visibly relaxed. She looked pleased with her triumph before she arranged her features into an expression of sympathy. "I'm sorry your wife died," she said to Alex in a softer tone, patting his arm. "I hope you understand why I had to ask. Chelsey has been through a lot. I don't want her to get hurt."

"I fail to grasp how my marital status could hurt Dr. Mallon," Alex said, frowning. He lifted his gaze to Chelsey, making certain she noticed his emphasis on *Dr.* Mallon. "I assure you I would never injure Chelsey— I'm here to grant her wishes. My services will be a direct benefit to her."

"Jeez, what an ego." Betty rolled her eyes, then laughed as they walked toward the car. "You're going to grant Chelsey's fondest wish, huh? And going to bed with you will be a big benefit to her." She shook her head and slid into the car. "I'll say this for you, Alex. You have to be a real stud to make a claim like that. You're giving yourself a lot to live up to." She met Chelsey's eyes in the rearview mirror. "Lucky girl," she murmured with a grin.

Chelsey gripped the steering wheel and stared straight ahead, feeling wildly exasperated. She had lied about Alex to her best friend who was now convinced that Chelsey was having a secret affair with an ego-driven sex machine. A long, frustrated sigh escaped her lips. She slid a narrowed look toward Alex in the seat next to her. He was running his fingertips over the plush seat covers and sniffing the night air with oblivious pleasure, unaware of Betty's misconceptions.

What next? she thought as she turned the key in the ignition, then drove down Broadway toward the Campus

Theater. An evening with a genie, she decided uncomfortably, was like playing hopscotch on a mine field.

THE MOVIE THEATER was jammed with marvelous sensory impressions, and Alex was eager to sample them all. The smells in particular delighted him, blending a rich mixture of women's perfume, men's cologne, carpet shampoo, candy and other scents he couldn't readily identify. Above it all drifted the pervading enticement of the popcorn machine, a seductive hot buttery smell that made his mouth water.

"But we just finished eating a mountain of pizza!" Chelsey protested when he insisted on buying buckets of popcorn, soft drinks and boxes of chocolate-coated candy.

"I've never tasted these things," he explained.

"Where have you been?" Betty inquired. "In outer Siberia?"

Foods had altered dramatically since his day. Variety and taste were vastly improved. Ordinarily Alex didn't spend enough time in the reality plane to sample much of anything. He was determined not to waste this rare opportunity to taste, touch and inhale everything there was to taste, touch and inhale. A century might elapse before he was offered another chance like this one.

Once they were settled in the dimly lit theater, Chelsey leaned against his shoulder and whispered curiously, "Have you been to a movie before?"

She wasn't wearing perfume but her natural scent was clean and fresh, distracting enough that Alex had to forcefully remind himself of her question. "I know about movies, of course, but I haven't actually sat in a theater and watched one, no," he said finally. Being reminded of his lack of actual experience pained him.

Resentment diminished his pleasure in the scent of Chelsey's skin and in the crunchy taste of the popcorn. Only after the lights dimmed and the screen flared did he set aside a bitter roster of grievances and focus his concentration on the experience at hand.

Instantly Alex forgot the concerns of a moment ago. The opening scenes of *Robin Hood: Prince of Thieves* stunned his mind into shocked attention. Chelsey had explained that this was a film about a thief who robbed from the rich and gave to the poor. Nothing had prepared him for a depiction of the Crusades. Leaning forward in the theater seat, he scanned the screen intently, feeling a deep and building anger at the superficial portrayal of the pivotal event in his life. What he watched on screen was a tidied-up, prettified depiction that was far from what the Crusades had actually been. Where were the horrific battle scenes? The screams of dying men, the smell of blood and urine and rotting flesh? Where were the mountains of bones and amputated limbs, the exhaustion and disillusion, the cries to heaven?

No, he thought, it hadn't been like what he was watching on the screen; it had been like this.... Totally absorbed, he shifted the image on the screen to a scene immediately following the battle at Baldaz. This is what it had been. Ragged thieves scavenging a scorched field littered by mutilated and dying men, plundering the men's valuables even as they pleaded for a scrap of shade or a sip of water to ease their last thirst. And dazed, vacant-eyed men, stripped of youth and illusions, stumbling over fallen comrades, shock, horror and exhaustion carving their bloody faces.

Not wanting to see, but unable to resist, Alex shifted the scene to the south of the battlefield, near the city walls, and examined himself astride the white stallion that had belonged to his liege lord. His bloodied sword hung limp in his hand. His tunic was filthy and stained, hanging in tatters. Tangled hair—matted with dust and another man's blood—obscured his vision.

Isabel rode pillion behind him. She leaned against his back, her arms clasped around his waist. Her flaxen hair, her vanity, had swirled loose from her braids; her eyes were as colorless and blank as his own as they silently skirted the carnage of a battle inexplicably lost.

Curling his hands into fists, Alex leaned forward in the theater seat and stared. Isabel. Once her name had sung to him. How could he have forgotten how young she was? Shock clenched his stomach as he realized she was plain of face and sharp featured. To him she had been beautiful, a prize among women. Emotion had thrown a veil across the slyness in her slanted eyes, the deceitful twist of a mouth too thin and cunning.

"How odd. I don't remember any of this," Chelsey murmured, staring up at the screen.

"I'd forgotten how bloody and gritty the opening is," Betty murmured in agreement. "These scenes are so real they make me squirm. When does Costner show up?"

Alex didn't hear. His gaze remained riveted to the screen, his memories whirling backward across centuries. He passed swiftly over his capture and his anguish as Isabel was dragged screaming from the stallion. The scene leapt forward to those last searing moments in Selidim's palace.

Yes, there was the small curtained room where he had been tortured and beaten, exactly as he remembered, authentic in every detail. Torment in the midst of silken opulence. And there was Selidim and his hawk-nosed vizier, Mehmed. Alex let the vision of Selidim grow to fill the screen as hatred blackened and scalded his mind.

Selidim, magnificent in snowy robes, his turban en-
crusted with a king's fortune in jewels. Selidim, mystical
prince, victorious general, husband to a thousand wives.
Selidim, philosopher, scholar, conjurer. Selidim, magician, tormentor, guardian of dark secrets.

Selidim's heavy lips curved in a poisonous smile. "Where
is your God now, Crusader, the God you would impose on
us?" His smile thinned. "It appears that you, who would
force your wishes on others, now stand deserted, at the
mercy of an infidel's pleasure." Cold flame flickered in eyes
as black as the void.

"His punishment, oh Magnificent One . . ." Like an ancient bird, Mehmed hopped from one slippered foot to the
other.

Selidim leaned so near that Alex could see the grid of
veins reddening his eyes, the pockmarks pitting his handsome dark face, could smell the scent of honey and al-
monds floating on his breath. "Two were captured. One
shall live. You decide, Crusader. Do you live . . . or does the
woman?"

"Kill me." Alex barely recognized the croak issuing past
his cracked lips. "You have no quarrel with the woman. Let
her live."

"Such nobility, such innocence. Such devotion to chiv-
alrous ideals, yes, Crusader?" Selidim's black eyes narrowed in chill amusement accompanied by a grudging
flicker of respect which Alex had not identified at the time.
"Do you truly suppose the woman worthy of your sacri-
fice? You are a fool, Crusader. You forfeit your life in
tribute to a false God and false philosophy."

"She is worthy. Let her live." Alex heard the depth of
conviction in his shattered voice, the blind and unques-
tioning faith in the goodness of his beloved, his Isabel, his
wife.

Selidim clapped his jeweled hands. At once there was movement behind the curtain as someone was led into the room at Alex's back. Selidim leaned near him again, his whisper a long, malignant hiss. "You inflict your wishes at the point of a sword, Crusader. You claim your religion, your philosophy, your ideas and ideals are superior to all others and you would impose them through blood and subjugation. I say to you, listen and hear the destruction of one dream, one ideal, then ask if all your ideals are equally as false."

The vizier shoved a silk scarf into Alex's mouth, then bowed to Selidim and drew the curtain aside that Selidim might enter the next room. Alex stiffened and his heart leapt as he heard Isabel's frightened cry.

Selidim murmured softly to her, then spoke in a voice Alex was intended to overhear. "Two were captured. One shall live. You decide, little jewel. Will you offer your life so the Crusader may live? Or will you stand by my side and watch your Crusader die?"

"Take him," Isabel whispered. "I will make you happy, sire. Kill him, not me. I beg of you. Not me. Not me."

An elbow shoved Alex to the far side of his theater seat, intruding on the remembered anguish which had blackened to hatred, then eventually to indifference, as slow centuries passed. After scrubbing a hand across his face, Alex turned his head to look into Chelsey's indignant stare.

"Stop screwing around," she whispered fiercely. "Put the Robin Hood movie back on the screen!"

"I don't remember *any* of this." Betty's hand had frozen in midair above her box of popcorn. "You know...if that actor wasn't so bloody and beat-up, he'd look a little like Alex."

"Shhh!" An irritated chorus erupted from the seats behind them.

Alex stared, watching Selidim return through the curtain, his black eyes burning with triumph. He could not bear to hear Selidim's pronouncement of punishment. The scene flickered and faded, then Kevin Costner's boyish smile jumped onto the screen.

"Wait a minute," someone whispered behind them. "What happened to that other guy?"

Alex stumbled to his feet, spilling his bucket of popcorn. He grabbed Chelsey's hand and strode up the darkened aisle, pulling her behind him. In the lobby he bent over the drinking fountain and splashed cool water on his face.

It had all happened over a thousand years ago, yet for a moment the memories had come crashing back, still painfully vivid, still possessing the power to carve him into little slices.

The poison that circulated through his spirit was the knowledge that Selidim had been right. Alex had been a fool to dream noble dreams. Self-interest ruled the world, not self-sacrifice or lofty principles. Nobility of spirit was a false conceit. Love was only as strong as its first selfish challenge.

Chelsey grabbed his arm and spun him to face her. "How could you! You promised you wouldn't do anything weird, then you did that stuff at dinner and now you're rewriting movie scripts to amuse yourself! Damn it, Alex!"

She stared up at him. And the anger abruptly drained from her expression. She stumbled backward a step and her fingers flew to her mouth.

"Oh my God. That Crusader didn't just resemble you—it *was* you! Alex . . . that was your story!"

"I need a drink," he said roughly. "Something stronger than that pale weasel piss you people call beer." He knew it would annoy her, but right now he didn't care. A flagon of strong dark ale appeared in his hand and he drank steadily until beads of sweat rose on his brow and his lungs screamed for air. He tossed the flagon toward the ceiling where it disappeared, then wiped the back of his hand across his mouth. "I apologize," he said finally, avoiding her wide, stunned gaze. "I didn't intend to alter the film. But they depicted it falsely, and I just..." He stared across the lobby at the popcorn jumping inside the machine. "The past...it overwhelmed me."

"In living color," Chelsey added softly, pressing her hand against the muscles twitching in his arm. "I'm sorry, Alex." She drew a breath. "Isabel looked very young. I'm sure she loved you, but she was frightened, and a long way from home."

"In those days seventeen was a ripe age. Isabel was a widow when I married her."

His arm was rock-hard beneath Chelsey's fingertips, as hard as his expression. Not thinking, Chelsey reached a hand to his face, wanting to comfort him for a loss that right now seemed as fresh to him as yesterday.

The instant she touched his face, all her inner systems stopped, as if they had received an electric jolt. The past dropped from his eyes and he stared down at her with a gaze so focused and intense that Chelsey's mouth went dry.

Hastily she pulled her hand away and wet her lips. "What happened to you? Did Selidim kill you?" She waved a hand, unable to meet his steady stare. "Well, of course he must not have killed you, but—"

Betty popped out of the theater doors and walked toward them, shaking her head. "I must be getting old. I've seen that movie twice but I don't remember half of what we've seen so far." She made a face. "Early senility. I wonder how many outfits I've forgotten at the cleaners?"

Chelsey examined Alex's face. "Betty, would you mind terribly if we deserted you? It's been a long, very strange day. I think Alex and I need to talk."

"Talk? Or make a few wishes come true?" Betty winked. "Go ahead. Don't worry about me, I'll hook a ride home with Professor Markley and his wife."

"Thanks." Chelsey gave her a hug.

When she turned to take Alex's arm, she noted the faraway look in his eyes and understood his thoughts had turned backward again.

And she was feeling jealous of a woman who had been dead for over a thousand years.

CHELSEY AND ALEX DIDN'T speak during the drive back to Chelsey's rented house but both were aware of the strong physical current that flowed between them, enhanced by the close confines of the small car. It was as if a magnetic tug had leapt between them, creating an invisible attraction they both tried to ignore.

Once Chelsey started to speak, but noticed his hands were clenched into fists on his thighs and changed her mind. She wondered if the differences between their lives and experiences made her seem as exotic to him as he was to her. Perhaps that explained her strange heightened awareness of his slightest move. Or perhaps it was a primal recognition of male and female that originated deep in the cells. Whatever was happening, it made her nervous and uneasy.

Neither reached for the door handle after Chelsey switched off the ignition in her driveway. They sat together in the summer darkness, listening to the ticking sound made by the engine as it cooled.

It was a pleasant Colorado evening. The sky was clear and velvety dark, spangled by distant stars. The night air had cooled enough that Chelsey's sweater felt good against her skin. Insects strummed love songs from the safety of dark trees and bushes. The scent of lilac and cut grass was strong and poignant. From the house next door came the muffled gaiety of the "Tonight Show."

"What happened to Isabel?" Chelsey asked quietly, dropping her hands from the steering wheel.

Alex leaned his elbow out the window, drummed his fingertips against the roof of the car. Chelsey had the feeling she was sitting beside a coiled spring. His memories upset him, but she sensed something else running beneath the obvious. A powerful and perhaps dangerous awareness had been released when she touched his face in the theater lobby. For both of them.

"Selidim..." he said in a harsh voice. Stopping, he waited, then began again. "Selidim decided Isabel was disruptive, an influence he did not wish for his harem. Less than a year after the scene you witnessed, Selidim ordered her drowned in the seraglio pool as an example to his wives and concubines."

Chelsey nodded, familiar with the ruthless cruelty of Alex's period. She heard him rub a hand over his face, but she didn't embarrass him by watching his anguish. Instead she stared at the summer moths batting themselves against the porch light globe. "I'm sorry."

"Why?" he asked after a moment, shifting in his seat to look at her. Chelsey felt a bolt of lightning shoot through her body when he met her eyes. "It happened over eleven hundred years ago."

"It happened. Obviously it still upsets you," she said, looking away from him and rubbing her arms. What was happening here? She felt hot and cold, nervous inside. The realization that if she moved only a little she would be touching him made her feel apprehensive and thrillingly aware of his maleness.

"It's odd," he said softly, looking at her mouth. "I haven't thought about Isabel in centuries."

Chelsey hesitated. "Did you love her very much?"

A bitter laugh scraped the back of his throat. "Love is the grandest of all illusions and the easiest to puncture. Self-interest is the only true reality. Self-interest will conquer love in any contest."

"I don't believe that."

"Then you have never experienced a conflict between self-interest and the illusion of love."

Stung by the implication, Chelsey's chin lifted defensively. "If you're suggesting that I've never been in love, you're wrong. I'll admit it wasn't a grand passion, but it was real enough." The pain had certainly been real when it ended.

"I said only that your love has not yet been tested against self-interest."

"Perhaps not," Chelsey conceded, trying to be fair. Heat rose in her cheeks. "But I know in my heart that I would not have made the same choice as Isabel."

"With all respect, Mistress Mallon, I suggest you're speaking with the haste of idealism rather than the logic of reality. Until you have actually faced a similar choice, you cannot state with true certainty how you would choose." His voice and expression softened. "Chelsey, do you honestly believe Isabel made the wrong choice? Self-interest and selfishness are protective mechanisms. Isabel's instinct for preservation gave her ten months of life that she would not otherwise have enjoyed. Can you condemn her for wanting to live?"

"That wasn't your choice," Chelsey bluntly reminded him.

"I was a fool."

"I don't think so."

Chelsey surprised herself by wanting very much to stroke his hand resting on the car seat beside her. Learning of Alex's story had softened her perception of him. She knew she was responding strongly to his personal tragedy and to the intimacy her new knowledge imparted. Her impulse was to extend that warmth into something greater that she couldn't put a name to. Or didn't want to name. Still, she resisted touching his hand because her instincts also sensed danger. She shied from the explosive power of a single compassionate touch.

"Alex, before we go inside, there's something I want to say." She paused to gather her thoughts, pushing aside the images of bubbling sexuality that impressed her as wildly hopeless and inappropriate. "I greatly admire your capacity to forgive. Regardless of your generosity toward Isabel's memory, she betrayed you. Isabel betrayed the ideals you believed in, she betrayed your faith in her and your loyalty. She betrayed all that the two of you meant to each other. And she betrayed your love for her. Yet somehow you found a way to forgive and make her choice seem logical and acceptable in your mind. I don't think many men could do that."

The glow from the porch light illuminated his smile. "Most men don't have eleven hundred years to work it out. I'd like to believe I deserve your praise, but I don't."

"What's wrong with this picture?" Chelsey asked. His smile made her skin feel taut and tingly. "My surly swaggering genie with the belligerent attitude is suddenly modest? I don't believe it. And I don't believe it required eleven hundred years to forgive her. You forgave her almost immediately, didn't you?"

"Perhaps," he said after a minute. "You leg is tired, isn't it?"

"You're trying to change the subject." But it was his story. She had no right to press. "Yes, my leg is throbbing and achy." It surprised her that they could mention her bum leg so easily, without Alex looking uncomfortable and without her feeling acutely self-conscious or apologetic.

"What I'm longing for right now is a long, soaky bath and a good night's sleep." When she thought back to arriving at Wickem Hall this morning—was it only this morning?—it seemed like an event that had occurred in another lifetime to a different person. So much had happened since. Chelsey suspected she wouldn't be—couldn't be—the same person she had been before Alex whirled into her life. Shaking her head, she reached for the door handle. "On second thought, I doubt I'll get much sleep tonight. I'll probably be awake until dawn, thinking about wishes."

"Shazam."

Her fingers closed around air. Instantly they were standing in the upstairs hallway outside her bedroom door. Senses reeling, Chelsey flung out a hand and steadied herself against the papered wall. Her cane dropped from suddenly boneless fingers.

"God! That's...really hard to get used to!" The abrupt transition sent her heartbeat flying into overdrive. She clapped a hand over her breast, feeling the rapid pounding against her palm. When she realized the gesture had drawn Alex's intense interest to her breasts, she felt her cheeks heat and made herself drop her hand. Her cane lifted of its own accord from the carpet and nudged her hand until she grasped the curved handle.

"Thanks," she said in a voice that emerged sounding higher than her own. "I hate to sound ungrateful," she added with a wobbly smile, "but did you put the car in the garage and lock the downstairs door?"

"Shazam," he said, returning her smile. Chelsey wondered why she had ever thought Alex incapable of good humor. He had a gorgeous smile, and when he was relaxed he smiled often.

Performing a graceful flourish with his fingertips, he dipped into a salaam. For the first time, the gesture was light and easy, free of resentment or shades of mockery. "Your car is in your garage, mistress. Your house is secured for the night."

"Thank you. I—" Her remark was interrupted by the sound of running water. Alex was filling the bathtub for her. The fragrance of jasmine-scented bath oil floated into the hallway. "You know," she said with a sigh of genuine pleasure, "you're spoiling me. I think I could get used to having a genie around."

"I could get used to being around."

They gazed into each other's eyes and smiled. Gradually Chelsey's pounding heart called her attention to how close together they were standing. Near enough that she could inspect at close range the thick fringe of dark eyelashes framing his remarkable eyes. Close enough to warm herself within the male heat radiating from his large, sexy body. Because Alex was lean and magnificently proportioned, she tended to forget how big he was and how overwhelming his height and size could be.

Ordinarily Chelsey resisted any situation that might make her feel fragile or in need of protection or assistance. But Alex's height and solid muscled torso made her feel fragile by comparison. His male heat and swelling masculine power made her feel suddenly helpless against the magnetism that drew her hand upward toward his face.

Embarrassed, she straightened abruptly and dropped her hand. After clearing her throat with a self-conscious sound, she hastily stepped backward. "Well," she said, sounding overly brisk and cheerful. "It's a bath and bed for me. I suppose you'll be going into your lamp."

"I beg your pardon?" His thick eyebrows moved together in a puzzled frown.

"The silver cup lamp," Chelsey repeated, suddenly uncertain. "Won't you be using it tonight?"

"Chelsey, I'm sorry but I don't have the faintest idea what you're talking about."

Silently, she cursed the late night reruns of "I Dream of Jeannie." Although Chelsey had a sudden awful suspicion that she was going to sound like an idiot, there was nothing to do but blunder forward. And who could tell? Maybe there was an outside chance that she was right. She fervently hoped so.

She fiddled with her cane, not looking at him. "You live and sleep in the silver cup lamp, don't you?"

He stared down at the top of her head. "Let me see if I understand what you're saying. Is it possible that you believe something this size," he waved a hand down the length of his body, "will fit into something the size of the silver cup lamp? Which I could carry in my pocket?"

Chelsey had guessed right the first time. She was an idiot.

"Let us assume for a moment that I could indeed shrink myself to the size of your little fingernail. Why would I then want to go inside the cup lamp?" His frown deepened. "Do you imagine there's a miniature inn concealed within the lamp? With stamp-sized beds? Is that it?"

Embarrassment flamed upward from Chelsey's throat. "All right, so I don't know where genies sleep. Pardon me, I must have dozed off during Genie Lore 101."

An effort toward patience puckered his brow. "The silver cup lamp is merely a summoning device." He thought a moment. "Think of the lamp as a garage-door opener.

The device opens the door, that's all. Your garage-door device does not power your car, nor can you park your car in it. It does one thing and one thing only. It opens the door. The silver cup lamp does one thing and one thing only. It summons your genie." A broad grin split his lower jaw. Amusement twinkled in his eyes. "Did you honestly imagine I lived in the lamp? That I could shrink or enlarge myself at will?"

Bright crimson fired Chelsey's cheeks. "Look, twenty-four hours ago I would have sworn there was no such thing as a genie! How am I supposed to know where you sleep?"

"How was this sleep-in-the-lamp idea supposed to work?" His eyes were sparkling brightly now, dancing with humor. Chelsey suspected he held back a shout of laughter. "Was I supposed to hunker over the lamp, say shazam, then hope I dropped into the opening when I suddenly shrank? Did any fanfare accompany this feat? Maybe a burst of flashing lights or colored smoke? The clash of tiny cymbals? Or do I shrink myself, then depend on my master or mistress to pick me up with a pair of tweezers and lower me into the lamp? Frankly, that sounds perilous."

"All right," Chelsey said, narrowing her eyes and lifting her chin. "You've made your point." She spun on her heel and walked down the hallway. Halting in front of the guest-room door, she pressed the handle and stepped inside. "You can sleep here. There's an extra pillow in the closet if you want it."

He walked around the room, running his palm along the bureau top, leaning to glance out the window, testing the pillow. Finally he walked to the door and leaned his head out, judging the distance to Chelsey's bedroom door.

"This won't be acceptable."

Now it was Chelsey's turn to strive for patience. "Why not?"

When he looked at her, his smile had vanished. "I must remain within the sound of your voice. That is the rule."

"Alex, I sleep like the dead. I promise I'm not going to wake up at three in the morning, snap my fingers and make a wish. You can sleep here in perfect confidence that I'm not going to be making any middle-of-the-night wishes!"

"The rule cannot be broken. I must remain within the sound of your voice."

She hadn't mistaken the stubbornness hinted in the strong angle of his jawline. He spoke firmly in a voice that allowed her no argument or persuasion.

Chelsey stepped into the hallway and eyed it uncertainly. The hallway was short, narrow and uninviting. "Well, you can't sleep on the floor. I think we're stuck. I don't know where you can sleep and still adhere to this idiotic rule."

"I'll stay in your room, of course. With you."

# Chapter Four

Because Alex suspected Chelsey would vigorously protest if he stated his intentions, he didn't seek her consent before gently easing her into a natural sleep. Had he not assisted, he suspected she wouldn't have slept a wink. He sensed her nervousness and racing thoughts, and she was obviously uncomfortable about trying to relax in bed while a strange man watched from a chair not three feet away.

Alex considered assuring her that he was a man of honor and had never violated a woman or taken advantage of a woman's vulnerability.

But that wasn't entirely true. In fact, as Alex stood in the darkness at the foot of Chelsey's bed and studied her sleeping form, he knew he was violating her trust by gazing at her as she slept. But he could not help himself.

She was so beautiful. In sleep her defensiveness dropped away like a shadow from a rose, as did the brisk, businesslike manner she adopted to hold people at a distance. She looked younger, softer, more womanly.

A moment ago she had kicked aside the sheets, and Alex noticed her ankle-length summer nightgown had traveled upward to a point about an inch above her knees. The neckline had dropped to expose one smooth shoulder and the tops of her breasts.

He sucked in a hard deep breath. When he opened his eyes again, Alex made himself focus on her legs instead of her lush breasts. Her right leg was long and sensually curved, tapering to a slender ankle, so perfect that he yearned to trace the contours with his palm. As her two legs did not lie close together, the shortness of the left was not apparent. But her left leg was thinner, not as beautifully shaped or curved. That she insisted on wearing nothing but slacks and chose ankle-length nightgowns suggested that, regardless of her professional accomplishments, and no matter how strenuously she might object to his conclusion, Dr. Chelsey Mallon defined herself in terms of her body.

It was unfortunate that her definition was negative, because Alex thought her body was magnificent, beginning with her heart-shaped face, translucent skin, and her intelligent eyes, whose color reminded him of rich dark earth. A halo of ginger tendrils fanned across her pillow, framing twin crescents of lashes that shadowed her cheeks and her slightly parted lips.

When she softly sighed and shifted on her side, he let his narrowed gaze travel slowly down her body. The seductive arch of her hip had lifted and folds of her light nightgown settled into the curving valley of her waist. For a long moment Alex stared at the sweet promise of hip and waist and the glimpse of pale thigh beneath. Finally he raised his eyes to the full rounded globes of her breasts. His hands clenched by his sides. He ached to discover if her breasts were as firm yet as soft as they appeared. If her nipples were pink or brown; if they rose like tiny thrusting pebbles to greet a man's caress.

His arousal was swift and powerful, almost painful in intensity. Silently turning on the balls of his feet, he ground his teeth together and faced away from her, trying to recall when he had last bedded a woman.

Over the centuries he had encountered mistresses who had invited him into their beds, had commanded him. He was a man; he had accepted their invitations. He had done his best to give them a night to remember, a night of fantasy and rapture.

But each time, the summons from a mistress came as a surprise, not as a result of his own instigation or calculation. Never had he gazed at a mistress and thought of her as a woman first, nor had he speculated how it would feel to hold and stroke her or make love to her. When invited into a mistress's bed, her sex had aroused him, not the woman herself.

Until now. Chelsey Mallon was different.

She was the first woman in centuries whom he had begun to regard as more than an object to serve. Because of his extended time with her, Alex was beginning to view Chelsey Mallon not only as his mistress but as a woman, a very desirable woman, and as a person who intrigued his interest.

Such an occurrence had not happened in a very, very long time. If ever.

When Alex attempted to recall the masters and mistresses he had served, they emerged as nameless, faceless links on a long dark chain. Part of their anonymity was the result of preference. Largely their anonymity resulted from the brief span of time he spent in their company. They passed uneventfully through his consciousness, blurring into obscurity.

Until this emergence with Chelsey Mallon, the longest he had spent in the reality plane had been twelve hours. Unlike Chelsey Mallon, most of his masters and mistresses knew at once how they would spend their three wishes.

Seldom did the process require more than two, possibly three hours.

Because Chelsey had given him the gift of extended experience, he knew he would never forget her. She would not become another obscure link in the long chain.

She would remain unique in his grateful mind because of the time she had granted him, because of her beauty, and because he physically wanted her as he had wanted no other woman.

After gazing at her with hungry, smoldering eyes, Alex forced himself to move away from her. He walked into the hallway and cocked his head, listening to the silence that had settled over the house. Because it was a quiet night, he discovered he could move farther from her than he would ordinarily have been able to. If he strayed beyond the range of a master's voice, the air around him thickened, became almost tangible and pressed him back. An unpleasant urgency built in his nerve endings, nearly painful, until he returned to the prescribed range.

But tonight's stillness permitted him to explore most of her small house except the kitchen, adding to his knowledge about her. She liked plants and books, especially textbooks, history books and books about people who had overcome adversity. Few of the objects in her room had been chosen for display, but rather for comfort. He assumed that sentimental attachment accounted for a collection of stones, the composition of which indicated widely varying origins. Pottery shards of no value suggested mementos of digs that had been important to her. Her doctorate was framed and given a place of honor on the dining room wall. A basket of yarn and knitting needles waited on the floor beside a well-worn chair. He could approach the kitchen near enough to glimpse a flower press on the end of the counter.

There were no signs of a man either past or present.
That pleased him.

"DID YOU SLEEP WELL?" Chelsey asked, mounding her pillows behind her back, then examining the breakfast tray that had appeared above her lap. There were eggs Benedict, blueberry crepes, croissants, a pot of steaming hot chocolate and a vase holding the most perfect red rose she had ever seen. She combed her fingers through her hair and hoped she didn't look as disheveled as she usually did in the mornings.

"I dozed for about thirty minutes."

"That's all? Don't genies need sleep?"

Her question made him smile. "Yesterday I would have said no. But now I'm not as sure. I was surprised that I slept for thirty minutes."

"You don't know if you need sleep?"

"I've never been in the reality plane long enough to find out."

Chelsey considered his answer for a minute, then decided to forgo further questions until she was more awake.

"So what did you do all night?" Averting her face, she spread butter and jam over a croissant. She could not believe she had actually managed to fall asleep with Alex sitting next to her in the dark. It had been the weirdest and most uncomfortable sensation. She, wearing a thin nightgown with nothing underneath; Alex, fully dressed beside her. She had listened to his quiet breath, remembering his naked chest and the look of his smooth hard skin. Wondering. Then wondering some more.

He shrugged. "Once the house quieted, I discovered I could move farther from you than I originally thought. I spent most of the night downstairs in the living room."

"Really? Doing what? Did you watch TV? Read?"

A light shudder of distaste tracked down his spine. "No. During the eighteenth century I developed an interest in fencing, so I practiced lunges and parries for a while. Then I arranged a banquet based around menus I found in one of your magazines. I spent most of the night grooming a horse." He related these activities in a matter-of-fact tone, as if there was nothing unusual about them. "I miss riding, but more than riding, I miss caring for a horse. It's a deeply satisfying set of tasks. Unless grooming a horse is something you have experienced and enjoyed, the pleasure is impossible to describe."

Chelsey closed her mouth and slowly lowered the croissant to the tray. She concentrated on keeping her voice level. "Alex—you're saying you had a *horse* in my living room?"

"I grasp your concern. Let me assure you that I restored everything exactly as it was before. To see your living room now, you would never guess that last night it briefly served as a fencing gymnasium or as stables."

She nodded slowly, staring at him. "What would my landlord have seen if . . . No, I don't want to know." She blinked and fought beyond the idea of a horse prancing around her living room. "Then you gave yourself a banquet. Seriously, Alex, how can you eat as much as you do? Why don't you gain four hundred pounds?"

His smile dazzled her. "Actually, I don't need to eat at all. I've forgotten what hunger feels like."

"But—"

"Don't ask me to explain—I can't. But food isn't necessary. Eating is, however, a great pleasure. The taste, the different textures and flavors. I can indulge that pleasure without feeling full or sated, and without changing weight."

"Lucky you," Chelsey murmured enviously.

He watched her sample the items on the tray, then inquired, "Have you made any decisions about making a wish?"

"Is there a rush?"

"Absolutely not." The swiftness with which he assured her made Chelsey suspect that he was in no hurry, either.

"Actually," she said, feeling excitement rise in her eyes, "I've decided on my first wish."

Alex sat straighter, and his expression instantly sobered. He inclined his head. "I await your command, mistress."

Chelsey pushed back a lock of hair, then moved the breakfast tray aside. Happiness competed with the excitement sparkling in her dark eyes. "It's a perfect wish. But it would be easier to explain if I showed you. Give me a few minutes to shower and pull myself together, then we'll take a short drive. No," she added quickly raising a hand. "No help this time. I want a real shower." She studied him a minute. "I just had a thought. Would you like a shower?" The intimacy of the invitation brought a rush of pink to her face. Her uncharacteristic shyness deepened as she recognized the smoky look smoldering in his suddenly speculative eyes. "I don't mean with me," she explained, sounding more snappish than she had intended. "I meant by yourself. You keep talking about wanting to experience physical sensations. I just thought . . ."

"I would appreciate the opportunity to feel water running over my skin more than I can tell you. Thank you." The smoky look still glowed in his eyes, not as intense as a moment ago, but intense enough that Chelsey felt her cheeks heat and her heartbeat quicken.

"Uh, look. Why don't you go first." Now that the image of showers and nakedness flickered in her mind—and possibly in his—Chelsey felt too self-conscious to slide out of bed in her nightgown in front of him. "There are extra towels on the shelf over the commode."

Excitement danced in Alex's eyes, and he darted an eager look toward the bathroom door. "You don't mind if I go first? You're sure about this?"

"Go." Would that all men were as easy to please, she thought, smiling at his enthusiasm. She reached for the tray. "I'll finish breakfast."

But she couldn't swallow a bite. Alex left the bathroom door open so he would hear if she uttered an unexpected wish. Before the mirror fogged, Chelsey caught an arousing glimpse of firm, rounded buttocks and heavy male thighs. A deep valley ran down his spine, bordered by thick ridges of muscle. She stared, then made herself look down at the breakfast tray, swallowing hard.

The image of Alex's naked backside was so powerful and disturbing that Chelsey didn't hear the doorbell. When she finally became aware of the persistent ringing, she started, then leapt out of bed and threw on a light robe, wondering how long someone had been standing on her porch before she heard the sound of the bell. Grabbing her cane, she hurried down the staircase and pulled open the front door.

Her landlady and next-door neighbor gave Chelsey an uncertain smile. Marge was in her mid-fifties, plump, and spent most of her time worrying about things that never happened. When she couldn't nibble to accompany her worrying, she twisted a tissue between her fingers as she was doing now.

"I'm sorry to bother you," Marge said, looking at Chelsey's robe, "but—and I know this is going to sound strange—it's just . . . Well, you see, it's Marvin." She drew a long breath and shifted her gaze to a spot somewhere beyond Chelsey's right ear. "Last night Marvin swore he saw your car vanish into thin air." She steadfastly refused to meet Chelsey's eyes. "I know that sounds nuts, and I guess it is, but the thought of a car vanishing kept bothering Marvin. I mean, he was so sure it had happened. Anyway, he kept worrying about it, so he finally gave up trying to sleep, got up about one o'clock, put on his robe and came over here to look inside your garage windows to see if your car was there or if it had really vanished."

"My car is in the garage, Marge."

Marge nodded. The tissue began to shred between her fingers. "Marvin said the front of the house had changed. It was larger. Much larger. And I know this sounds insane, but Marvin swears on his mother's grave that he heard horses inside. He made me swear that I'd come over here as soon as you were awake and ask you about it. He's absolutely positive you had a horse in your house last night." She looked down at the tissue in her hands. "This is really embarrassing, but..."

Chelsey opened the door wide so Marge could see inside. She phrased her answer carefully. "If there was a horse in here last night, he managed not to break a single item or overturn a thing. He didn't damage the floor or walls. Would you like to step inside and check for yourself?"

"Mistress Mallon!" An angry shout roared from the staircase. "If I've told you once, I've told you a dozen times that I must stay within the sound of your voice! Damn it, Chelsey!"

Marge stared over Chelsey's shoulder. Her eyes widened and her mouth dropped open. Chelsey spun to see Alex striding down the staircase, his hair dripping wet above a furious expression. But that wasn't the worst of it.

He was stark-naked.

And there was something about Alex's perfect, powerful body that made him seem more naked than any other naked man Chelsey had ever seen. He was totally, incredibly, so damned *naked*.

His dark hair was slicked back and dripping. Tiny bubbles of soap slid down his shoulders as if his skin were lightly oiled. His wet body glistened and flexed in the morning sun, the statue of an angry Greek god come to life.

But what drew Chelsey's helpless glance was the arrow of dark soapy hair that streaked across his muscled chest and pointed down to... She blinked hard, then looked again. "Good God," she whispered. He was large and powerful all over. She couldn't help staring any more than Marge could. Behind her, Marge released a long, choked sigh.

Alex seemed oblivious to their shock. He stood in the middle of the staircase, glaring furiously, splendid in his certainty that he was in the right, waiting impatiently for Chelsey to explain or apologize. Tiny rainbow droplets ran a zigzag course through the dark hair adorning his thighs, legs and arms. His naked skin caught the morning light and gleamed with male power and beauty. He was absolutely magnificent.

Chelsey couldn't tear her eyes away from him. She wasn't sure whether to laugh or cry or throw off her robe and chase him back upstairs. A hysterical bubble lodged in her throat. She touched her fingertips to her eyelids and wondered frantically what she would say to Marge. Finally she did the only thing she could think to do. She brazened it out.

"Alex, I'd like you to meet my neighbor and landlady, Marge Craddock. Marge, this is Alex Duport, my...my friend." Brazenness wasn't her style. Chelsey fervently wished the floor would open and swallow her. "I hope you'll pardon us for being a little underdressed," she said, giving Alex a furious glare. She wondered if the hysteria in her voice was as obvious to Marge as it was to her. "We're getting a late start this morning."

When she dared a peek between her fingers, Alex was moving down the staircase, arranging a charming smile on his lips. He now wore white chinos and a blue chambray shirt. Only his feet were bare.

"How do you do, Mrs. Craddock," he said, bending to take Marge's hand in his. Marge looked thunderstruck. He raised her limp fingertips to his lips. "It's a pleasure to make your acquaintance."

Marge's eyes had dilated. She looked to be in shock. Maybe it was having a blindingly handsome man with a foreign accent kiss her hand. Maybe it was seeing a naked man with a physique like an Olympian god. Maybe it was the fact that one minute Alex had been standing before them naked and furious and the next instant he was dry, dressed and smiling at her.

The instant Alex moved away from them and stepped into the living room, Marge swallowed and whispered. "He...he was buck naked, then just like that he was dressed! I saw it but I don't believe it."

"I beg your pardon? Did you say Alex was naked?" Chelsey couldn't think of any other way to handle this situation. She was desperate. "You think Alex was... Oh my." She tried to look surprised, shocked and amazed that Marge could even imagine such a thing.

"He was!" Marge hesitated, her mind telling her that what she had seen was impossible. "Wasn't he?" A flicker of uncertainty appeared in her eyes as she studied Chelsey's carefully questioning expression.

Chelsey hated herself for doing this. She frowned, striving for a look of concern, then placed her hand on Marge's sleeve. "Marge, are you and Marvin taking any kind of medication? Something where hallucinations might be a side effect?''

Confusion pinched her landlady's face. The tissue she'd been holding drifted to the porch in a spray of confetti. "I'm taking estrogen. And Marvin is taking those new megavitamins...." Her voice trailed. She peered through the door at Alex who smiled back at her with perfect innocence. "No," Marge whispered. "It isn't possible. I must be... But it was so *real*."

"Perhaps you and Marvin should have a checkup," Chelsey suggested, easing the door shut.

When Marge had gone, shaking her head and muttering, Chelsey collapsed against the closed door and breathed deeply for a full minute. When she opened her eyes, she stared at Alex.

"I can't believe I tried to make Marge think that she was hallucinating." Her stare deepened. "And I wouldn't have believed how much one person—you—could screw up another person's life—mine—in so short a time."

The smile Alex had manufactured for Marge vanished, replaced by the arrogant scowl Chelsey had observed when he first arrived. "If anyone is to blame, it is not me. How many times must I explain the rules?"

"Are you suggesting that what just happened is *my* fault?"

"It was you who wandered off while I was in the shower!"

Chelsey charged forward until she stood toe-to-toe with him, her chin jutting. "Look, you, I didn't ask to have a genie pop up and complicate my life. I was just doing my work, plugging along, not expecting or asking for anything." Thrusting her hand in front of his face, she started ticking down her fingers. "Since you arrived, I've got a completed inventory that I can't begin to explain, I've lied to my best friend who now believes I'm having a secret affair, about three hundred people are going to swear they saw movie scenes that don't exist, my landlord and landlady think they're losing their minds, and you're running through the house buckass naked, causing me enormous embarrassment. So far all I've gotten out of this deal is breakfast and a whole lot of complications!"

He leaned over her. "It was your suggestion that I take a shower."

Chelsey refused to be intimidated. Rising on her tiptoes, she returned his angry stare. "Let's get something straight right now. I don't mind not getting something for nothing. If you bipped back to never-never land right now, it wouldn't cause me a minute's regret. I was getting along just fine before you showed up and I'll get along fine after you leave. But I mind like hell the problems you're creating that I'm going to have to deal with! What do your insufferable rules have to say about *that?* About the problems you're creating!"

His scowl loomed over her. "Most people are happy to have a genie at their disposal."

"Maybe when I start seeing some wishes granted, I'll be happy, too. But right now, Alexandre Duport, you're nothing but trouble and a pain in the neck, one giant headache!"

He spoke through his teeth, bending closer until their noses almost touched. "Naturally my fondest desire is to provide for your happiness, Mistress Mallon. So let us proceed to your first wish."

"Excellent! Good! Let us do that." Chelsey pulled back from him. "Forget what I said earlier. Do your magic stuff and give me one of those instant showers and shampoos. I'd like my beige linen slacks and silk blouse, please, and—" When she looked down she was dressed as requested except for her shoes. "You may be enamored of high heels, but I'm not," she snapped. "Give me my own built-up sandals. And say shazam, damn it."

"Shazam, damn it."

She glared at him. But now she was wearing her own specially constructed shoes. "Thank you," she said between her teeth as she passed him on her way to the kitchen for her purse and car keys.

"You don't have to drive," he said, following her. "I can just—"

"And tip a dozen old people into heart attacks when they see two people materialize out of thin air? No, thank you! We'll travel by conventional means." She saw him eyeing her car keys with avid interest. "Forget it. No, never, not a chance, not in this lifetime! God knows what you might do to my car. It's a clunker but it's paid for. I don't want some guy from another century experimenting with my car, and that's that."

THEY ONLY HAD TO TRAVEL a few blocks to reach McKenzie's Nursing Home, but it was a hair-raising ride.

Alex slammed to a halt in front of the low flagstone building, taking up two parking spaces. He cut the engine and leaned back. "Driving isn't as easy as it looked."

Chelsey willed her hands to stop shaking. Amazement trembled in her voice. "I can't believe I let you talk me into this." She closed her eyes and dropped her head against the seat back. "When you smashed that woman's fender, I wanted to kill you."

"I repaired the damage to both cars," Alex said in a tight voice.

Chelsey covered her face with her fingers. "It was... Did you see her face when she realized her car had healed itself?"

She couldn't help it. Suddenly she was laughing so hard that her sides ached and tears ran from her eyes. Alex frowned, then he was laughing, too.

When Chelsey had composed herself, she opened the car door and slid outside, looking at him over the top of her newly mended and painted car. "Seriously, Alex. No more funny stuff, okay? We go inside, you grant my wish, and that's all. We leave, and no one's the wiser. No extra magic. Right?"

"Right." He studied the neat, low building and the landscaping. A mischievous glint sparkled in his eyes. "Tell me, don't you think those flower beds would look more appealing if the flowers were all blooming?"

Chelsey halted on the path and gave him an appalled glare. "I mean it, Alex. Don't you dare do anything to those flowers!"

"I was joking."

She studied his dancing eyes. "I knew that," she lied, feeling vastly relieved.

"What is this place?" he asked, opening the door for her. Chelsey prayed that no one noticed the door open by itself. Her shoulders dropped. Alex was a hopeless case. Even when he tried not to use magic, he couldn't help himself. It was second nature.

"McKenzie's is a home for elderly people who can no longer manage on their own." She gripped her cane, then strode toward a receptionist seated behind a desk overlooking a large, comfortably furnished lawn terrace. "We're here to visit Dr. Florence Harding."

The receptionist, a blue-haired woman in her early sixties, gave Alex the once-over, ending with a coy fluttering of darkened lashes. "Dr. Harding is in the crafts room. I'll show you where it is."

"I've been here many times," Chelsey said. "I can find the way."

She led Alex down a carpeted corridor, past an exercise class and a music class, to a large, sunny room that smelled pleasantly of paint and glue. Touching Alex's arm, she paused in the doorway.

"Do you see the white-haired woman wearing a gray skirt and print blouse?"

Alex looked puzzled. "The handsome woman sitting beside the window?"

"Dr. Harding was the first person to believe in me. No," Chelsey amended after a moment's thought, "that isn't right. Dr. Harding was the first person to help me believe in myself. I met Dr. Harding when I was in high school. High school was a difficult time." She shook the memories away. "Dr. Harding took me out of myself by introducing me to history and archaeology. I'll never forget...she took our class on a field trip to help excavate some dinosaur bones in the foothills. After a couple of hours of kneeling on rock, my leg hurt like hell and I wanted to quit. Dr. Harding wasn't having any. She fixed me with one of her famous looks and said briskly that I could be bitter or better—which was it going to be? Before I could answer, she stated firmly that in her opinion, I was more than just one leg, I was her best student and she expected great things from me. Wasn't it time that I started expecting something from myself?"

Chelsey smiled affectionately at the woman across the room. "She told me I could concentrate on my mind or on my leg. It was my choice. If I allowed my leg to make my decisions, I would live a very narrow life indeed. Dr. Harding changed my way of thinking and changed my life. I stopped being just a leg and became a person."

"Did you really, Chelsey?" Alex asked gently.

She hesitated, feeling the pink rise in her cheeks, then she brushed his question aside. "I think so. At least, for the most part. Anyway, Dr. Harding was a brilliant, compassionate woman who changed the lives of many people, not just mine. Her paper on Roman concrete is still the definitive work on the subject." She turned to look directly at Alex. "She's eighty years old. Until last year she was sharp as a tack. Now she has Alzheimer's disease. She doesn't recognize me, she..." Chelsey bit her lip and stopped speaking. She couldn't bear to list the depressing symptoms.

But the symptoms didn't matter anymore. They were about to vanish. Excitement grew and replaced the depression that always accompanied a visit to McKenzie's Nursing Home. She drew a long, deep breath, preparing herself.

"I'm ready, Alex. Pay attention. I wish..." A gold coin appeared between her fingers, growing unnaturally warm. "I wish that Dr. Harding's Alzheimer's would disappear and her mind would be as sharp as it has always been." Eyes shining, she gazed up at Alex and extended the coin. "Take it."

"Chelsey, I cannot grant your wish."

"No, listen," she said urgently. "I've thought this out. You're going to claim this wish does not benefit me. But, Alex, you're wrong. Nothing would make me happier than to see Dr. Harding sharp and alert like she used to be. If being happy doesn't benefit me, then I don't know what does. Happiness is a legitimate benefit. You have to grant this wish!"

"The rule is specific. It doesn't say you must benefit. The rule states that you must benefit *directly*. Curing Dr. Harding's Alzheimer's would directly benefit Dr. Harding—you would receive only a fleeting secondary benefit."

"Alex, please." Chelsey gripped his arm, pleading with him. "I beg you. Grant me this wish. You can have the other two wishes back, all I want is this one. Please. Please, Alex. I know you can grant this wish if you only would."

Alex stared at her in frank amazement. Nothing like this had ever occurred before. No master or mistress had ever begged to waste a wish for the sole benefit of another person. But her earnestness and sincerity could not be doubted. He looked into Chelsey Mallon's pleading eyes and felt cracks shoot through his philosophy regarding human selfishness.

"Chelsey, if I could do this for you," he said slowly, "I would. But I can't."

Her fingers dug into his arm. "Look at her. She was one of the most brilliant minds in archaeology. She loved to read and work puzzles. She was an amateur artist. Now she can't even remember her own name. She can't read or paint anymore. She just sits there, confused and in mental pain. You can help her, I know you can! Please, Alex. I'm begging you!"

He clasped her shoulders as tears brimmed in her eyes, then spilled over her cheeks. "Chelsey, listen to me. I admire you more than I can say for wanting to help Dr. Harding, but I can't accept this wish. The rule states—"

Jerking backward, she twisted out from under his hands. "The hell with the rules! If you won't grant this wish, then…then I want to speak to your supervisor or the head genie or whoever it is who made up these stupid damned rules! Do you hear me, Alex? I want to speak to the boss genie and I want to speak to him now!"

"There is no such person." His mind raced. Since this problem had not arisen before, he didn't actually know if the rule could be bent. "Give me the coin," he said finally. "I don't think it's possible, but I'll try to grant your wish."

"Thank you!" Immediately she thrust the gold coin into his hand and held her breath expectantly, her face blazing with hope.

"This is not in your best interest," he said, looking at her. "You understand that."

"Just do it!"

He studied her expression for a moment, then flexed his shoulders and turned, clearing his mind. He stared hard at Dr. Harding. Concentration narrowed his eyes, his body tensed. He willed forth the indefinable burst of energy that signified a wish had been granted.

Nothing happened. The sensation of forces gathering in his mind and body did not occur; he felt no alteration of his energy level. Dr. Harding continued to gaze out the window with vacant, uncomprehending eyes.

Silently, he turned to Chelsey and gently dropped the coin into the pocket of her slacks where it promptly disappeared. "I'm genuinely sorry."

Angrily she dashed the tears from her eyes. "What good is it to have a genie if you won't grant any of my wishes? This isn't fair!"

"Chelsey—"

But she didn't wait. Furious, she spun on her heel and ran out of the building. For the first time, she looked awkward to Alex. The sight of her trying to run and manage her cane unexpectedly squeezed his heart.

This was a unique and puzzling woman. She was defiant one moment, stunningly generous the next. Running away from him, she looked achingly vulnerable. But she could also be stubbornly fierce. He sensed she was intrigued by him, possibly drawn to him, yet she pushed him away. He didn't recall meeting anyone like her.

He reached the curb in time to watch her jump into her car and speed away from McKenzie's with the intention of leaving him behind.

Striving for patience, he appeared in the passenger seat beside her. "As I've explained several times, the only wishes I can grant are those—"

She ground her teeth and edged her body away from him. "Don't tell me again. In fact, don't even talk to me! I have nothing to say to you."

"I didn't make the rules. I only—"

"The thing is, I let my hopes and expectations build, I *believed* in you, that you could do it, then you trot out some insane rule and blandly announce you can't grant my wish. How would *you* feel if someone made extravagant promises, but when it came time to deliver, they wouldn't do it?"

"You're in the wrong lane. There's a car coming straight at us." Driving and riding in an automobile were nerve-racking experiences, exhilarating but perilous. It amazed him that the streets were not littered with crashed cars and broken bodies.

"Don't try to change the subject, damn it," Chelsey snapped, jerking on the steering wheel. "I'm furious, okay? I'm trying to think of a word that wraps together frustration, fury, disappointment, impatience and a dozen other depressing terms. This just is not fair! You're supposed to serve me, right? You're supposed to make my dreams come true, right? Well, let me tell you something, Alex. You aren't doing it! As far as I'm concerned, I drew a dud genie!"

What she was saying stung his pride. He hated being a genie, despised catering to humanity's base desires, resented his perpetual servitude and loathed to the depths of his soul being deprived of life and reality. But no one—not one single master or mistress during the course of eleven hundred years—had *ever* so much as hinted that he had failed them. Or suggested that he was shirking his duty. Not once had a master or mistress accused him of betraying their trust.

Chelsey sped into her driveway, stamped on the brake inches from the garage door, got out, slammed the car door behind her, then threw up the garage door and shot the car inside, braking a hair's width from the back wall. Alex realized his fingers were digging into the upholstery.

"I need to calm down," she whispered, gripping the steering wheel. She drew several long, deep breaths. "You do whatever you want to. I'm going to dig in the yard until I feel human again."

"I am trying to serve you, mistress," he said stiffly, staring at the back wall of the garage. It was infuriating that she blamed him for rules that he hadn't made and had no choice about obeying. "It would benefit us both if you would accept and adhere to the rules."

"I mean it. Don't talk to me." She narrowed her eyes. "I have a big date tonight, Alex. An important date. I'm warning you right now. If you do anything—and I mean *anything*—to mess up my date with Howard, I'll . . . I'll . . . I don't know what I'll do, but it will be drastic. So don't mess with me. Right now I'm more upset than I've been in a very long time. Don't make things worse."

His jaw clenched and his eyes narrowed. "My only desire is to serve you and make you happy, oh wise mistress."

"Don't give me that genie gibberish. What you say and what you do are two different things. I want your promise that you will not interfere with my date with Howard. That you won't do any weird magic stuff while he's here. That you won't embarrass me or do anything awkward that I'll have to invent a lie to explain. Promise me, Alex."

He ground his teeth together, furious that she assumed the worst of him. "I desire nothing but your happiness and pleasure," he said tersely. "I exist to serve you."

"That is a promise you had damned well better keep!" she said sharply, getting out of the car and slamming the door.

He followed her inside, placing as much distance between them as it was possible for him to do. She was too angry to notice that he had not promised a damned thing, and he didn't intend to. Regardless of what she thought about his job performance, he couldn't disobey the rules.

Entering the back door, he gave one of the kitchen chairs a kick.

Who the hell was Howard?

## Chapter Five

"How do I look?" Chelsey inquired nervously, smoothing her palms over the hips of a black silk pantsuit. A glitter belt hugged her waist. Her silk camisole was the same tawny ginger as her hair. As she liked the loose, wild curls that Alex had given her yesterday, she had kept the style, dressing it up for tonight by brushing back one side and securing it with a glitter comb.

"You instructed me not to speak to you."

She looked across the living room. "I'm still mad at you. But not as much."

Working in the yard had eased Chelsey's anger, but had increased her nervousness. While she planted geraniums along the back fence, Alex had knelt near the porch and experimented with flowers he wanted to remember. At one point her entire backyard, except for a circle around her, was filled with rye plants. When Chelsey jumped to her feet, pointing at the two-story houses overlooking her backyard, Alex had apologized and explained that peasants had grown rye around the village where he grew up north of Paris. He wanted to see and smell the rye fields again.

Aside from that moment and the moment when Chelsey had tersely announced she was going upstairs to take a long, relaxing bath, they had not spoken.

"You look beautiful," Alex said in a husky voice. His smoldering gaze lingered over the ginger-and-black silk that molded the curves of her body. Finally his gaze returned to hers. "May I offer you a glass of wine?"

"Thank you." Blushing at his close inspection, Chelsey turned toward the grandfather clock. Howard was never late.

Hastily she reviewed a mental checklist. Toothpaste, makeup, mouthwash, a change of lingerie for tomorrow. It all fit inside a large purse. She preferred the purse to an overnight bag, in case she had misunderstood Howard's intentions. Chelsey didn't think she had, but it was better to be on the safe side than risk embarrassment.

"Who is Howard Webber?" Alex asked, crossing his ankles on top of the ottoman.

Now she noticed Alex was dressed more formally than she had previously seen him. He wore a lightweight cream-colored turtleneck beneath a charcoal jacket that made his eyes seem more blue than blue-green. Navy slacks and shoes completed the outfit.

"You look nice tonight, too," Chelsey commented, trying not to stare. Alex looked gorgeous, like a male model. "This wine is very good. What is it?"

"It's a Spanish vintage. It was a great favorite during the late eighteenth century."

Chelsey checked the clock again. She tried to convince herself that she wasn't feeling apprehensive about going to bed with Howard. They were friends. He already knew she didn't have a perfect body. There would be an awkward moment or two, then everything would be fine. Maybe it would even be wonderful.

"We'll tell Howard the same story we told Betty, okay? You're an old friend from back east, we met in college, blah, blah, blah." She gave Alex a slightly narrowed look. "It's crucial that you don't slip and call me mistress. And please, no magic while Howard is here."

Alex moved to stand beside her, studying her fingers playing nervously with the wineglass. "Are you in love with this Howard person?"

She bit her lip and gazed into the amber wine, feeling uneasy that Alex stood so close. He wore cologne tonight, a fragrance she didn't recognize. The faintly musky scent made her think of rumpled sheets and bodies twined together.

She moved backward a step. "The relationship seems to be moving in that direction." A frown puckered her brow. "It's too soon to tell if it's love." Maybe after tonight.

"But Howard Webber is important to you."

She inhaled Alex's cologne and thought about feverish whispers and exploring hands. If the sofa hadn't hit the back of her knees, she would have moved backward another step. She swallowed and tried to recall what they were discussing. Howard.

"Howard's been a good friend at a time when I need all the friends I can get. When the university regents met to discuss...what happened last summer, Howard appealed to them on my behalf." Her eyes dropped to Alex's firm, wide mouth. When she realized she was staring, she made herself turn toward the front window. What was keeping Howard? "He's been very supportive during a difficult period."

"You aren't talking yourself into something, are you? Perhaps mistaking gratitude for something else?" Alex asked gently. His glance traveled slowly down her body. "Your blouse is the same silky color as your hair."

"It is?" she asked weakly, meeting his eyes. His eyes were as deep and blue-green as the Mediterranean. She could drown in those eyes.

Chelsey straightened abruptly and gave herself a shake. What on earth was she doing? Fantasizing about one man minutes before she planned to go off to spend the night with another.

Frowning, she tasted her wine, then lifted her chin. "I think Howard and I are developing a relationship that's important to both of us." Alex was temporary; Howard would always be there for her. She needed to keep that distinction uppermost in her mind. "Howard cares about me. Does it really matter if my feelings began with gratitude? Of course I'm grateful to him." She paused, trying to focus. "A lot depends on tonight." She thought about the items in her purse, then darted a look at Alex. "Look, are you absolutely sure that you can't read people's minds?"

"I sense things," he answered, smiling. "But I can't read minds, no."

"What kind of things do you sense?" Chelsey demanded.

He shrugged. "I know if a person is good or evil, if his or her intentions are beneficial or malignant. I can usually tell if a person is lying. Occasionally the knowledge is specific—usually it's more of a general impression."

Chelsey thought about that. Anxiety overwhelmed her better judgment. "What do you sense about me?"

Could he tell that his cologne reeled through her senses and made her feel hot all over? Did he know that the rich timbre of his voice occasionally sent a thrill up her spine? Was he aware of how often she recalled him standing naked on the staircase? A warm blush tinted her throat as she waved a hand. "Never mind, I don't want to know."

Stepping forward, he cupped her chin in one hand and looked deeply into her eyes. His touch paralyzed her, made her nerves fizz like the end of a frayed cord. "You are a genuinely good person, Chelsey," he said quietly. "Something troubles you deeply, something I don't know yet. And you don't have the confidence in yourself that you should have."

His gaze dropped to her mouth. Staring at her as if mesmerized, he ran his thumb across her lips. Time seemed to stop. Chelsey's breath halted in her chest, and her eyes widened helplessly. She could not have stepped away from him even if she had wanted to. His fingertips were light on her skin, but they possessed her, drew her closer to the hard heat of his body. She stared at his mouth, absorbed by the contours of rough promise, and felt her own lips part in expectation. The wineglass trembled in her fingers.

The doorbell rang.

For an instant neither of them moved. They continued to stare into each other's eyes, drawing the moment out.

Finally, her heart pounding, Chelsey made herself step past him, careful not to brush against his body. She had the absurd idea that if her body touched him, something explosive and earthshaking would happen.

"Saved by the bell," she said lightly, hearing the quaver in her voice. Howard, she reminded herself firmly. Howard is your future. Not Alex; not a genie. She glanced toward the front door, drew a breath, then whispered, "Remember . . . you gave your word. You promised not to mess this up for me."

After straightening her shoulders and arranging a smile on her lips, trying to behave as if she were sophisticated enough to leave an intense moment with one man and go off with another, sophisticated enough that dinner followed by a night in a hotel was nothing extraordinary, Chelsey stepped to the door.

"Howard! On time as usual. Please come inside, there's someone I want you to meet."

A slight pucker of annoyance dimmed Howard's smile, and he made a point of consulting his pocket watch. "Our dinner reservations are for eight, and it's a forty-minute drive...."

"This will only take a minute. I'd like you to meet an old college friend. Alex has an archaeology grant from Harvard." Each time she told the lie, it rolled from her tongue a little easier. There was something depressing in that. "Alex, this is Howard Webber. Howard heads Colorado University's English department."

Chelsey watched as the two men shook hands, warily taking each other's measure. Her heart sank. Standing next to Alex, Howard looked short, bland and uninteresting. His sandy hair was thinning on top, something Chelsey hadn't previously permitted herself to notice. Nor had she taken note of the smug quirk of his thin lips or noticed how small his eyes were. Although it was a warm night, Howard wore a wool tweed jacket with suede patches on the sleeves. The stem of a pipe poked out of his pocket. He held himself like a man utterly convinced of his own importance, a man infinitely superior to his peers.

Chelsey gave herself a sharp mental shake. Howard might not resemble a film star and he might be a bit pretentious and overbearing, but he was her friend. After tonight, he would be much more. Howard had stood by her when others had not. He had defended her to the university regents. Did it really matter that he liked to quote Hegel, Kierkegaard and Nietzsche in everyday conversation? Or that he preferred Chelsey to leave her cane at home when they went out? Howard cared about her.

She could see that he and Alex had taken an instant dislike to each other. As Chelsey anxiously watched, they examined one another like prizefighters sizing up an opponent.

"Well," Chelsey said, summoning a cheerful tone. "I'll just get my purse, and we'll be on our way." She hesitated, then chose her brass-handled cane, the one she preferred for evening. She hoped the cane wouldn't embarrass Howard too much, but her leg was aching from kneeling all afternoon in the garden. She had been too angry at Alex to plan ahead.

Taking Howard's arm, she let him hasten her to the front door. "Don't wait up," she called to Alex. Then she cast an uneasy look at Howard, trying to guess his thoughts. "We'll be late. Very late."

"Is Duport staying here, with you?" Howard asked in a low voice. When Chelsey nodded, his thick eyebrows clamped into a frown of disapproval. Chelsey suspected she would hear more about this later. Howard paused, then turned at the door to glare back at Alex. His arm tightened around Chelsey's in a proprietary gesture. He had to tilt his head back slightly, but he met Alex's steady eyes. "We'll be back after brunch tomorrow. I'm sure you understand."

A silent sigh dropped Chelsey's shoulders. On the one hand, she was secretly pleased and a little surprised to discover Howard's jealousy and possessiveness. On the other, she would have preferred not to reveal their plans so pointedly. Especially not to Alex.

Alex returned Howard's stare. "It makes no difference to me when we return," he said.

"Good," Chelsey said, stepping forward and reaching for the door handle. She froze. Surely Alex had not said *we*. Turning slowly, she leveled a long, now-hear-this stare. "There are leftovers in the fridge," she said evenly. "For your dinner. I'm sure you'll find plenty to do this evening, to occupy yourself while you're here. Alone. Do you understand?''

"I understand perfectly." He was so tall and so handsome and so damned sure of himself.

"Good," Chelsey said, holding his gaze. "Goodbye then," she called before she closed the door firmly behind her, feeling vastly relieved to escape before something went wrong. But she spoke too soon. She and Howard had not taken three steps before Alex spoke from directly behind her. Chelsey and Howard both jumped and whirled around.

"I believe you know the rule," Alex continued in a pleasant voice, speaking as if their conversation had not been interrupted.

"What rule?" Howard asked. He stared at Alex. "How did you get outside?"

Angry crimson flared upward from Chelsey's throat. She removed her hand from Howard's arm. "You go ahead. I'll be right behind you. I need to have a word with Alex." Her smile was grim.

Still staring at Alex with a puzzled expression, Howard pulled out his pocket watch and tapped a finger against the glass, reminding Chelsey that time was passing and they were running late. He looked as if he wanted to add something, but changed his mind and did as Chelsey asked. Each step signaled annoyance as he walked toward a green Ford parked at the curb.

When Howard was out of earshot, Chelsey whirled. "What do you think you're doing?" she asked furiously, speaking between her teeth.

Alex pushed his hands in his pockets and gazed down at her with a bland expression. "We're going out to dinner. Isn't that correct?"

"Don't play innocent with me! As you perfectly well know, that is not correct. Howard and I are going out to dinner. You are staying here. You are not invited." She stared at him. "Alex, don't take advantage of a weak moment. I'm not sure what happened between you and me a few minutes ago, but it changed nothing. Howard may be my future. I could fall in love with him. Now, don't mess this up!"

"As I have explained numerous times, oh forgetful mistress, I must remain within the sound of your voice."

"Not this time. This is a date, Alex, an important date. Tonight... Well, just take my word for it that tonight is very special. I thought I made that abundantly clear. Howard and I need to be alone."

"We have no choice." Alex spoke in a polite but firm voice. He glanced at Howard, who was standing beside the car, glaring at his watch. Alex's eyes twinkled and danced. "If it distresses you to have me ride inside with you, I'm willing to ride outside. I could still hear your voice if I sat on top of the car."

"Fun-ny," Chelsey snapped. She glanced at Howard, aware that his irritation increased by the second. Howard hated to wait, hated to be late. He was not a patient man. "I swear on all I hold dear that I will not be making any wishes tonight! Alex, you *cannot* come along!"

"My obligation is to remain by your side at all times." A twinkle of infuriating amusement accompanied his stubbornness.

Angry and starting to feel frantic, Chelsey clutched his lapels and gave him a shake. "Listen to me. What do I have to say to make you agree to remain here and leave us alone tonight?"

"There is nothing you can say, mistress. Where you go, I go."

Frustrated beyond reason, Chelsey stamped her cane on the walk. "Alex, this is crazy! You can't come with me on a date!"

"I regret to say the point is not negotiable."

Like hell he regretted it. He was enjoying the trouble he was creating. Before Chelsey exploded, Howard called to her, "We're going to be late!"

"I know, I know. I'll just be a minute." Leaning forward, she glared up into Alex's eyes and begged him. But it was hopeless. Chelsey recognized the unyielding truth in his gaze and in his posture. He was polite, he regretted everything, he was oh, so sorry. But he wasn't going to budge. "Damn it!" She could plead and argue from now until the next ice age and it wouldn't do any good. Alex's holy rules would not be broken; he would not yield an inch. Chelsey swore beneath her breath. "I hate this! Wait here," she said furiously, jabbing him in the chest with her finger. Leaning heavily on her cane, her thoughts racing, she stormed down the sidewalk toward Howard.

"Exactly what is going on here?" Howard demanded, scowling up the walkway to where Alex stood with his arms crossed over his chest. Alex wore a knowing smile that was designed to infuriate Howard. "Who is that bozo, anyway? And why is he staying at your place? Hasn't he heard of hotels?"

"Howard, we have a little problem." Reaching, Chelsey smoothed her hand down his jacket lapel. "You see..." As she had been doing since Alex popped into her life, she searched frantically for a plausible lie, hating the necessity. "The thing is, Alex is going through a rough time right now." She drew a long deep breath. "His wife died, and...well, I don't think he should be left alone."

"If he's so damned broken up, then why is the bastard smiling? And why does he look at you like he's undressing you in his mind? Is something going on between you two?"

Chelsey threw a venomous glance over her shoulder. Howard was right. Alex was smiling as if he knew a secret that Howard didn't. In another age a smile that insulting, that challenging, would have called for swords and the naming of seconds.

She spoke through clenched teeth. "Alex is an old friend, that's all."

"Then why haven't I heard you mention him before?"

"He may be smiling on the outside, but he's mourning on the inside." Chelsey fought the desire to dash up the walk and assault Alex with her cane. She and Howard weren't even out of the driveway and already the evening was turning sour. They were both in dark moods which Chelsey was about to worsen. She made herself do it because she could see no other choice. "Howard, I think it would be a nice gesture if we invited Alex to join us for dinner. He really shouldn't be alone."

"What?" Howard's mouth dropped open, then snapped shut. "Chelsey, I've been planning this particular evening practically since the day I met you!" Howard's gaze skimmed her lips, dropped suggestively to her breast. "I thought you understood. I also thought you shared my feelings...."

"I do!" At least, she thought she did. She wanted to. Chelsey bit her lip hard. "It's just that... Look, wait here. I'll talk to Alex again. There has to be a way to work this out."

"If he's nothing but an old friend, as you claim—" Howard drew back and raised a suspicious eyebrow "—then he'll understand that we want to be alone. He won't make a problem."

Chelsey winced. She understood Howard was challenging her to prove that she and Alex were only friends. He was sensing something fishy.

Leaving Howard standing beside the car frowning at his watch, she hurried up the walkway and gripped Alex's arm. Desperation darkened her eyes.

"Alex, listen to me. Are you absolutely, positively sure there is no way I can go on this date without you tagging along?"

"None," he confirmed, smiling pleasantly. Chelsey was beginning to detest the reasonableness in his smile.

"I'd hoped it wouldn't come to this, but...there is a way around this problem. I just thought of it. All I have to do is use my wishes."

His smile vanished and he frowned. "Chelsey—"

"Here's my first wish," she said, speaking rapidly and urgently. "I wish you had never appeared in my life. Are you listening?" A coin came into her hand. "I wish you would go back to your lamp or wherever you came from. I wish you would disappear and let me get on with my life. Adieu, Monsieur Duport, it's been fun. Goodbye." She stared into the amusement dancing in his eyes, and waited for him to vanish. When he didn't, she sighed. "Okay, Alex. Why are you still here?"

"Wishing your genie away is not in your best interests. It does not benefit you."

Behind her Howard began drumming his fingertips on the roof of the car. Chelsey could feel his stare and his growing anger.

"Okay, we'll try again. I wish for a diamond ring, I wish for great hair, I wish for a long, wonderful, uninterrupted evening alone with Howard. Those are my three wishes, here are the coins." Grabbing Alex's hand, she closed his fingers around the coins. "Grant me the wishes quickly, then take a hike while I still have a prayer of salvaging this mess. Better luck on your next mistress or master. Adieu. Adios. Goodbye and farewell.''

He smiled down at her, clinking the coins in his hand.

"Damn it!" She cast a nervous glance back at Howard. "Why aren't you gone?"

"It does not benefit you to squander your wishes on a hasty impulse."

"I am so frustrated I could scream!" She stamped her cane on the walk, then shoved back a lock of hair. "I plain don't believe this! Are you saying you won't grant three bona fide, legitimate wishes? You can't do that! Where do I go to file a complaint?"

"You're making a mistake, Chelsey. Are you aware that Webber plans to seduce you? The bastard has it all planned. The restaurant he's taking you to is located in a hotel."

"Augusta's is one of Denver's finest restaurants! And we're going to forfeit our reservations because of you!"

"After dinner Webber plans to take you upstairs to a hotel suite he has already rented. He plans to seduce you."

"Alex, I'm begging you. It's been a year and a half since I was last seduced. Can you understand what I'm saying? I *want* to be seduced. I can't wait to be seduced. I'm dying to be seduced! So get the hell out of the way and let it happen!"

"Howard Webber is not worthy of you. He's dung on a camel's tail."

Chelsey hastily checked her own watch. If Howard stepped on the gas and they made all the lights, they would only be fifteen minutes late for their dinner reservation. "Howard may not be a paragon of virtues, but neither am I. Alex, I'm begging you. Grant my wishes and let me go."

He bristled, swelling up before her eyes. "You are indeed a person of virtue, mistress. You are a beautiful!

woman with many fine qualities. Any man would be proud to call you his own." His dark head lifted to glare at Howard. "It pains me more deeply than you can guess that you wish to surrender yourself to a piece of camel dung like Howard Webber. But if that is your preference, then so be it." Inclining his head, he dropped into a deep salaam. "I shall make myself invisible. You will not be aware that I am present."

"Chelsey?" Howard's voice spiraled toward a shout. "This is getting ridiculous!"

"That won't work!" Chelsey's voice was as wild as her eyes. "I don't want you in the hotel room with Howard and me even if you're invisible! I'd feel— I don't want you there at all!" She pressed a hand against her forehead. "This is hopeless. Please, Alex," she whispered, her voice a plea. "Don't do this. Please let me have this night alone with Howard. Howard is the first man in a long time who... Please, I'm begging you not to ruin tonight."

He touched the back of his hand to her cheek, his touch gentle, almost sympathetic. Almost. "Dear mistress, the rules must be obeyed."

"You and your crazy rules are ruining my life!" And there was no way out, no acceptable solution. "This isn't going to work, is it?" Conceding the obvious and not waiting for an answer, Chelsey walked slowly back to Howard's car. Her purse strap hung heavy on her shoulder. Now she felt foolish about the items inside, the toothpaste and lingerie. The plans and hopes.

"Well, are you satisfied?" Howard asked angrily. "We've missed our dinner reservations."

"I'm sorry, Howard, but I think we'll have to postpone our special evening."

"I beg your pardon?" He stared at her. "Are you telling me that you're choosing him over me?"

"That isn't true. But it is true that I can't leave him right now." At some point between pacing back and forth between the two men, Chelsey had dropped her cane. Her leg was throbbing. With surprise she noticed twilight had faded to full darkness. "Believe me, I wish I could leave Alex behind. You'll never know how much I wish it. But I can't. It's impossible."

"I was right. There is something going on between you two!"

Alex moved up behind her, then stood in front of Howard, placing Howard at a distinct disadvantage. Alex was taller and leaner. More handsome, better dressed. His smile was cold and didn't reach his eyes.

"Allow me to explain," he said, speaking to Howard. Contempt flickered behind his hard gaze. "I am not permitted to leave my mistress's side until I have made her most secret desires come true."

"You bastard!" Howard said between his teeth.

"Alex, you are absolutely wrecking my life," Chelsey groaned. His choice of words and the look he gave her were deliberately sensual, deliberately intended to provoke. She closed her eyes in despair and her hands curled into fists. "Why are you doing this?"

Alex continued to stare a challenge at Howard. "I am obligated to remain within reach of my mistress's most tender whisper. Should her sweet lips murmur a wish, I must be near enough to hear it."

A dark plum color infused Howard's cheeks. He glared an accusation at Chelsey. "If you wanted to break it off, all you had to do was say so. You didn't have to humiliate me!"

"Howard, please! It isn't like that! I can explain everything if you'll just—"

"Forget it!" Outrage stiffened Howard's frame. His lips pressed together so tightly they disappeared. "I've heard all I need to hear."

"Howard, please listen." Despair pinched Chelsey's features. "I know how unbelievable this is going to sound, but Alex is—"

"You picked your moment, didn't you? You let me think we were going to have a 'special evening.' I'll bet you and your 'friend' had a lot of laughs planning this!"

Horrified by what Howard was saying, by what was happening, Chelsey watched helplessly as he marched around his car to the driver's side. She started to follow, but Howard shot her an icy smile across the roof of the car.

"Well, don't flatter yourself, Chelsey honey. I planned to dump you after tonight. You didn't really believe I'd settle for a cripple, did you? I can do a lot better than you."

Chelsey's head jerked as if he had slapped her. Shock froze her in place as Howard slid into his car and sped into the darkness. She stood on the curb, pressing her hand against the pain that filled her chest then expanded to fill her body.

"Revenge is a valid direct benefit," Alex said sharply, stepping up beside her. Anger shook his large frame. "You have only to wish it, and Howard Webber will suffer a fatal accident. He will never insult you or anyone else again."

A second wave of shock shot down Chelsey's spine. She stared up at him with wide, damp eyes. "I don't understand you. You're willing to murder a man if I wish it...but you wouldn't permit me to enjoy a romantic evening that would have harmed no one. What kind of monster are you?"

"You heard what Webber said. He intended to use you, then abandon you."

"He was speaking in anger! He thinks you and I are lovers, that we were deliberately toying with him, making a fool of him."

"He was also speaking the truth. He's small, petty and cruel. I knew everything about Howard Webber the instant I shook his hand."

"Stop it! I don't want to hear this." Bending, Chelsey found her cane in the grass, then, moving with as much dignity as her aching leg and devastated pride would permit, she returned to the house. By now she knew a locked door was no defense against a genie, but it made her feel marginally better to slam the door.

"You're far better off without Webber," Alex said, appearing beside her. "You deserve better."

"Do I?" Chelsey shouted, spinning to face him. "Howard was right. I am a cripple!"

That Alex had witnessed her humiliation devastated her. Alex, who was making a shambles of her life.

Tears sprang into her eyes and spilled down her cheeks, adding one more embarrassment to an evening overflowing with humiliation. Mortified, Chelsey grabbed the banister and fled up the staircase.

"Leave me alone!"

All she wanted was to wash her face, put on her oldest, most comfortable bathrobe and curl into a solitary ball on her bed. She hadn't felt this wretched since her mother made her attend her high school prom. Watching the others dance while she sat on the sidelines had driven a dagger into her heart. She felt the same humiliation now, the same hideous embarrassment of being publicly rejected.

Holding back the tears, she slammed her bedroom door behind her.

ALEX PACED IN THE HALLWAY outside her door, seething with jealously and righteous indignation.

How dare that self-centered, puffed-up, malicious little bastard even think of putting his hands on Chelsey.... The thought of it enraged him.

It wasn't enough merely to thwart Howard Webber's intentions. He wanted to punish Howard Webber and punish him decisively. As he recalled the deliberate cruelty of Webber's parting comments, Alex's jaw clenched and the blood pounded in his head. Watching Chelsey return to the house, holding her head high with quiet, painful dignity, was enough to make him shake with the need for revenge.

Pacing back and forth, he tried to think of a way to compensate Chelsey for her undeserved pain and her failed expectations for this evening. Although he detested sharing anything in common with Howard Webber, Alex conceded that he was as much to blame for Chelsey's pain as Howard was. If it had not been for Alex and the rules that bound him, Howard would not have deliberately insulted and wounded his mistress.

His obligation was to serve, not to agitate. To gratify, not to anger. But all he had accomplished so far was to upset Chelsey and disappoint her.

The admission made him feel wild inside. He wanted to blot out her bad experience with Webber. He wanted to restore her self-image and make her smile again. Damn it, he wanted her to be happy.

Somehow Chelsey Mallon was different from all the others. She had gotten under his skin and stirred something inside.

When he'd first met her, Alex had thought she was pretty and attractive, but he didn't recall thinking of her as stunningly beautiful. This omission now seemed incredible to him. When she was happy, Chelsey Mallon was the most beautiful creature he had ever observed. She took his breath away. Her smile could have launched the thousand ships attributed to Helen of Troy. Her sparkling eyes captured the sunlight with twin flames. No one observing her vivacious smile could resist smiling in return.

And there was much more. She possessed a quiet bravery and a generous heart. She combined spirit and vulnerability. Temper and compassion.

"Chelsey?" He knocked on her bedroom door.

"Go away!"

Had he remembered to list pride and stubbornness when he listed her unique qualities? The obstinate tilt of her chin was justified. She didn't capitulate easily, he thought, smiling. But then, neither did he. Their battle of wills was well matched.

"Chelsey, come here, please. I'm not going to stop knocking on your door until you come out."

"I mean it. Go away and leave me alone!"

"I have a surprise for you."

"I don't want a surprise! Give me a break, Alex. Just go away."

He rapped his knuckles on her door. "Chelsey?"

A long silence ensued during which he called to her again. Finally he heard her swear. A moment later the sound of angry footsteps approached the door.

"Shazam," he muttered, straightening his tie.

She flung open the door, her face furious. She wore an old bathrobe and her feet were bare. "This better be important, Alex, because—" Her angry words ended on a gasp and her eyes flared wide with astonishment. "Good God," she whispered, staring past him. "What happened to the hallway? Where did it go? Alex... where are we?"

# Chapter Six

They stood on the marble terrace of an Italian villa that had once belonged to a friend of Alex's, a fellow crusader. Soaring stone arches framed ribbons of moonlight glistening across the Mediterranean Sea. A warm night breeze floated off the waves, stirring the bougainvillea that dripped like crimson lace from huge terra-cotta urns.

"Since Roman antiquities are your specialty, I thought..." Here and there he had scattered marble pedestals topped by Roman artifacts. The air of Southern Italy shimmered with the luminous quality he had discovered nowhere else. Italy seemed a logical choice for her.

The delight in Chelsey's wide eyes told him that he had guessed correctly. His surprise had succeeded.

Lustrous marble tiles, stone balustrades and a warm moonlit sea were as romantic a vision as he could conjure. And he had not forgotten that Chelsey had missed her dinner. Positioned in the center of a high curving archway facing the sea was a long, lace-draped table. Paper-thin china and heavy silver gleamed beneath the soft radiance of scented candles.

"You shall have your romantic dinner," he announced firmly. Stepping forward, he took her hand and wrapped it around his arm, leading her forward.

"But, Alex..." She wet her lips then spoke in another whisper. "I'm not dressed for—"

"Shazam."

In an instant her terry bathrobe vanished. He dressed her in Grecian gauze, a petal-draped hem reaching to her ankles as he knew she would prefer. He gave her gold sandals and a gold bracelet that circled her upper arm. The low neckline and filmy material drew his gaze to her breasts, and he sucked in a low, hard breath. She was so beautiful. It required enormous willpower not to pull her into his arms and ravage that trembling mouth.

Chelsey didn't notice the hard intensity of his narrowed gaze. She peered down at herself with pleasure and wonder, then held the gown out from her body, letting the material slip through her fingertips like cobwebs. She raised a quick, self-conscious hand to her hair. Before she could speak, Alex dressed her hair in a tumbled upsweep, restraining the springy ginger curls with a gold circlet that rested at the top of her forehead. A few unruly tendrils escaped the circlet and curled beside her cheeks and at the nape of her slender neck.

"This is... It's... I don't know what to say," she murmured. She tried to smile, the effort self-conscious. "Did you give me the right makeup to go with this splendor?"

"Yes." But he hadn't. Her heart-shaped face required no artifice beyond a slight darkening of the lashes. Her skin was smooth and lovely, her mouth naturally rosy.

Raising the hem of the gown, she examined the gold sandals and thin straps that crisscrossed her calves. For a moment Alex believed she would protest his choice. She started to speak, but changed her mind. Instead, she took his arm again and allowed him to escort her to the table.

Alex could easily have provided a built-up shoe like she usually wore, but he deliberately decided against it. When she emerged barefoot from the bedroom, he had instantly noticed the shorter leg gave her a provocative, slightly rolling gait that he found wildly seductive. His eyes had been riveted to her undulating hips and sexy walk.

Swallowing, he mounted a heroic effort not to dwell on those perfect curving hips and fought to ignore the yielding softness of her breast brushing his arm. Concentrating, he made himself focus on the scents of the food and the perfumed fragrance of the air instead of the sweet apple scent rising from her skin and hair.

After holding out her chair, he stepped backward away from temptation. "Is everything to your liking, mistress?" The array of serving dishes marching down the long table included everything he had imagined she might enjoy.

"Oh yes," she answered softly, gazing toward the moonlight shimmering on the sea. Silver-capped waves whispered up a pebbled beach and foamed around a rock outcropping. A swollen moon filled the sky like a plump lemon resting on black velvet. "Alex..." She touched her fingertips to her throat and gazed up at him, her eyes as soft as her voice. "Is this real? Or am I dreaming?"

He smiled, hungering to kiss her. "It is real."

"I don't know how to thank you for all this." Her hands rose, then fluttered back to her lap. "It's just... It's magical. The sea, the flowers, the moonlight shining on the marble, all this...." A gesture indicated the table and candelabra, the urns and stone arches, the scented air, her gown.

"It isn't necessary to say anything," he said, pleased by her dazed reaction. Clearly she was not thinking about that bastard, Howard Webber. "Enjoy your dinner, mistress." Inclining his head, he stepped backward, hoping to fade into the shadows. But he was unable to take his eyes off of her.

Candlelight alternately disclosed then shadowed her face and the tops of her breasts, softly illuminating her skin, enhancing the satiny glow of strawberry and pale ivory tones. Her eyes were fringed pools of dark liquid. The warm night breeze toyed with loose curls framing her graceful throat. Hungrily, Alex stared at her beauty and felt his stomach tighten sharply.

For several minutes she sat very still, gazing out at the waves and moonlight. Once she lowered her head and raised her fingertips to her eyes. At length she reached for her wine and returned her attention to the table. But Alex didn't begin to relax until he watched the tension drain from her shoulders and thought he glimpsed a smile.

"Alex?"

In an instant he was at her side, worried that he had overlooked some crucial element. "Mistress?"

A flash of exasperation compressed her features. "What is it going to take to break you of that habit? Please don't call me mistress! It's causing me no end of problems."

"For which I apologize," he murmured, bowing to conceal a smile. "How may I serve you?"

"Everything you've done is wonderful—enchanting, in fact—and I'm deeply grateful."

"But . . . ?" A frown drew his heavy eyebrows.

She smiled, and at once he relaxed, thinking how absolutely lovely she was. He wondered if she guessed how wildly desirable she was. He suspected she had no idea.

"There's something missing. Usually a romantic dinner is more successful if two people are present, don't you agree?" A twinkle of humor returned to her wonderful dark eyes. "Dinner for one sort of defeats the whole idea. Will you join me?"

"I would be delighted." Being uncertain of her mood, he hadn't anticipated that she would welcome company. Especially his. It flattered and pleased him that she did.

"No, don't sit way down there. Sit here beside me so we can talk." Tilting her head, she squinted down the length of the table. "I've seen tables like this in films and I always thought it was a lonely arrangement."

He took the seat to her right and draped a snowy napkin across his dinner jacket and slacks. "Will you have mushrooms or shrimp or escargot?" he inquired.

"The mushrooms, I think." She watched him serve the mushrooms, then shrimp for himself. "Why did you look so surprised when I asked you to join me?"

"I assumed you were still furious with me. And rightly so."

"Alex..." She dropped her head and frowned at the lace cloth. "About tonight..."

"I'm deeply sorry for my role."

A sigh lifted her magnificent breasts, and he almost spilled the shrimp platter. "You were only following your rules."

"Chelsey, is it necessary to discuss this? I'd hoped to help you forget it."

"There are a few things that need to be said." She drew another full breath that molded the gauzy material of the gown around her full breasts. Alex stared. He could almost see her nipples through the filmy material.

"I was wrong to get so angry, and I apologize. I'm still learning about genies. It sounds stupid now, but I didn't think your rules would apply to a date. I know," she added, raising a hand. "You've made it clear that you have no control over the rules—they must be obeyed. I didn't think the situation through. I should have verified my assumptions. Then, when they proved wrong, I should have phoned Howard and postponed our evening."

"Postponed?" he asked, searching her eyes. "Or canceled?" He was doing it again. Intruding in her life.

She turned to face the night sea, gripping her napkin in her hands. Circles of pink bloomed on her cheeks. "I was trying so hard to convince myself that I could fall in love with Howard. Trying so hard to be the person Howard wanted that I didn't ask myself if Howard was what I wanted." She turned and met his eyes with a clear gaze. "Obviously, he isn't."

"I'm glad to hear it."

"Everyone I know will be." A suggestion of regret hovered around a half smile. She shook her head, then sampled one of the mushrooms before she leaned forward to steal a shrimp off his plate. Her unconscious theft charmed him as much as the sudden, breathtaking glimpse of her cleavage.

"Howard is a closed chapter, and I have you to thank. I guess I always knew he was a mistake. But after he defended me to the regents..." She shrugged. "He kept pushing for a relationship, and I coasted along, letting it happen. I was grateful, plus he didn't seem to mind that..." The color deepened in her cheeks. "That isn't important anymore."

Alex refilled their champagne flutes. "What happened last summer in Istanbul? Why was it necessary for Howard, or anyone, to defend you?"

When she tilted her head back, the breeze caught the tendrils at her neck and teased them across her smooth, bare shoulders. "I wish I didn't have to tell you about Istanbul." Hastily she lowered her head and raised her palm. "That's rhetorical, not a real wish. But I have decided on my first real wish, and it's connected to what happened last summer. So I guess I'll have to tell you." A plea appeared in her eyes. "But not now, not tonight. Alex, this moment is too magical to spoil. We'll talk about Istanbul tomorrow, okay?"

"As you prefer." Someone besides Webber had hurt her. He saw the pain and embarrassment in her eyes before she looked away.

During dinner they restricted their conversation to safe topics that carried no emotional charge. Both shared an interest in history, and Alex listened avidly to Chelsey's anecdotes about digs and historical finds. He contributed a few anecdotes of his own, delighted when he made her laugh. They traded memories of traveling in Italy, Greece, and the Middle East. They discussed art and music. Alex told his camel story; Chelsey told her train story. They talked about interesting people they had met or known, compared their favorite foods.

After dinner, Chelsey gave him a smile that electrified his skin. She gazed into his eyes. For a minute, all Alex could think about was sweeping her into his arms and molding her womanly heat against his hard body. She looked pliant and yielding, soft eyed and moist lipped. His body ached from wanting her.

"Tell me about you," she said softly, folding her arms on the cleared table and giving him an attentive, speculative look that required another effort of will not to misunderstand. Such seductively intent gazes had undone many a man. "I know you were a crusader. Once you had a wife. Now you're a genie. Tell me more about the man who is going to make my wishes come true."

He shrugged, glancing away from her feathery long lashes, soft lips and the glowing skin he wanted to stroke and caress.

"Alex?"

"There isn't much to tell. My father was a blacksmith, my mother raised eight children of which three survived to adulthood. I was the second-oldest son. My family lived in a cottage in a farm village about sixty miles north of Paris. It might as well have been a million miles. I knew only one man who had traveled more than fifteen miles outside the village, our liege lord, Baron Duvoux. When Duvoux called for men to join his Crusade, I was among the first to appear at the fortress."

"Were you a religious man? Was that why you were eager to enlist in a Crusade?"

"I wasn't especially religious," he answered. "But Duvoux was, and I believed in Baron Duvoux and in his philosophy and ideals. Duvoux took an interest in me—I was educated at the manor with his sons. What I wanted was to discover what existed beyond the perimeters of the rye fields. I wanted to see and know the world. I wanted to experience all that life could offer a man with no wealth and few prospects." He smiled at the memory.

"Ah," Chelsey said, returning his smile. "The second-son syndrome."

"In my day only the first son could inherit. Not that there was much to inherit in my family. The prospects were uncertain for Jean and dismal for myself and my younger brother. There were many who joined the Crusades in search of adventure, glory, or, like myself, a future."

She touched his hand and gazed into his eyes, speaking softly. "It was Selidim who made you into a genie, wasn't it?"

He nodded, idly lacing his fingers through hers. Her hand combined strength and softness, another of the contradictions that fascinated him.

"Mehmed argued for having me drawn and quartered, but Selidim possessed a more subtle hatred. He sought a punishment worse than death—he wanted disillusionment and his own form of justice. To Selidim, I represented all the crusaders who arrived in waves to subjugate his people, to impose a foreign philosophy upon him and his subjects. He turned the tables by deciding that I would spend eternity bound in servitude to others, granting wishes instead of imposing them." His grim smile did not reach his eyes. "To Selidim, this was punishment founded in basic justice. There is a certain ironic elegance to his reasoning."

"Selidim possessed the power or the magic to do such a thing?" Chelsey whispered. "Obviously he did, but...?"

"I can't explain how it was done. I don't know. But yes, the dark arts exist, and Selidim had mastered them."

Her eyes were so intent, so large and dark and filled with sympathy, that Alex felt as if he were drowning in soft brown velvet. His thighs tensed and his jaw tightened. He wanted her with an urgency that was becoming physical pain.

"What happens when you are not serving a master or mistress? Where do you go?"

"I can't explain, at least not the physical place," he said, frowning at her lips. "I don't know. It's like being submerged in a floating dream state." He looked away from the distraction of seductive lips and eyes, seeking words to describe the indescribable. "I dream the world as it's happening. I saw Columbus land in the New World, observed Napoleon's march to Moscow, witnessed the ovens at Dachau. I observed the triumphs of Washington, Jefferson, Lincoln, Kennedy.... I watched it all as if in a dream. The wars and broken treaties. The inventions, the industry, the progress. I dreamed it."

After a pause, she asked, "Is that why you seem so modern and up-to-date? It isn't that you're out of touch with the world—you're aware of all that occurs. But you only dream it?"

"The frustration of the dream state is the lack of sensation. I observe and hear, but I cannot taste or smell or touch. It's as if—" he searched for an adequate comparison "—as if you lived within your television set. The figures are negatives. They have no weight or substance, no compelling reality. You can observe and learn, but you can experience nothing sensory, can affect nothing. After a time, you begin to question reality itself. What is it? Does it exist? In the dream state there is no pain, no pleasure. No sense of time passing. No hunger, no weariness, no comfort or discomfort. There are no sensations beyond the inadequate facilities of memory."

Shock knit her brows. "I can't imagine existing like that."

"If the dream state were all there could be or would be, perhaps such an existence would be tolerable. But there are moments of emergence into the reality plane, two or three hours when I'm summoned to a reminder of all the richness of experience that I can no longer enjoy. This world—" he flexed his shoulders and spread his hands "—is so bright and noisy and ripe with scents and tastes and textures. It's so raw and splendid and *alive!*"

For a long moment, she sat looking at him without speaking. "It must be terrible to return to the dreaming."

"Returning is agony," he admitted simply. There was no bid for pity in his voice. "I promise myself I will remember the scent of a wood fire or the fragrance of a rose or the earthy good smell of a horse's sweat. I think it's not possible to forget the sweetness of summer wine or the rich tang of Greek olives and cheese. Or the taste of bread. I'm certain I will recall the difference between a dog's warm fur and the silky hair of a child. Always I am wrong. There is no memory more elusive than that of a scent or a taste or a touch. They tantalize but evaporate and cannot be retrieved."

"I'm sorry." Her sympathy filled his vision. The scent of her skin reminded him of apples on a summer day. Her hand gripped his. "How long must this punishment endure? When will Selidim release you?"

A harsh laugh shattered fantasies of kissing her until she grew dizzy in his arms. "Selidim has been moldering in his tomb for centuries. He was not fool enough to wish eternity for himself. Eternity is a punishment."

"I don't understand," Chelsey said, frowning. "If Selidim is dead, then who imposes your rules?"

"The rules simply are. They were never explained, yet I knew them." He stroked his thumb across the back of her hand. "This experience with you, this prolonged stay in the reality plane, has been enlightening. I'm learning new rules."

"Heaven help us," she said, smiling and rolling her eyes.

He returned her smile. "For instance, I didn't know I required sleep."

"Thirty minutes isn't sleep. It's a catnap."

"And I've discovered I can eat without feeling sated."

A deep, smoky look appeared behind his eyes, and Chelsey's heartbeat quickened. She imagined him wondering if there were other things he could do without feeling sated.

Dropping her head, she caught a breath and studied their clasped hands. His hands were large and strong, yet the fingers were tapered and elegant. A few silky dark hairs showed between his wrist and cuff. "How long can you stay in the reality plane? Are there rules governing that?"

"The problem hasn't risen before." He gazed at her, hoping to memorize her lovely face. Her hair formed a slight peak at her forehead, enhancing the heart shape of her face. "I'll know if a governing rule emerges. I'll feel an inner pressure."

One delicate, ginger-colored eyebrow lifted, and she laughed, her eyes soft and shining in the candlelight. "You must have thought I was an idiot when I mentioned that nonsense about you sleeping in the cup lamp."

"Not an idiot." He paused, then grinned. "But you have to admit it was a peculiar idea." She was so lovely that he couldn't look away from her.

"No one has ever made that suggestion before?"

"I've never been in the reality plane long enough that where I slept or if I slept was a concern. Moreover, past ages have been more willing to accept a genie than this age seems to be. There were fewer questions."

When she smiled, her entire face lit from within. "You could search the world over and I doubt you'd find three people who would admit to actually believing in genies."

Returning her smile, he lifted her hand and pressed her palm over his heart. "As you can see, genies are very real."

Their eyes met and held. An aeon passed and worlds collided while two people gazed into each other's eyes and glimpsed dark whirlpools of promise.

That's how it felt to Chelsey as she pressed her hand against the rock-solid warmth of his hard chest. As if time had stopped to allow this moment to expand and expand until she thought the growing tension between them would cause her to fly apart inside. In self-defense, she finally cleared her throat self-consciously and gently withdrew her hand. She lowered her gaze and laid aside her napkin. "Thank you for tonight, Alex. This was absolutely lovely. Most of all, I appreciate what you were trying to do."

"Did I overlook anything?" He was still staring at her with those blazing blue-green eyes that asked so many questions and promised so much.

She glanced at the sea beyond the urns of flowers and released a sigh. "This is so perfect. The only thing missing was music." A teasing twinkle enlivened her lovely dark eyes, lightening the moment. "Frankly, the conversation was so interesting that I didn't notice until now."

"Shazam," he said, humoring her with the nonsense word.

A forty-piece orchestra appeared on a dais at the far end of the terrace. Chelsey laughed out loud and clapped her hands as the haunting strains of a Viennese waltz reached them across the expanse of moonlit marble tiles.

"Wonderful!"

Taking her fingertips, Alex drew her to her feet and led her to the stone balustrade overlooking the sea. He should have remembered music. Music and dancing were an integral part of a romantic evening. Of course she would expect music.

Turning her to face him in the moonlight, he paused for an instant to look at her, then gently guided her into his arms, intending to dance. But the stunning warmth of her woman's body momentarily paralyzed him. This, above all things, was impossible to remember in the dream state—the yielding softness of a beautiful woman's curves, her warm seductive scent, the quickening of breast and breath, the explosive passion hinted in shining eyes and parted lips.

He held her firmly against his body, against his hard instant arousal, while tides of erotic sensation rocked his senses.

The instant Alex guided her into his arms, Chelsey experienced the force of a lightning strike. She, too, felt paralyzed. His hand seared through her gown as if the gauzy material had fallen away, and his fingertips explored her naked skin. Her blood heated and raced through her body with a tingling sensation. A deep hot tremor began in the pit of her stomach and thrilled through her limbs. With her trembling hands on his shoulders, she gazed into Alex's smoldering eyes, and her mouth went dry as she read his desire. Something stunningly physical was happening that had never happened to her before.

She could feel each single fingertip on her back, gentle yet masterful, sensitive yet mapping the feel and heat of her, sending earthquake tremors through her nervous system.

Standing hip to hip with him, she could feel his body hard against hers, as taut and urgent as the physical hunger blazing in his eyes. An answering passion swept through Chelsey's body like a soaring flood tide. Because she could not help herself, because suddenly she desperately needed to touch him, Chelsey lifted a shaking hand and stroked her fingertips across his jawline, then traced his lips, surprised to discover the firm contours disguised a softness she had not expected. Her touch sent a shudder down his body and he groaned softly.

"Alex, I feel . . ."

Gazing into his eyes sent the world spinning around her. His personal magic electrified the air and his eyes and hands and body, and it electrified Chelsey, as well. She felt his restrained power, felt as if her nerve endings were fizzing and throwing off sparks. She gazed into his smoldering eyes and trembled with wanting to taste his kiss.

Alex's intense gaze held hers as he lifted a hand and gently raised her chin. Not looking away from her, he lowered his head until his mouth almost touched her lips, until their breath mingled and tension crackled between them.

Then he paused, a pause that sent her nerves into a frenzy, and one dark eyebrow lifted.

"Yes," she whispered when she understood. "Yes."

Finally his lips softly brushed hers, teasingly, tentatively, as if he expected her to resist and pull away from him. When she offered no resistance—could not resist—Alex's arms tightened around her and he kissed her again. This time he pulled her tightly, almost roughly, against his tall hard body. This time his mouth was not soft, but demanding, hot and eager on hers, claiming her, possessing her.

Chelsey could not have resisted him if her life had depended upon it. Never had she been kissed like this. Never. Alex's kiss, increasingly hard and insistent, shot a burning brand through Chelsey's body, scorched across her nervous system. Her knees weakened and she swayed dizzily against him, gripping his shoulders for support. Then his tongue parted her lips, and she gasped as he plundered the sweetness within.

When they drew apart to gaze into each other's eyes, Alex tightened his arms and held her so close she could feel his heartbeat pounding against her breast, could feel his powerful arousal. He pressed his face into her hair with a low groan.

"If you only knew how long it's been since I've wanted a woman as much as I want you...."

Chelsey felt weak from the force of a sudden explosive passion. Never had a man's kiss or a man's touch affected her as Alex's kiss had. Never had she experienced this kind of erotic urgency, this passionate blend of confusion and desire, this melting dizziness at a man's caress. Only his powerful hands on her waist kept her from falling—that and the strength of her growing desire.

"Alex," she whispered, "Alex," needing to say his name aloud, hearing it emerge as a soft moan of yearning and wonder. "Alex." There was urgency and discovery in her whisper, surprise and desire.

This time when he kissed her, there was no hint of holding back. His mouth was as hard and demanding as his body, possessive on hers. His large hands molded her hips, forming her body tightly against his. Her arms wound around his neck, her fingers twisted through his hair. She could not think, could not breathe, she could only feel the hot wild sensations flooding her secret places. The sea and sky fell away and nothing existed but Alex. Alex. His mouth, his eyes, his large hands exploring her body and her own breathless response and burning desire.

Chelsey had never before felt this sudden volatile need and flooding passion, this sensitivity to a man's slightest nuance and to the contrast of his hard masculine body crushing her feminine softness. The yin and yang of oneness. Never had she been so powerfully aware of her own physical desires.

Kissing, frantically touching each other, swaying to the music, they clung together, fingers flying, stroking and discovering, lost in the magical wonder of what was happening to them.

It seemed so natural when Alex's hand slipped around Chelsey's waist, when he cradled her hand close to his chest and stepped forward as the music swelled and enveloped them.

Chelsey stumbled.

Cold reality washed over her. She returned to her senses as abruptly as if she had been splashed with a bucket of ice water. Shock and repugnance trembled down her body.

Alex wanted to *dance*.

White-faced and shaking, she flattened her palms against his chest and sharply pushed him away from her. The gesture was automatic and involuntary. She could not have prevented it even if she'd wanted to.

"I don't dance!" she snapped furiously, her voice a choked whisper.

That Alex would expect her to dance devastated her with a force as painful as Howard's comments. With her shorter leg and without her special shoes, she couldn't possibly dance. She would be graceless and awkward, stumbling after him in a clumsy parody. An object for ridicule and laughter.

"I don't know how to dance. I can't."

It was so obvious that he should have guessed, should have known. Feeling betrayed and confused, Chelsey spun and hurried toward the nearest door, knowing she looked clumsy and ridiculous, praying that the door led back to her bedroom.

When she saw her old bathrobe folded across her spread, she dashed inside and slammed the door behind her. Leaning against the door, she drew a long, shuddering breath that ended on a sob. Throwing herself on the bed, she curled into a ball and pressed her palms against the hot tears stinging her eyes.

If only. Damn it ... if only.

Her traitorous imagination revealed what it might have been like. Alex, tall and handsome, holding her, his attention focused intently on her. Chelsey, willowy and fluid in his arms, her gauzy hem floating behind as he whirled her around and around the marble terrace. Moving together in faultless harmony, a poem of symmetry and grace. It would have been an enchanted waltz to end a perfect evening.

So lovely. So impossible.

"Chelsey?" Alex rapped on her bedroom door. "Chelsey, I'm sorry. It didn't occur to me that you don't dance. I'll teach you."

What kind of fool did he think she was? Did Alex believe she was a masochist who enjoyed humiliating herself? That she welcomed fresh opportunities to look clumsy and awkward?

A dozen angry retorts sprang to Chelsey's tongue. But what was the point of sarcasm? Would it change anything to reveal that she would rather be tortured than go lurching around a dance floor?

"Forget it," she said in a dulled voice. She was too upset, too beat down, too lacking in energy to fight any more battles tonight. She hoped he wouldn't argue.

"There's no reason why you can't—"

"I'm tired, Alex," she snapped, cutting him off. "Thank you for dinner and for trying to help. Right now I just want to go to sleep." She couldn't believe that Alex was cruel, wouldn't allow herself to consider such a possibility. He had committed a thoughtless error, that was all.

After a long pause, he called softly through the door. "Good night, Chelsey." A current of disappointment flowed beneath his voice. That was what Chelsey heard the loudest. And that hurt the most. She had not lived up to his expectations.

Hot color flooded her cheeks. Alex had no right to expect anything from her. She didn't care what he thought about her. Alex Duport would only be a brief interlude in her life; that's all he could be. Tomorrow Chelsey would make her first legitimate wish, and soon her genie would disappear. A year from now she would look back and wonder if she had imagined all of this.

Chelsey's chest tightened and she bit her lip sharply. She lay in the darkness, staring up at the ceiling and remembering the exciting thrill of his large hands exploring her body, the passionate brandy-tasting kisses. No man had ever made her feel so utterly desirable. Already she understood that for the rest of her life she would compare all other men to Alex.

And none would be his equal.

# Chapter Seven

The Flatirons were Boulder's most distinctive feature. The vertical slabs of reddish limestone reared into the Western sky like jagged, giant lengths of sidewalk set on end. When Chelsey needed a quiet place in which to ponder a problem, she headed for the mountain meadows rolling back from the top of the Flatirons.

She clenched her jaw and shifted down, not looking at Alex. They had hardly exchanged three words this morning. Last night he had been a charming, attentive companion, wildly sexy. This morning he was still wildly sexy, but he'd gone gothic on her. Chelsey imagined she could see a chip on his shoulder, could definitely see the wariness in his brooding eyes. Distance and a hint of hostility had returned to his posture and voice.

Okay, maybe he was right to be angry. He had tried to do something nice for her and she had ended up spoiling the evening. But there was more than the dancing incident and their continuing misunderstandings to make them both edgy and tense today.

There was the second thing: the memory of deep, feverish kisses and frantic touches.

From the corner of her eyes, Chelsey could see Alex's hands and long legs. He wore bleached jeans and a white shirt opened at the collar wide enough that she could glimpse a few curls of crisp dark hair. Occasionally, taut muscles jumped along his neck and shoulders, and she was aware that his gaze frequently returned to her own jeans-clad thighs.

Her fingers tightened on the steering wheel. There had been one stunning moment last night when she knew she would surrender to him. She had, in fact, expected the evening would end in rapturous lovemaking, and she had wanted it to end that way. She'd had a narrow escape.

In the bright light of day, logic kicked in. Making love to Alex would have been a mistake, a crazy lapse of judgment. Alex was a genie, for heaven's sake. There could be no commitment from his side, no tomorrow, no future. All he could offer was pure sex.

Which, she thought, sliding a glance toward his thighs, wasn't all that bad. This uncharacteristic thought shocked her, and a long sigh escaped her chest.

They didn't speak until they had almost reached the meadow that Chelsey thought of as her own. She cleared her throat and cut a sidelong look toward the passenger seat, deciding she might as well get the apologies over with. Alex sat beside her with his eyes closed, inhaling the clean, cool scent of pine and fir. The breeze tumbled his longish hair. He looked as if his thoughts were a million miles away. And he was heart-achingly handsome.

Chelsey drew a long breath and released it slowly, pushing away thoughts of his kisses and her own breathless response. "Look, Alex, I'm sorry about last night. You're feeling angry and unappreciated, and you have every right to feel that way. You did something lovely for me and I responded by ruining everything."

"I am here to serve you, mistress," he said without opening his eyes. "The fault was entirely mine. I failed to anticipate correctly. You have no need to apologize for anything."

"Yes, I do." She kept her gaze on the road, trying to sort through the stew of frustration and regret that bubbled in her thoughts. The important thing about last night was the hungry passion that had exploded between them. Even now Chelsey couldn't help responding to Alex's sheer physical impact. Seeing his heavy thighs from the corner of her eyes make her feel weak and hot inside, shaky and a little unsure of herself. But she sensed they wouldn't talk about that. They would talk about the other important thing—her bad behavior.

Her hands tightened on the wheel, and she didn't look at him. "I had no right to suppose you'd know that even the thought of dancing is painful and embarrassing for me. I guess I assumed you knew that being unable to dance is the limitation I most regret." When he said nothing, she stumbled on. "Slow dancing looks so dreamy and graceful. Fast dancing looks like great fun." Still he didn't speak. "I tried it once. I was awkward, graceless. Let's just say I avoid dance floors as if they were poison. I guess you didn't know, Alex, I'm sincerely sorry that I exploded. It's just that the evening was so perfect, so wonderful. Then... And it shocked me. I reacted very badly and I apologize."

He opened his eyes and studied the pink on her cheeks. "I'm only a genie, Chelsey, not a mind reader. Before I appear to a new master or mistress there's a brief span of cognizance in which I see the new master's life in very broad strokes. I knew you were an orphan with no surviving family. I knew you were a professor of archaeology at the university and had published three respected papers. I understood that you'd suffered a childhood illness which left you feeling crippled."

Chelsey winced and pressed her lips together.

"I'm sorry, but that's how you see yourself. The point is, I don't know the details of your life or your emotions unless you choose to share that information. Sometimes it seems you ignore your handicap entirely, refusing to give in to discomfort or pain. Other times you impose limitations that don't seem logical to me. If I offended you, all I can do is apologize."

Instantly Chelsey bristled. Her knuckles turned white on the wheel. "All my limbs are functional and I'm not in a wheelchair, but I *am* disadvantaged. There *are* things I can't do or things I prefer not to do because I'd look like a clumsy fool and open myself to ridicule. But I'm the one with the bum leg, Alex. It's up to me which challenges I choose to tackle and which I don't. Those choices don't have to be logical to you or anyone else!"

"Look, Chelsey, before this gets out of hand, let me say that I admire all you've overcome. It isn't easy being alone in the world. You've had to fight for everything you've achieved and you haven't had much outside help. You've managed to overcome physical discomfort and accomplish goals that must have seemed daunting in the beginning." She felt his stare. "All I'm suggesting is that you may have a few blind spots. It's possible that you impose a few false limitations on yourself."

"Really?" she snapped, jerking the wheel through a hairpin curve. She didn't like the direction this conversation had taken. "I doubt Howard Webber would agree that a person with one short leg has no limitations."

"Chelsey, I never said—"

"And Howard never made me feel like a coward because I wouldn't humiliate myself by trying to dance!"

"You know that was never my intention," he said coldly. "But if you believe it is, then again—I apologize."

An icy silence pushed against the warm air rushing in the windows. Chelsey let the silence continue until she couldn't stand it another minute.

"All right, damn it. I'm sorry," she said angrily, confused by a tangle of emotions. "Somehow I feel I've been maneuvered into arguing in favor of being regarded as severely handicapped, an image I've resented and fought against all my life." A humorless smile tightened her lips. "How did that happen?"

"You tell me."

"I can't." She shoved back a lock of hair that had tumbled across her forehead. "What I can tell you is that I've never in my life had as much trouble communicating with someone as I do with you. It's so frustrating! All I've done since you popped into my life is apologize for one thing after another. And when I'm not apologizing—then you are. I don't understand this, and I hate it! What's going on here?"

He was silent, swaying with the motion of the car as the tires bumped over rocks that had fallen into the rutted fire road.

"I'm probably to blame," he said finally.

"Please." Chelsey took her eyes from the road long enough to scowl at him. "I hate it when you go into the genie routine that insists the customer is always right. Sorry, Alex. That isn't honest and that isn't how it works in the real world. It takes two to argue, two to have a misunderstanding. I'm right in here, doing my part to screw things up. We're not going to find a solution to our communication problems if you insist on taking the blame. Especially when you don't really believe you're at fault. You're just accepting the blame to smooth things over."

It was a long speech, and she paused for breath and a chance to get her emotions back in control. But it made her angry when Alex patronized her by acting like a genie. Which, she realized, was about as reasonable as getting angry at a dog for barking.

For the first time today, Alex smiled. "This time I'm not just smoothing things over."

Chelsey rolled her eyes and muttered.

"Hear me out. It's genuinely possible that I'm the source of the communication problem. I don't have occasion to use communication skills very often. Frankly, there's a lot I've forgotten about the turmoil of human emotions, the confusion, uncertainty and ambiguity. The frustration of trying to please someone and understand them is something I don't deal with on a frequent basis. Believe me, granting wishes is a snap compared to negotiating the battlefield of simple conversation."

"Okay," Chelsey conceded, somewhat mollified. "That makes a certain amount of sense. And I guess it would help if I'd quit making assumptions. If we both do. At least we can try. Deal?"

"It's a bargain."

The worst of it was over, Chelsey thought with relief. With the apologies behind them, they could go on without the cool silences that were making her acutely uncomfortable. Already she sensed a thawing from Alex's side of the car.

For her part, her traitorous mind suddenly conjured the memory of Alex standing naked on her staircase. She swallowed hard and thrust away the image of long lean lines, of tight muscles and buttocks. She had a depressing suspicion that all her life she would wonder what it would have been like to make love to him.

But Alex wasn't the only person with rules; she had a few of her own. Chelsey Mallon had never had a one-night stand in her life and that was a rule she didn't intend to change. Sex was not casual to her. Sex meant commitment. Sex was the beginning of forever and happily ever after. Unfortunately, Alex could never make a commitment to a woman. And certainly no sane woman would commit to a genie. At best Alex could be only a fleeting passion. And that didn't work for Chelsey.

"I'm going to fill in a few of those details you mentioned," she said, concentrating on the twisting, rutted road. "It's time to explain last summer." And it was definitely time to change the direction of her thoughts. "I know what I want to wish for. But I keep wondering if I've made the wisest choice. There are so many possibilities that it's difficult to decide. I'm about to spend one, probably two, of my wishes. And suddenly I'm having second thoughts."

Immediately Alex sat up straight and shifted in the seat to look at her directly. "Are you ready to make a wish, mistress?"

"Soon. Within the hour."

"Excellent."

Chelsey noticed he kept his voice carefully emotionless. She didn't have a clue as to what he might be thinking. Did he regret that he was soon to be one wish closer to his return to the dream state? He had to be thinking that.

Frowning, she eased the tires over a pile of rocks in the road, then stepped on the gas to urge the car over the next rise. The last wish was going to be very difficult to make, knowing that it would condemn Alex to leave the reality he so obviously craved and loved.

And she would miss him when he left her. A lot. The admission surprised Chelsey although it shouldn't have. Her association with Alex had been brief and often confusing, but it was also intense and highly emotional. Their unusual circumstance was forging a bond that bypassed ordinary conventions. Also, Chelsey could think of no other person who could have the impact on her life that Alex was exerting. There were the wishes, of course. And the awakening of physical desire. And because of Alex she would never again dismiss unlikely claims as silly or impossible. Maybe there really were UFOs and alien visitors. A week ago she would have scoffed; now she wasn't sure.

*Yes, Chelsey, there is a Santa Claus.*

She smiled, her smile fading as her thoughts returned to the wishes. "There's something I was wondering about." A blush heated her cheeks and she couldn't bring herself to look at him. "If I... Could I wish for someone to love me?" The color in her cheeks flamed to a bright, embarrassed scarlet. And it was Alex's fault, she thought defensively. It was he who had reminded her so sharply of physical and, yes, emotional needs. He who had awakened dormant yearnings.

"I'd suggest you make the wish specific." Alex spoke in the same carefully expressionless voice. She couldn't guess what he was thinking. "I suggest you phrase your wish along these lines—I wish that Mr. John Smith would love me until I die."

"And Mr. John Smith would then love me forever? He wouldn't have a choice about it?"

"John Smith would love you for as long as you specify in your wish. He would have no choice. He would love you regardless of whatever you said or did."

"That's what I was afraid of," Chelsey said grimly, driving the car onto the meadow. She cut the engine, then sat a moment, gripping the steering wheel and looking out the windshield. Wild iris bloomed near a stand of aspens, tiny purple daisies sprang up in clumps on the mountainside. Lush meadow grass rippled beneath a light breeze, growing nearly as tall as her calves.

"Is that your first wish? For someone to love you?"

Although Alex tried to disguise any hint of emotion, Chelsey identified an appalled undertone. She turned to examine the concern darkening his eyes and laughed out loud.

"No, I'm not thinking of Howard. I'm not thinking about anyone, in fact. It's just that wishing for love seemed like a legitimate wish. However, I don't want someone who's forced to love me because a genie cast a spell on him. I want to love and be loved—like everyone else—but I want it to be honest. It has to happen naturally. If you made some poor guy love me, I'd always wonder if he would have loved me without the spell."

Alex stared at her. "You amaze me."

"Really? Why is that?" she asked, sliding out of the car and drawing a deep breath of clear air that was free from the smoke and smells of the city.

Alex closed his car door and walked around to stand beside her. "What difference would it make why the man loved you? Being loved would feel the same, wouldn't it?"

"I don't think so. Unconditional love is wrong. Love ought to be conditional on both people trying to be lovable." Bending, Chelsey reached into the back seat and removed an old blanket and a picnic basket. She pushed the basket into Alex's hands, then picked up her cane and set off across the meadow toward a spot where aspens and firs grew in a large semicircle.

After she spread the blanket and poured coffee from the thermos, she beckoned Alex toward the edge of the rocks.

"We're standing almost on top of one of the flatiron formations," she explained, smiling softly. "Isn't it lovely?"

Behind them, the Rocky Mountains soared, some still white-capped from late-winter snows. The plains stretched in front of them, a flat patchwork quilt that extended as far as the eye could see, eventually blurring into a distant bluish haze.

"That's Kansas," Chelsey said, pointing east with her cane. "I'm sure we can see it. And there's Utah," she said, nodding to the west. "Ahead of us is Wyoming. This spot is our own Olympus. From here we can see the whole world, but it can't see us."

"Really?" he asked, smiling.

"Probably not, but I like to think it." She sipped her coffee, gazing toward the far horizon. "Up here, with this vastness in front of me, my problems seem very, very small and not terribly important. Coming here puts things in perspective."

Her mouth tightened with dread as she walked back to the aspens and firs and sat down on the blanket. She hated telling him about her problem. She hated talking about last summer with anyone, but especially with Alex. From the first, she had experienced an odd desire for Alex's good opinion. She wanted him to like and admire her, but her story wasn't very admirable.

"I'm listening," he prompted, stretching out on the meadow grass instead of choosing the blanket. His long fingers probed the dirt, and he chewed on a stem of grass. His eyes narrowed against the thin sunlight, almost translucent, and she felt his steady gaze on her lowered face.

Chelsey drew her knees up and wrapped her arms around them, looking toward Wyoming. She held her breath a moment, then began.

"Last spring, I received a letter from Dr. Julian Porozzi inviting me to be his assistant at a dig outside Istanbul. I was thrilled to be selected since I'd had a serious case of hero worship for Dr. Porozzi. On the down side, the dig itself wasn't interesting, even though it was Roman. A dozen or more teams have excavated the site over the years—there

# NO RISK, NO OBLIGATION TO BUY...NOW OR EVER!

## GUARANTEED

### PLAY "ROLL A DOUBLE" AND GET AS MANY AS FIVE FREE GIFTS!

## HERE'S HOW TO PLAY:

1. Peel off label from front cover. Place it in space provided at right. With a coin, carefully scratch off the silver dice. This makes you eligible to receive two or more free books, and possibly another gift, depending on what is revealed beneath the scratch-off area.

2. Send back this card and you'll receive brand-new Harlequin American Romance® novels. These books have a cover price of $3.50 each, but they are yours to keep absolutely free.

3. There's no catch. You're under no obligation to buy anything. We charge nothing – ZERO – for your first shipment. And you don't have to make any minimum number of purchases – not even one!

4. The fact is thousands of readers enjoy receiving books by mail from the Harlequin Reader Service® months before they're available in stores. They like the convenience of home delivery and they love our discount prices!

5. We hope that after receiving your free books you'll want to remain a subscriber. But the choice is yours – to continue or cancel, anytime at all! So why not take us up on our invitation, with no risk of any kind. You'll be glad you did!

# THE HARLEQUIN READER SERVICE®: HERE'S HOW IT WORKS

Accepting free books puts you under no obligation to buy anything. You may keep the books and gift and return the shipping statement marked "cancel." If you do not cancel, about a month later we will send you 4 additional novels, and bill you just $2.71 each plus 25¢ delivery and applicable sales tax, if any.* That's the complete price, and – compared to cover prices of $3.50 each – quite a bargain! You may cancel at any time, but if you choose to continue, every month we'll send you 4 more books, which you may either purchase at the discount price...or return at our expense and cancel your subscription.

*Terms and prices subject to change without notice. Sales tax applicable in N.Y.

BUSINESS REPLY MAIL
FIRST CLASS MAIL    PERMIT NO. 717    BUFFALO, NY

POSTAGE WILL BE PAID BY ADDRESSEE

HARLEQUIN READER SERVICE
3010 WALDEN AVE
PO BOX 1867
BUFFALO NY 14240-9952

NO POSTAGE
NECESSARY
IF MAILED
IN THE
UNITED STATES

was virtually no possibility of finding anything interesting. Our team would only be taking measurements. Very dull stuff.''

Alex rummaged in the picnic basket until he found a chicken leg. Chelsey frowned, remembering she had packed chicken salad but not fried chicken.

''In the end, the opportunity to work with Dr. Porozzi outweighed the disappointment of reworking a finished site. Porozzi's name would add prestige to my résumé, and the university was willing to offer a sabbatical for however long I required....'' She shrugged. ''At the time, accepting the offer seemed like a sound decision.''

''But...?'' he asked, watching her face over the chicken leg.

''Nothing worked out like I thought it would.'' She managed a glum smile. ''Julian wanted the money from the grant and the sponsors, but he wanted to stay in Istanbul and play footsie with his new lover. He didn't care about the dig. He knew it was worked out. All he wanted from me was to supervise a crew of students whom he'd hired at dirt wages to satisfy the minimum requirements of the grant. He dumped us in the desert, told his men to unload our supplies, and that was the extent of his involvement.''

Alex dug a hole in the ground with his finger and buried the chicken bones. He offered Chelsey a chicken-salad sandwich and found a large slice of chocolate cake for himself, which Chelsey hadn't packed either.

''I put the students to work measuring the foundations,'' she said, turning the sandwich between her fingers. ''All except a bright kid named Scott Markem. Scott and I kept from going nutty by excavating what looked like the stones of an alley floor. It wasn't exciting work, but it was a damned sight more interesting than standing in a boiling sun holding a tape measure. And there was the possibility that we might find some pottery that had been overlooked.''

"What happened?"

"By the middle of the fifth week, Scott and I had uncovered about three, maybe four feet of the alley floor. At that point the length of floor caved in. It wasn't a floor at all, it was a ceiling.''

Interest flared in Alex's eyes. "Something important was in the room below?"

Chelsey nodded, setting aside her untouched sandwich. "It was a major find,'' she explained in a dulled voice. "Inside the storeroom were four marble busts in such prime condition that much of the original paint still remained. Unquestionably they were from Nero's period and were later confirmed as the work of Aristes Marcellus, one of the most gifted and celebrated sculptors of his period. Complete surviving works are exceedingly rare and highly prized. On the private market, a genuine Marcellus is worth a king's ransom. And we found four of them.''

"Let me guess,'' Alex said, sitting up. "Dr. Porozzi returned to the scene.''

"Oh yes,'' Chelsey said, frowning, trying to soften the bitterness thinning her voice. "I phoned him at once, so excited I could hardly speak. He advised me to sit tight. Tell no one else. No media, no announcements, no publicity until he had personally verified the find.'' She paused, frowning down at her hands. "He arrived with a half-dozen international news teams.''

"I see this coming,'' Alex said quietly. "I'm sorry, Chelsey.''

"Porozzi knew the busts came from a period that was my specialty. He didn't doubt the busts were authentic—he didn't need outside experts to verify them. The delay he requested, and which I fell for, was so he could notify the world press and take credit for the find. Scott Markem vanished from the account. For the most part, so did I. I stood on the sidelines, stunned, and listened as Dr. Porozzi told the press how he had suspected the existence of the busts, how he had relentlessly pursued the search, and how he had finally uncovered them.''

In the ensuing silence, a deer peeked out of the firs, blinked at them, then silently vanished. "The press loved the story, and Dr. Porozzi's fame grew by leaps and bounds. You couldn't pick up a major newspaper or turn on CNN without seeing a photo of Julian standing in front of the busts. His story grew also. He claimed he had been searching for these particular busts for twenty years. Had narrowed the search to Ballan. Blah, blah and blah.''

"So that's what happened. Some bastard took credit for your work."

"I wish that was all there was to it. And it wasn't really my work. It was a lucky accident that was as much to Scott's credit as mine.'' Chelsey continued to stare at her hands, biting her lip. She would have given anything to end the story right here. "There's more. It gets worse.''

"Chelsey, if you—"

"I don't want to tell you any of this! But I have to so you'll understand my wish.'' She drew a breath, frowned, and stared at her twisting hands. "All four busts vanished.''

"Vanished?'' Alex folded his long legs beneath him and hunched forward, his eyes fixed on her face. For once, he wasn't touching or stroking something while they talked.

"Like a puff of smoke. One day the busts were in the Caraki Museum, awaiting a special private showing, and the next day all four were just...gone.''

"What happened to them?''

She bit her lip so hard that she tasted blood beneath her teeth. "Someone stole them. There was another flurry of press coverage. Only this time Dr. Julian Porozzi was not smiling. He gave the world cameras a steely-eyed look and pointed out that only four people had a key to the Caraki Museum. The curator, a trusted assistant named Mustafa, himself... and me."

"Oh."

"Yeah." Chelsey let her head fall backward and stared at the cloudless sky. "Logic says the curator didn't steal the busts. Why should he? He already had them. And Porozzi was the one who discovered the theft. So it came down to Mustafa or me. I was everyone's favorite suspect."

"Why?"

"Why?" She shrugged. "First of all, Mustafa had an ironclad alibi for the night the busts were stolen. In fact, everyone had an alibi for that night except me. Plus, rumor had it that I was angry and hurt at not being given more credit for the find. The tabloids hinted that Dr. Porozzi and I had an ugly falling out. I guess the prevailing theory was that I wanted to embarrass Porozzi and enrich myself. The bottom line is... my reputation is ruined. There's no proof that I stole the busts, but just about everyone assumes that I did. I'll never receive another professional grant. No trade journal will publish my papers. I'm damned lucky I wasn't fired from the university. The decision to keep me came down to one vote. Only the intervention of people like Howard Webber and Betty Windell saved my job. They argued that nothing was proved, that I was innocent until proven guilty, all of that. But I've lost all credibility. That's why I'm doing inventories this summer instead of doing what I love best—working on a dig. You'd have to search far and wide to find anyone more persona non grata than I am."

Alex stared at her. "You didn't steal those busts," he stated flatly.

Tears sprang into her eyes and she ducked her head. "Thanks," Chelsey whispered. "I wish my colleagues had as much faith in my integrity as you do."

"They're fools and they are dead wrong."

"They don't think so. And you have to admit it looks bad."

Pushing to her feet, Chelsey approached the edge of the rocks and leaned on her cane, staring at the seemingly endless plains. There were thousands and thousands of people out there who had never heard of Chelsey Mallon or the stolen Roman busts. It was good to be reminded of that. When she had regained a measure of composure, she called to Alex over her shoulder. "Alex, if I asked that my reputation be restored...would that be a legitimate wish, and could you grant it?"

His large warm hands framed her shoulders, startling her. For an instant Chelsey resisted, then she leaned back against his solid chest, accepting the comfort he offered. She rested her chin on his arms when they came around her. With Alex holding her, she could almost believe that everything would be all right.

"Does the opinion of other people matter that much to you?" he asked gently, speaking against her ear.

"If I don't have my good name," she answered quietly, "then I have nothing."

"Your wish is legitimate and I can grant it." He paused for a moment. "I cannot alter history, so I can't go back and prevent the busts from being stolen. But I can grant a wish that the busts be found and the thief exposed. I can ensure you a public apology and vindication. Is that your wish?"

"Yes." Chelsey hesitated. "And no."

Turning her in his arms, Alex smiled down at her. "I've never had a master or mistress who struggled so hard to make three wishes."

"I don't want to make a mistake," she said, looking at his mouth. A melting feeling stole over her as if his touch were transforming her to hot, bubbling liquid. Gently she extricated herself from his arms. "Alex, I need to think this through. Give me a few minutes alone, will you? It's quiet here, you'll hear me call when I'm ready."

Lifting a hand, he smoothed a strand of hair back behind her ear. He looked as if he wanted to deliver a speech, but all he said was, "As you wish," before he walked away from her.

CHELSEY SAT on the meadow floor, her arms clasped tightly around her raised knees, watching Alex and the black mare. The sunlight was hot on her bare head. The scent of pine and crushed grass surrounded her, along with the lulling drone of insects.

As always when she came to this meadow, her inner turmoil had diminished and she felt in balance again. Watching Alex helped, too. She had never met anyone as aware of small sensory pleasures as Alex Duport, and his appreciation heightened her own.

To him the warm sunshine that Chelsey took for granted was a tangible joy to gather around himself. The pines and firs and tiny spring flowers were not scenery to Alex, but living things deserving of all the awe that life and beauty inspired. Each twig, each blade of grass, had something unique to offer, was singular in texture and structure and in its place within the universe. Eagerly Alex tried to touch and taste and experience all of reality's bounty.

She watched him now, standing in the middle of the meadow, leaning against the black mare, stroking his large hand along her neck. Chelsey could hear his soothing murmur, the deep richness of his voice, but the words were indistinguishable.

As she watched, Alex swung up on the mare's broad back, the motion so natural and graceful it appeared almost liquid. When he twisted his fingers in the mare's dark mane and bent over her neck, the elation on his face was so transfiguring that Chelsey made herself look away, embarrassed to intrude on a moment so private and intensely joyful.

When she looked up again, Alex and the black mare were flying across the meadow grass, moving through air and sunlight as if man and horse were one. The sight was so beautiful, so natural and right, that it took Chelsey's breath away. He rode leaning forward, his hair streaming behind him, his powerful thighs clasping the mare's back. Tears filled Chelsey's eyes. Never had she witnessed anything so magnificent, so utterly harmonious and moving as this splendid blending of illusion and reality.

She didn't know how long she sat transfixed, her mind empty of all but the erotic beauty of man and horse cantering across the meadow grass. She might have sat there all day, hardly daring to breathe lest she shatter the image rushing toward her.

Alex drew up beside her, his face flushed with exhilaration, his eyes joyful and triumphant. The mare pranced and tossed her head before coming to heel in front of Chelsey. The sensual scent of horse flesh and male sweat rose in Chelsey's nostrils, stirred something primal and raw in her stomach.

She was acutely aware of the sexuality of man and beast, the power of fusion and flying hoofbeats that pounded the earth like her own heartbeats.

Alex swept her body with those smoldering brooding eyes as she slowly rose to her feet in front of the mare's tossing head. His gaze challenged as he wordlessly extended his hand to her.

Chelsey had never ridden a horse before, let alone bareback, but she didn't hesitate. As if in a trance, she stepped forward and gripped Alex's hand. Instantly she found herself seated in front of him, her buttocks snugged tight against his crotch.

"Relax," he said in a husky voice, his arms coming around her. "Lean against me." His solid warmth enclosed her, and strong elegant fingers twisted in the mare's mane. Chelsey closed her eyes, listening to her heart thunder in her ears, feeling his hard body cupped around her.

Alex made a sound beneath his tongue, and she felt his thighs tense. Then they were racing like the wind across the meadow, which seemed to expand and lengthen. She, too, gripped the mare's flying mane as wave after wave of exhilaration swept over her and the pounding hoofbeats drummed in her ears and heart and brain.

It was wonderful, thrilling and wildly arousing. The warm breeze rushed past her face and hair. Alex's solid heat wrapped around her. Massive muscle flowed beneath her body and his. She felt Alex's breath on her cheek followed by the flame brush of his lips. His powerful legs clasped the horse as his hands slipped from the mare's mane to frame Chelsey's waist then slid upward. His large, hot hands cupped Chelsey's breasts and pulled her back against his chest.

As if at a signal, the mare slowed to a walk, then halted beside the blanket. And Chelsey surrendered to the chaos erupting inside her as Alex's hands gently kneaded and stroked her aching breasts. His breath flowed hot against her temple. She felt his hardness against her buttocks where he held her tightly against him.

And she wanted him even if it could be nothing more than raw, urgent sex. Regrets be damned. The passion pounding in her temples and at the base of her throat could not be denied.

Alex slipped from the mare's broad back and extended his arms to her. Wordlessly, Chelsey let him lift her from the horse and slide her down the long, hard length of his body. Her arms wound around his neck, and she strained against him as his mouth came down hard to cover hers.

"Yes," she moaned, her voice husky with need. "Yes, Alex."

He tangled his hand in her ginger hair and pulled her head back to look deeply into her eyes as if judging the depth and honesty of her desire.

Then he swung her up into his arms, his mouth hungry on hers, and he carried her to the blanket and laid her across it. Not taking his burning gaze from hers, he reached for her shirt, his fingers shaking slightly as he opened the buttons then flung her shirt aside before he reached for the snap on her jeans.

Chelsey's hands knocked against his as she reached for the buttons of his shirt, frantic in her eagerness. They both laughed, then their smiles faded and they hastily flung aside the rest of their clothing.

Finally, finally, they were both naked beneath the warm morning sun. Chelsey looked up at Alex's magnificent rampant body and sucked in a deep moan. A thrill partly of fear, partly of pleasure, rocked through her body. He was so large and powerfully built, so hard and splendid and beautiful that she didn't at first realize that he was staring at her with the same awestruck look as she stared at him.

"You are so beautiful!" he whispered in a thick voice. Kneeling in front of her, he extended his hands and gently, almost reverently, cupped her breasts, drawing his thumbs across the quivering tips. "So utterly and wonderfully beautiful!"

The sun burnished his body to a rich golden color, gleamed in the thicket of dark hair covering his chest, shone in the tousled strands falling across his forehead. Chelsey raised trembling hands and pressed them flat on his chest, thrilling to the swell of muscle that flexed taut at her touch. Her breath caught in her throat, sounding almost like a sob, when he leaned forward to kiss her breasts and tease his tongue around and around the nipple until the almost painful pleasure of his teasing made her want to scream and pull him on top of her.

"Lie back," he whispered, his hands supporting her weight as he eased her down on the blanket. "Let me make love to you."

But if she lay flat, he would see her bare leg. She tried to protest, tried to sit up suddenly, but Alex hushed her with a kiss and pressed her down on the blanket. He spread a sheet of fiery kisses down her body, moving lower and lower until he was kneeling on the end of the blanket near her feet.

Chelsey waited for that inevitable little pause. Her heart thudded painfully against her rib cage and she didn't open her eyes, not wanting to see his face. And then ... and then she felt his fingertips caressing her left leg, raising her ankle to his lips. He kissed her toes; his warm, gentle hand stroked the withered calf. And he murmured words of praise for her beauty, for the perfection he imagined he saw.

Tears slipped from beneath her lids and her heart swelled so full she thought it would burst. "Oh, Alex," she whispered. Blindly, she reached for him, pulling him down on top of her and covering his face with frenzied kisses of gratitude and desire.

But this was not her realm to dominate. Alex returned her frantic kisses roughly, with force and passion, but his restraint was greater than hers. He would not come to her until he decided the moment, until she could not wait another second, another instant, not until she was thrashing and quivering and pleading with him to take her.

Pressing her back on the blanket, he moved slowly over every inch of her body, doing things with his tongue and hands that Chelsey had never dared imagine. When finally he returned his attentions to her thrusting, swelling breasts, she was drenched in perspiration and her heart was pounding in her chest like a mad drummer.

"Alex, please!" she gasped, reaching for him. But it was too late. An orgasm tore through Chelsey's body like a riptide, and her body arched beneath his hands, lifting to his mouth and fingers. Her plea drowned in moans of rapture and release that left her shaking and feeling faint.

Then and only then, when the recurring waves of intense pleasure had begun to recede, did Alex press his knee between her damp legs, gently guiding them open. He kissed her deeply, then thrust his hips forward, and Chelsey gasped as his powerful fullness entered and filled her. Her eyes closed and her sated body reawakened and arched to meet each possessive thrust. Again and again he rocked into her, taking her higher and higher with the magic of his powerful male body until a scream burst from her lips and a profound shudder rippled through her being. Only then did he satisfy himself, exploding into her with long, deep strokes before his damp head fell forward on her shoulder.

"My God," she said softly when she could speak. "I never dreamed sex could be like that." She pressed her face into his naked shoulder, inhaling the musky male scent of his perspiration. Never before had she been so uninhibited. The memory brought a rush of scarlet to her throat and cheeks. "It really and truly does not matter to you, does it?" she asked softly.

"What?" One hand lazily stroked her shoulder, the other rested on the curve of her hip. She heard the hint of drowsiness in his voice.

"My leg," she whispered.

Gently Alex turned her in his arms until she faced him. "You are one of the most beautiful women I have ever known. Beauty is more than the curve of an ankle or the shape of a leg. It's more than silky skin or sparkling eyes. Beauty is that rare combination of form and spirit. It's warmth and courage and a tilt of the chin. It's a blend of sensuality and intellect, a mix of laughter and loveliness. You are these things."

Because she didn't want him to see the sudden tears brimming in her eyes, Chelsey pressed her face into the crease at his neck until she could control an outpouring of emotional gratitude.

"Did you do something magic to me, or was what we just experienced honest and real?"

His laugh carried across the meadow. "The only magic came from you," he said, kissing the top of her head. "And, Chelsey, you were magic. I will never forget you."

"In your case, never is a very long time," she said, smiling against his chest.

In her case, never wouldn't be as long, but Chelsey knew she would never forget him. For Alex, she had broken her most stringent rule. But she didn't regret it. It would have been tragic to go through life without fully knowing or understanding the depth of pleasure a man and a woman could enjoy together.

The problem lay not in breaking her rule, but in what followed after. Already Chelsey felt the stirrings of a crazy commitment to Alex. Already she felt the strengthening of bonds.

Which, she thought with a tiny sigh, was merely a high-handed way of saying that she was falling in love with him. And falling in love with a genie was a dead-end road.

Alex caressed her damp curls and smiled down at her. A mock sigh lifted his chest. "I hope neither of us is going to apologize for making love."

Chelsey laughed and kissed the dark hair glistening on his naked chest. "Nope, no apologies. Not for something as wonderful as this was."

Sitting up, she tilted her face to the sun and smiled. The last time she had exposed her naked body—or more accurately, her seminaked body—to the sun had been in junior high school.

She looked down at her body stretched out beside Alex's on the blanket. His long legs were golden, covered with thick, silky dark hair. Her legs were milky white.

"You should get out in the sun more," he teased, following her gaze.

"Mmm." For the first time in her life she had not ended a session of lovemaking filled with embarrassing questions she couldn't bring herself to ask. Alex thought she was beautiful. He had said so, and she had seen his belief in his eyes.

"Oh, Alex," she said softly. "You will never know what you've done for me today."

"I haven't done it yet," he said, misunderstanding. Sitting up, he reached for his jeans. "Then you're ready to make your first wish?"

Chelsey laughed and shook her ginger curls in disbelief. She had forgotten about the wish.

"Yes," she said, feeling reluctant to dress, exhilarated by the unique feeling of sunlight warming her bare limbs. Regretting the necessity, she slowly dressed, pleased to notice that Alex watched her with an expression of pleasure.

Finally she was ready. Sitting cross-legged on the blanket, she faced Alex and drew a breath, trying to focus on wishes instead of kisses and naked bodies. "Do we have to do anything special? Are there any rules or procedures about making the wishes?"

"No," he answered softly, his eyes on her face. "Merely state your wish. Be precise."

Chelsey drew another long breath and concentrated. A sense of unreality fizzed around her, making her feel strange inside.

"I wish..."

# Chapter Eight

A gold coin appeared between Chelsey's fingers, catching the sunlight. The longer she held the coin, the warmer it felt against her skin.

Alex sat on the blanket in front of her, his muscled arms crossed over his chest, his intent blue-green eyes fixed on her face. This was not her lover of a moment ago. This was the powerful gothic man who had appeared in her workshop at Wickem Hall, an exotic visitor from a faraway place lost in the mists of time. The man before her was mystical and foreign, a stranger to Chelsey and to her world. His intensity awed her and frightened her a little.

"I await your command, mistress. State your wish specifically."

Chelsey swallowed hard, feeling slightly foolish.

"I wish to know the present location of the four marble busts sculpted by Aristes Marcellus which Scott Markem and I found in the ruined Roman city of Ballan about twenty miles outside of Istanbul." She thrust the coin forward as if it had begun to burn her fingers, an eventuality Chelsey thought was definitely possible. The coin glowed hot to the touch. It would be uncomfortable to hold much longer.

Alex glanced at the coin, but he did not take it from her. Instead his eyebrows soared like dark wings and he stared at her with a frown. "I need to be very certain this is the wish you want to make. Once the wish is granted, I cannot change it. I thought you intended to wish for the restoration of your reputation."

Chelsey placed the coin on the blanket between them, then gripped the handle of her cane, too nervous to leave her hands idle. "Someone set me up, Alex. I want that someone exposed, but not by magical means. I want him caught fair and square. And I want to play a role in clearing my name. Can you understand that?"

"No."

"I couldn't control the theft of the busts or the rumors that circulated afterward. I couldn't control the innuendos the journalists chose to print or what my colleagues believed. I couldn't control the university's reaction." She gave him a pleading look. "Is it so hard to understand that I want—no, I *need*—to have some control in solving this mess?"

"If you wish it, I can reveal the thief's name."

Chelsey shook her head. "I want to discover the thief myself. Someone did this to me. I want to be there when he's exposed. I want to look him in the eye. Don't waffle on me, Alex, not this time." Her sudden panic sounded like anger. She gave him her most piercing, most threatening stare, the stare that brought students and salesmen to their knees. "Knowing the whereabouts of the marble busts is the first step toward reconstructing what happened and restoring my reputation. I want that more than anything."

Alex hesitated then he inclined his head. "As you wish, mistress." Leaning forward, he accepted the coin.

Locking his gaze to hers, Alex raised his palm to the level of his chin. The gold coin gleamed and flashed in the sunlight. It appeared to pulse briefly, then burst into flames so hot and bright that Chelsey gasped and closed her eyes against the fiery glare. When she opened them again the coin was gone. There was no residue of molten gold, no burn mark on Alex's palm.

"Impressive," she murmured weakly. "Real genie stuff."

And very sobering. It was all too easy to forget that Alex was not a man like other men, that he was something unique and strange, a man not of this world.

"If you liked that," he murmured, his smile not reaching his steady eyes, "wait until you see this. But watch carefully, because I can do this only once."

"The rules," she guessed, her voice still small and whispery with an awed sense of discomfort.

"Yes. To repeat the showing will require another wish. So take all the time you require, be thorough in your inspection."

"Wait a minute." She flexed her shoulders and her fingers, then blinked hard and rubbed her eyes. "Okay, I'm ready. You're going to show me the present exact location of the marble busts."

Alex flattened his palms on top of the knees of his crossed legs and closed his eyes. His chest swelled and his upper arms bulged. The sunlight seemed to gather and coalesce around him until Chelsey could have sworn he glowed and became radiant. She had a crazy idea that he was exaggerating, performing a little razzle-dazzle for her benefit. She gave her head a shake, sending her secret smile flying, then she blinked hard to clear her thoughts.

At the same instant, Alex opened his eyes, and frowning, concentrated on the empty space between them. The air shimmered and appeared to thicken, assuming color and form.

A three-dimensional image formed into a hologram that hovered, then steadied, above the blanket. Chelsey pressed her hands together to stop them from shaking and leaned forward. The hologram image revealed two finely sculpted busts displayed on marble pedestals.

"Yes," she whispered, feeling a rush of excitement rise in the back of her throat. The busts flanked a velvet-curtained archway. "Those are two of the Marcellus busts. Where are they?"

The hologram collapsed, then reformed to reveal the imposing colonnades fronting a three-story building. Even before Chelsey read the name etched in marble above the entrance, she recognized the building. "It's the Lupberger Athenaeum," she murmured. "I know it well. It's a privately owned museum located in New York City, a block off Fifth Avenue near Central Park East."

"Take your time. Once we leave this vision, we cannot return to it."

"Go to the next," Chelsey instructed him eagerly, staring at the hologram.

The third bust shimmered into view. It, too, appeared to be in a museum. The bust rested on a marble shelf in a place of honor, dominating two other busts of lesser value which had not been created by Aristes Marcellus.

"Yes," Chelsey whispered. "Pull back to the outside of the building."

At once she recognized the London Museum of Roman Antiquities, which surprised her.

Both the Lupberger and the London Museum were noted for stringent standards. Both had impeccable reputations. To the best of Chelsey's knowledge, neither museum had endured a single breath of scandal. This suggested a brilliantly forged provenance had accompanied the Marcellus busts.

"Go to the last bust," she said, staring at the hologram so hard that her eyes burned and stung.

At first Chelsey didn't spot the final bust. The hologram revealed a small, dark storeroom crammed with items that appeared to be household cast-offs. She saw a sagging chair with exposed springs, a torn lamp shade, battered cardboard boxes and a leaning stack of old clothing. It wasn't until an invisible hand pulled away the sheet covering the bust that she saw it.

When she was absolutely certain that she was indeed looking at the final Marcellus bust, she nodded. "Go on. Let's see the outside of the building."

The hologram shifted in a swirl of colour, then resettled into a depiction of a narrow two-story white house with a red tile roof. Other houses just like it crowded in at the sides. The front door opened onto the street. Judging from the rooftops behind, the row of houses sat on a street that ran downhill. There were no markings on the house, no street numbers or anything to identify the building.

"I need more," Chelsey said uneasily, daring a quick look at Alex. "Can you show me a street name? And a city name?"

"I'm sorry."

Chelsey's heart sank. In a flash she identified the flaw lurking behind her three wishes. A genie could grant a wish, but only the wish as stated. He could provide neither more nor less than what was contained in the statement of the wish. He could not make assumptions as to what the master or mistress intended to accomplish with his or her wish. Alex had told her this by warning her to be specific, and Chelsey had tried. But she saw now that she had not been specific enough. It was sheer dumb luck that she had been able to identify the first two sites. Had all four busts been hidden in the storeroom of the house she was studying now, she would have wasted her wish.

"Do you recognize this house?" she asked Alex, hoping against hope that somehow he did.

"No."

"Istanbul? Egypt? Iraq?" The house could have been located in just about any warm climate in the world. Frustration wrinkled her brow. Her hands clenched into fists. "Think," Chelsey muttered, talking to herself. "Where could this house be? Is there anything unique about it?"

Staring until her eyes began to sting and water, she searched the hologram scene for clues. After rubbing her eyes, she tried again. But there was simply no hint of the greater location. There was nothing unique about the house. She had seen a thousand just like it in various parts of the world.

Frustrated and bitterly disappointed, she finally shoved back her mop of ginger curls and nodded to Alex. "That's it. I could stare at this house until I was ninety and still not guess where it's located."

The hologram flared, then faded away.

Chelsey struck the ground with a fist. "I see what you mean about phrasing the wish specifically. I screwed up, didn't I? Why didn't you tell me?"

He shrugged and spread his hands. "You said you wanted to know the exact location of the busts and that's what you were shown. You did not say you wanted to know the addresses of those locations. I've already told you, I'm not a mind reader."

She sighed. "You're right, of course," she admitted after a minute, trying to swallow her disappointment and focus on the locations she did recognize instead of the one she did not.

For some reason, Chelsey had expected Alex to look tired and drained after producing the hologram and granting her wish, but he didn't. He looked alert and curious, concerned about her.

"Did you see anything that was helpful?" he asked.

She turned her face toward the vast expanse of plains basking in the noon sunshine. "Yes. I know the location of three of the busts. That's more than I knew an hour ago. It's a beginning. I hope it's enough."

After a moment, she opened the thermos and poured them both fresh cups of coffee.

Actually she was glad she had the marble busts to occupy her thoughts. Without the marble busts to worry about, Chelsey suspected she might have drowned in the blue-green depths of Alex's concern. She wouldn't have been able to think about anything except the wild passion they had shared. Or how glad she was that they were still two wishes away from the moment when they had to say goodbye. She didn't want to think about that.

Standing, she leaned on her cane a moment, then walked to the edge of the rocks where she had a clear, unobstructed view of forever.

"What happens next?" Alex inquired, coming up behind her.

"We fly to New York and speak to the curator at the Lupberger Athenaeum," Chelsey answered absently. She was thinking about the concept of forever and how meaningless it was. Maybe for some people, forever could be compressed into a few days. She found herself hoping so. "We track the Lupberger's two busts back to their origination point. Once we've accomplished that, we'll find some answers."

"Shazam."

ALEX CAUGHT CHELSEY'S arm when she flung it near his face, steadied her, then bent to pick up her cane from the sidewalk.

He admired her, respected her, and God knew he desired her. But he didn't understand her. It would have been a relatively simple matter to resolve the theft of the marble busts and expose the culprit. He could have assisted her in phrasing a wish specific enough to accomplish the return of the busts and the restoration of her reputation. He only partially understood her desire to be personally involved in the denouement. She frustrated him, fascinated him and kept him continually feeling slightly off balance.

"Where are we?" she gasped, clutching his arm and staring around her with wild eyes.

"We're in New York City, standing on the sidewalk in front of Fifth Avenue." It surprised him that she didn't immediately recognize the site. Where else would she see so much traffic, both pedestrian and vehicular? Where else did the air seem tangible with the scents of humanity and excitement? Where each street was a canyon flanked by cliffs of glass and stone? "The Lupberger Athenaeum is across the street and a few doors up."

Chelsey looked so shocked that he immediately decided she needed a moment to orient herself. Taking her arm, Alex led her toward one of the park benches set back from the sidewalk. They passed a woman who had frozen in place at the sight of them, and was staring with huge eyes.

She gripped a shopping cart which seemed out of place alongside Fifth Avenue and the park. But the shopping cart and the peculiar assortment of items inside didn't surprise Alex as much as the layers and layers of clothing she wore. It was hotter on the pavements of New York City than it had been in the mountain meadow. He couldn't think why anyone would wear three dresses and two coats when waves of heat shimmered around the tires of the vehicles charging up and down the avenue.

"Sit here for a minute," he suggested to Chelsey, indicating a park bench. "Would you like something cool to drink?"

"Yes. A lemonade, I think," she answered in a whisper, glancing toward the striped awning of a hot-dog stand on the corner. "God, Alex. I wish you'd give me more warning when you intend to fling out your magic carpet! No, no," she said, raising a hand. "That's not a *real* wish. But I can't tell you how disconcerting it is to suddenly be transported somewhere unexpected! My heart is pounding like crazy."

He offered her a crystal tumbler filled with ice and lemonade. Instantly her eyes flared then narrowed, and she swiftly looked around her at the people on nearby benches and passing on the sidewalk.

"Don't *do* that!" she said sharply. "Someone will see." She passed a hand over her forehead. "Maybe genies have outlived their time. I'm not sure the modern world is prepared for you guys."

It occurred to Alex that perhaps she was correct. Certainly he hadn't experienced this kind of reaction in the past. His previous masters and mistresses had readily accepted his magic, had delighted in it to the extent that they wished him to demonstrate his magical powers for friends and acquaintances. It gave them pleasure to command a magician. He couldn't grasp why the same was not true for Chelsey, or that times had changed so greatly that magic was no longer valued. Did this mean that *he* was not valued? Magic was now as much a part of him as his arms and legs. He used it automatically, without much thought.

Disturbed but striving to please, he made the crystal tumbler disappear from her fingers.

"Oh God," she groaned.

"Chelsey. Do you want the lemonade or don't you?" he asked, hoping he didn't sound as exasperated as he felt.

"I want the lemonade," she admitted as the tumbler reappeared in her hand. She closed her eyes and made a choking sound. "But I wanted you to buy it. I don't want anyone to see things appearing and disappearing. Alex, we're surrounded by people. Someone is certain to see. I'm amazed that no one has gone crazy over us popping out of thin air!"

"No one is paying us any attention," he said reasonably.

This was true. Except for the overdressed woman with the shopping cart. She continued to watch them intently, still frozen in place. The shredded feather atop her red hat pointed toward them like a rusting sword.

"See?" Chelsey whispered. "That poor bag lady probably thinks she's hallucinating."

Alex wasn't interested in the bag lady. He was, in fact, paying scant attention to a discussion he considered irrelevant. Instead, he watched the dappled sunlight that filtered through the trees overhead and played across Chelsey's heart-shaped face. Sunlight and shadow heightened the angles of her features, making her seem alternately strong then soft, but lovely in both cases.

She was taller than Isabel had been, but small boned and delicately formed. Isabel had affected fragility because fragility was in fashion, but in truth Isabel had been a sturdy woman, big boned, and as strong and ruthless as a man. In contrast, Chelsey Mallon had perfected her distancing stares and a proud posture that projected confidence and self-reliance, but at her core lay an unexpected and genuine fragility that gripped his heart and twisted his emotions.

Already Alex knew that leaving her would crush something inside of him. Because no one had ever impacted his emotions as this woman did. She exasperated him, fascinated him, engaged his admiration, made him angry, drove him wild with desire. It would require centuries to recover from her, if ever he did.

She placed her hand on his arm and looked up at him. "Alex, thank you for trying to expedite things, but this won't work. This isn't the way to proceed."

Frowning, he gazed down at her. She was so intense and lovely that it was difficult to keep his mind on what she was saying. Her face looked now almost as it had when he began to make love to her. Anxious but eager, hinting of apology. Wanting to go forward, afraid to go forward.

The bag lady wheeled her cart closer to them, halting at a safe distance. "Hey there. How did you do that?"

"Don't you see," Chelsey continued, glancing at the bag lady, then back at him. "If I'm going to clear my name, there can't be any questionable circumstances. Like popping up suddenly in New York City. Finding the busts and exposing the thief is going to cause a stir. In case some journalist wants to check our involvement, we have to leave a paper trail."

"Such as?"

The bag lady edged closer. "Are you aliens?" The shredded feather atop her hat quivered with cautious interest. "What do you want with earth? Why are you here and what are your plans?"

Chelsey lifted her cane and stood up. "We're not aliens." She glared at Alex.

"What kind of paper trail are you talking about?" he asked.

"Airline tickets, passport stamps, hotel and food receipts. That kind of thing. And the times have to work out.

There can't be any mysterious gaps. I'm trying to restore my credibility, not compromise it further.''

The bag lady's eyes narrowed shrewdly. "Well, I wouldn't expect you to admit it, now would I? You're going to take over the world, aren't you! Well, that's all right with me. I say go ahead and take it over. Can I ride in your spaceship?''

"What are we going to do?" Chelsey asked helplessly. "She saw us appear out of nowhere, and she's not going away.''

Alex bowed and gave the bag lady his most charming smile. "Madam, I assure you that we have no interest in taking over the world.''

"Who are you?''

"I'm a genie, and this is my mistress.'' His explanation seemed simple enough. He was genuinely surprised when the bag lady hooted with disbelief.

"Alex, the minute she turns around, get us out of here. Please?''

Alex smiled at the shaking feather, then he gently turned the bag lady to face the street, sensing her resistance in his mind. She knew something invisible was turning her against her will. "Shazam.''

There was an instant before they reappeared on the blanket in the meadow, and in that instant he glimpsed Chelsey's look of yearning as she glanced toward the Lupberger Athenaeum. He understood then how difficult it was for her to follow her own procedures. In her heart, she longed to dash across the street and confront the curator at once. But a stubborn sense of integrity would not allow an impulsive move that might compromise her goal.

He caught her as she stumbled on a rock hidden beneath the blanket and held her tightly against him. Instantly he felt their chemistry ignite, responded to his powerful need for her. Tilting her face upward, he kissed her roughly, possessing her with his lips and tongue.

"I'M TURNING INTO a shameless hussy," Chelsey said, smiling softly and buttoning her shirt. She suspected she wore a slightly dazed and dreamy expression. After not making love for over a year and a half, she'd done it twice today. In broad daylight. It was enough to leave anyone feeling a little dazed and dazzled.

"Should I apologize?"

She laughed and planted a kiss on Alex's wide shoulder. "If you do, I'll be offended."

Leaning forward, Alex cupped her face between his large hands. His gaze traveled slowly over her face before meeting her eyes. "I can't get enough of you. You smile and I want you. You speak and I want you. You look at me and all I can think about is the silky touch of your naked skin against mine."

"Plus, you're storing up physical impressions," she said, teasing him to lighten the seriousness in his eyes.

He drew back. "Is that why you think I made love to you? Merely to experience the physical sensations?"

"Now, don't sound so offended. That's why most people make love. To experience the physical sensations." While he thought about that, Chelsey finished dressing, noticing that her body was still warmed by a rosy glow. Without intending it, her movements were almost seductive. For the first time ever, she didn't feel embarrassed or uncomfortable dressing in front of a man.

In fact, she felt content and happy, desirable and beautiful. She couldn't recall feeling anything like this in a very long time. If ever. And it was all because of Alex. She wished she knew who to thank for sending him to her. He was changing her life and her image of herself in subtle ways she would still be discovering long after he had gone.

"Making love to you is more than just wanting to experience the physical sensations. Although that's part of it," he added grudgingly.

Chelsey tossed his shirt to him and grinned. "Feeling a little defensive, are we?"

She felt wicked about taking pleasure in Alex's sulky expression, but he deserved a bit of discomfort. After all, he'd turned her life upside-down. Take today for instance. Today she had ridden a horse, made love twice, and she'd been to New York City and back. And it wasn't even dinnertime yet. If Alex felt a little off balance, well, he had it coming.

"It's you, Chelsey. I want to make love to you."

The smoky, speculative look in his eyes made her want him again. A blush stole up from her throat, and she turned her face away. She was becoming shameless. A wanton. The image secretly pleased her. She could just imagine what her students would think if they could eavesdrop on her thoughts. The ice queen as a wanton? No way.

"I think this is an area we'd do better not to examine too closely," she suggested, seeing that Alex was disturbed. "Some things should just be enjoyed, not analyzed. We'll drive ourselves crazy if we think about this too much. I'll start feeling guilty about sexual relationships that can't go anywhere, and you'll start feeling bitter about all you're missing in the dream state. We'll mess up the time we have left together, and I don't want that to happen. I want to enjoy every minute I have with you."

"I just don't want you to think that making love to you falls into the same category as grooming a horse or smelling a rye field, or—"

Chelsey burst into laughter. She was too happy to take offense at anything he said. Her eyes sparkled. "It never occurred to me that you might compare me to a horse."

"Damn it, that isn't what I said!"

"Come on," she called, heading toward the car. "We're going home. We have plans to make."

He spread his hands and tilted his head back to scowl at the sky. "Is it all women in general? Or just this particular one?"

"This particular one is going to leave you standing there without your pants if you don't hurry up," she called over her shoulder, laughing because it was a wonderful day, a sunshiny summer day, an Alex day. And she knew where the stolen busts were. It was a fine, fine day, indeed.

"What sort of plans are we making?" he asked, appearing in the passenger seat beside her, stuffing his shirttail into his pants.

"We need to make airline and hotel reservations." She swung the car in a circle, then pointed it down the fire road. "I have to stop by the bank." That thought gave her pause. After a minute she continued. "And we have to think of a way to explain you to the Lupberger curator. A colleague, I think. Which means we need a paper trail for you. We need to create a history for you that can be checked if necessary."

"Such as?"

"Such as everything. Birth certificate, high school and college records, social security number, driver's license, passport, job history. You know...everything. A history, and all the usual papers that everyone carries who isn't a genie."

He shrugged, stretched his arm across the seat back and played with the loose tendrils fluttering around her neck. "It's done. Anyone who cares to check will discover Alex

Duport, archaeologist and all-around ordinary person, colleague of Dr. Chelsey Mallon.'' He touched his back pocket. ''Complete with wallet stuffed with the usual papers.''

''Good.'' God, what his fingers did to her. Tiny electric thrills chased up and down her spine. ''Money is going to be the big problem in all of this. We may have to return to Istanbul. That's going to be expensive.''

''Most masters wish for wealth.''

''I could think about this more efficiently if you'd keep your hands to yourself.''

He laughed and pulled his arm back, turning his face to the air rushing in the window.

WITH A GENIE IN RESIDENCE, there was no need to leave the house. Chelsey wanted grilled salmon for dinner but felt too lazy to drive to the grocery store. It had been a long, eventful day and her left leg ached. Before she finished phrasing a shy request, a beautiful salmon had appeared on the kitchen counter.

''Thanks,'' she said, toasting Alex with the ever-full glass of French wine that he had also provided. ''If you'll put this on the grill, I'll pop some potatoes in the microwave and put together a salad.''

''I could—''

''No,'' she said, waving aside his offer. ''We'll use conventional means. I don't want to get spoiled.'' Then she smiled and tilted her head. ''But you could whip up something low-fat and wonderful for dessert, if you like.''

By now she knew Alex enjoyed performing everyday tasks like grilling the salmon. He would baste the fish with his fingers, test the heat of the charcoal and stand over the grill, inhaling the scent of the cooking salmon. Chelsey also realized she enjoyed watching him, and enjoyed pretending they were doing normal things that any couple might do—small, homey, insignificant things that mattered only to the couple involved.

Except they were not an ordinary couple. And the fish had appeared by magic. As had the wine. And Alex could not wander farther than the sound of her voice. And she was about to make her second wish, an event that would move them closer to saying goodbye.

The thought jolted her and diminished her pleasure. The threat of depression nibbled at the edge of her mind. She couldn't bear the thought of saying goodbye to Alex.

She was falling in love with him. The realization exhilarated her and scared her to death.

"Why so quiet?" Alex asked midway through their candlelit dinner on the small outside patio. "Is something the matter?"

Chelsey gazed at him across the table, her heart in her eyes. Sunset rays painted red highlights through his long, straight hair and sharpened his chiseled profile. This was one of those moments when she looked at him and saw the crusader in his proud posture and the stubborn angle of his chin.

"I was thinking about the next wish," she said, turning the lie into fact. "I checked my bank balances and I don't have enough money to cover too many unexpected expenses. Such as a trip for two to Istanbul." Pushing aside her plate, Chelsey reached into her apron pocket and produced a list. She totaled the figures again in her mind. "I think I'd be more comfortable if I had about two thousand dollars more than I do. I'm thinking I should wish for it."

Alex stared at her. "That's not sensible. If you're going to use your second wish for money, then wish for wealth, not two thousand dollars."

Chelsey shifted in her chair. "I don't know. Doesn't that sound ... well, greedy?"

He threw up his hands. "Chelsey, I'm not judging you. No one is. The wish is yours to use for your direct benefit."

"Selidim had this all figured out," she observed softly. "The wishes seem like a boon, but there's a subtle corruption involved. For you, it's a corruption of ideals. For me, it's a corruption of what I thought I was and what I thought I believed in. I didn't think I was a greedy person. But here I am secretly agreeing with you. I only need two thousand or so, but if I'm really honest with myself, I'd like to wish for a million."

"Wish for five million. Ten million. What difference does it make? It's your wish and you can use it however you like."

She met his eyes, then looked away. "This is going to sound idiotic, but I don't like having you know that I'm secretly lusting for a million dollars. It sounds so rapacious. But I guess I am. Whenever I think about it, I picture a house of my own, a new car, the possibility of financing a dig or an expedition. I get a little crazy with the idea."

Reaching across the table, Alex took her hand. "Look at me, Chelsey. Don't let what's happening to us get in the way of using your wishes to the fullest benefit for you." Something like pain flickered behind his eyes. "Soon I'll have to leave you. If you spend your wishes based on what you think I may or may not approve ... you'll have nothing but regret when I go."

Chelsey heard nothing after *Soon I'll have to leave you.* The words struck her like a dagger in the heart. It wasn't fair. All her life she had waited for and dreamed about a man like Alex. A man whom she could love and respect. A man who might love her, too, and make her heart feel whole. At last fate had given her such a man, but fate would snatch him away again.

"Oh, Alex," she said softly. Sudden tears swam in her eyes. "Don't you think I'll regret it when you go?" His image blurred. "This time with you has been the most exciting, the most wonderful time in my life."

He came around the table and gently pulled her to her feet, taking her into his arms. "Chelsey..."

The warmth of his thumb brushing away her tears made a shudder of longing race through her body.

His strong hands brushed the hair from her cheeks and cupped her face, tilting her mouth up to his. For a long moment he stared into her eyes. The intensity of his gaze seemed to reach deep inside her.

"If only..." he whispered. Then he kissed her, and it seemed to Chelsey that their passion and need for each other caused the universe to tremble.

# Chapter Nine

"I never thought I was the type of person to whom money mattered," Chelsey said. "But suddenly I'm thinking what a relief it would be not to worry about paying the bills."

Full darkness had descended, but they continued to sit outside on the patio. Alex examined Chelsey's face in the light of the candle flame. She appeared to be trying to justify or apologize for a wish made by one hundred percent of his masters and mistresses.

This woman astonished him. First she tried to give away her wishes by spending them for the benefit of others. Now she was struggling with the personal morality of making a wish that was universal in scope. Alex was not sure what was expected of him. Did she want him to persuade her in favor of wishing for money?

"If you're concerned about needing two thousand dollars to follow the trail of the busts," he said carefully, testing the water, "that is an amount I can produce as the expenses arise. But if we're addressing financial security, that's a different thing and a larger amount. That will require a wish."

Circles of pink bloomed in her cheeks. "Would you think less of me if we were talking about a million dollars?" At once she raised a hand to the pink deepening on her throat.

"No, don't answer that. All right, financial security is the issue here. And Alex, I don't want you to pay the two thousand dollars. Running off to New York City and possibly overseas is my idea, not yours."

He resisted an urge to roll his eyes. "Chelsey, it isn't as if the money were coming out of my personal account. I don't have a personal account. The money just appears when I need it. Besides, the idea of a quest is appealing."

His last comment was an understatement. Alex was a man who understood quests. Once he had grasped that Chelsey would not be deterred from tracking down the missing busts and that he would have the opportunity to participate, he found himself impatient to begin. First, the money question had to be settled.

Her chin jutted and a defensive look entered her eyes. "This is my quest and I should handle the expenses." A sheepish look stole across her expression. "The problem is, I can't pay without wiping out my accounts. So..." She drew a deep breath and met his eyes. "I'd just wish for the two thousand, but that seems a bit shortsighted. It seems that as long as I'm doing this, I should wish for a million. That's what everyone else does, right? I mean, it just seems sensible."

"But...?" He was becoming adept at spotting that inevitable but. He read it in the crease between her eyes and in the way she continued to move the wineglass in agitated circles.

"But there's a problem. And I can't see a way around it."

"The money won't appear in a heap on the floor, if that's what you're worrying about. It will appear in your bank or investment account, however you specify. All paperwork will support the figures. You'll experience no suspicion or scrutiny from anyone."

Once upon a time the actual coins would indeed have appeared in a pile on the carpet. He recalled masters and mistresses gathering coins from the floor before hiding them away. But those days were long gone. The world was more sophisticated now, and so were banking procedures. The paper trail Chelsey had mentioned earlier was doubly important in financial matters. The money had to be accounted for. Which was easy enough to do.

"If I suddenly turn up with a fortune that I didn't have yesterday, how will that look?" She pushed aside her wineglass and dropped her hands into her lap. "It will look as if I really did steal the Marcellus busts then sold them. I don't have any way to explain the money."

"There's no need for concern." He smiled and shrugged. "We'll structure the wish in such a way that you inherited ten million dollars five years ago. An impeccable paper trail will support that premise."

"Ten million?" Chelsey blinked, then stared at him. "Alex, let's not get crazy here. One million will do nicely. Besides, if I'm so rich, why didn't I mention my wealth last summer when rumors were flying that I stole the busts to enrich myself."

He grinned, enjoying the discussion. "The suggestion was so ridiculous that you didn't dignify the rumors with a response."

"Not bad," she said, nodding her head. "If we leak the information about my wealth, it could work in my favor."

"If you want wealth, I'd advise you to consider at least five million." When she started to protest, he leaned forward, pushing the candle out of the way. "If you want to finance your own dig, that's an expensive undertaking."

It astonished Alex that he, who had scorned the greed of humanity, was arguing strenuously for an amount higher than his mistress would have chosen if left to her own inclinations. But it was important to him that Chelsey be financially self-sufficient and not dependent on a job she retained through the grace of one vote. He didn't want to think of her ever wanting something she could not afford. When he thought about it, he realized he wanted her to have the life he would have moved the earth to give her if he had had the chance.

This realization brought him up short. His chest constricted painfully. For a brief instant he cursed the fate that had brought him to Chelsey Mallon. He cared for her; he cared deeply. More so with every hour that he spent in her company. His reward would be nothing but pain.

With a jolt he realized that Chelsey would also suffer if he continued along this course. He had only to look at the radiance shining in her eyes, needed only to recall the eagerness of her lovemaking to know that she was beginning to care for him as strongly as he cared for her.

Had they been any other two people, the knowledge that they teetered on the sweet edge of love would have made him want to shout with joy. But he was a genie. He could offer her no commitment, no future. He had no right to love a woman; it would be an act of cruelty to allow Chelsey to fall in love with him.

For a brief moment he closed his eyes, feeling a twist of pain deep inside. "Are we agreed on the amount of money you will wish for?" he asked tersely.

As hard as it would be, as much as he wished it could be otherwise, he had to ease back, had to reestablish a distance between them. He had to protect Chelsey from falling in love with him; he had to shield her from a hopeless love that could bring her nothing but disappointment and pain. This was the kindest, most loving gift he could give to her.

"I'll cede to your judgment," Chelsey said after a moment's consideration. "It appears you know about financial matters and I don't."

Her trust strengthened his resolve. She deserved better from him than a broken heart. Looking away from her lovely face, he concentrated on securing her finances.

"We'll frame your wish for five million dollars and we'll structure the paperwork to reflect the money was inherited five years ago." He explained how he thought the money should be invested. Chelsey shrugged and agreed. "I suggest you hire a financial advisor. Your portfolio will be in order, but a financial advisor familiar with today's markets and investments will undoubtedly prefer to make some changes. Plus you'll want ongoing management of your affairs."

The dazed look returned to her expression as if she were having difficulty making the high figure seem real. "You know, this is going to feel funny. I've never had to think about investments before." She smiled at him. "But it's going to be a nice problem. Much better than worrying about the utility bill. Will you help me word the wish so I don't overlook anything? I don't want to screw up again."

They worked it out together, scribbling across a notepad that Chelsey fetched from the kitchen.

"I think we're ready," she said finally, studying the written wish. "I wish..." A gold coin appeared in her hand.

Alex accepted the coin and watched it blaze in his palm. Personal magic required no effort on his part. But fulfilling the wishes required that he concentrate and tap into something outside of himself. There was no name for the something he tapped into; he thought of it as an omnipotent presence. Occasionally, when in the dream state, he pondered the thing or being that granted the wishes, sensing that granting wishes was merely a fraction of its purpose. It frustrated him that his mind was too small, too mired in the human state, to comprehend more.

"It is done," he said, opening his eyes.

"Really?" She looked doubtful. "Wait here a minute."

Three minutes later she returned with her checkbook and a thick portfolio that she'd found on top of her desk. "Look at this!" Excitement swirled in her brown eyes. "My checking-account balance is now thirty-two thousand dollars! And this portfolio! Alex, I'm rich! Rich!" She threw out her arms and spun on the toes of her right foot. "I can buy a CD player."

He laughed out loud. His inclination was to take her into his arms and dance her across the patio, sharing in her excitement. But her remembered how she felt about dancing, and more importantly he remembered his vow to withdraw from her. Clenching his teeth, he remained in his seat.

But he could watch her. When Chelsey Mallon was happy, there was no more beautiful woman on earth. It made him feel sick inside to think of leaving her or to think about another man touching her. It caused him despair to realize that caressing her or kissing her were acts of teasing and cruelty if he did so knowing his caresses would bring her only pain in the end.

"Is SOMETHING WRONG?" Chelsey asked after they had turned out the lights in her bedroom.

"Why do you ask?" The answer was evasive and sounded moody even to his own ears.

She sat up in bed and clasped her hands on top of the sheets. In the soft glow of the moonlight, he saw a flush of discomfort heat her cheeks. "I thought...well, doesn't it seem a little silly for you to sit over there in a chair? We could share the same bed. After all, we..." She ended by biting her lip and making a small confused motion with her hands.

"I'd only keep you awake. I won't sleep for more than an hour." That startled him. When had it become an hour? And what did it mean that his requirement for sleep, a surprise to begin with, had lengthened? "Once you fall asleep I thought I'd go downstairs and view your portfolio. Maybe practice my fencing."

She nodded and pushed back a wave of the ginger-colored curls. "I'm sensing that something isn't right between us, that something has changed...."

"Why would you think that?" he asked, stalling. It was his task to be sensitive to the moods of others. Chelsey was the first person he had met who was sensitive to his. It left him feeling exposed and more vulnerable than he was comfortable with.

She shrugged and one strap of her thin summer nightgown dropped off her shoulder. Alex ground his teeth together, trying to ignore moonlight gleaming on satin. "You seem different somehow. More like you were when I first met you."

"And how is that?" God, but she was lovely. The moonlight polished her skin to a pearly glow. She was an inviting combination of shadow and warmth, moisture and promise. His stomach tightened and he wanted her again.

"I'm not sure. Distant and brooding. Far away. Did I say or do something that offended you?"

"No! Not at all." He ran a hand through his hair. How could he tell her that he couldn't look at her without wanting to take her in his arms and kiss her until she was dizzy and moaning his name? How could he admit that he was falling in love with her, but knew love could only bring pain to them both? He had no right to declare his feelings to her. No right to take pleasure in the affection he saw growing in her eyes and in her expression when she looked at him. The last thing he wanted for Chelsey was pain or regret.

"Then what?"

He wanted to shout and storm and brandish his crusaders' sword at the cruelties of fate. He wanted to smash and ruin, to rampage and scream his frustration. Bitterness flooded his mouth with a dark taste. After centuries of loneliness he had found a woman—his woman. And he had been given a glimpse of what their life together might have been like.

But he could not have her. Not now, not ever. He was one slender wish away from the dream state, from oblivion. Life in all its richness would rush away and continue without him. He would lose her and everything they might have shared together.

He turned a hard face to the moonlight filtering past the gauzy curtains. Knots rose like stones along his jawline.

"Go to sleep," he said finally.

CHELSEY STRUGGLED with the question of whether to inform the university that she was leaving Boulder for a while. In the end she decided against it. No one would miss her. And if she were challenged later, she had the completed inventory to offer in her defense.

She did phone Marge, her landlady, who seemed relieved that she was leaving town for a week or so. And she phoned Betty to cancel lunch and tell her not to worry if she didn't hear from her for a while.

"Is Alex still visiting you?" Betty asked, trying to sound casual. "Are you two running off together? Is that what this mysterious absence is all about?"

"It isn't mysterious. I've received a tip about the Marcellus busts. Alex and I are going to check it out."

"What happened? Did you win the lottery? Or is Alex paying? Don't tell me a guy that gorgeous is rich, too!"

"I don't have to worry about money since... since my inheritance." This was the hardest part. Deceiving friends.

"What inheritance?"

"You know I don't like to talk about money. Listen, there is something I want to clear up with you." She leaned against the wall next to the phone. "You were right about Alex and me."

"I knew it! So what should I buy you for a wedding present?"

"It's not like that," Chelsey said, closing her eyes. Feeling the pain of wishing. "It won't last, Betty. We're geographically incompatible." Which had to be the understatement of the century. "I live here, and Alex lives... very far away." In genie-land. But she still couldn't bring herself to tell Betty the whole truth. "There's no way to work it out, so don't start offering suggestions. I'm okay with it. All I can do is just enjoy this while it lasts."

Next she phoned United Airlines, then a hotel near Central Park South. Even though their flight was booked for the following day, she packed a battered suitcase that had accompanied her around the world and was pasted over with peeling stickers.

And through it all, she worried about Alex. He followed her without speaking, his hands thrust into his pants pockets, his expression angry and brooding. It worried her most of all that he wasn't touching and stroking everything that came within his reach.

And he hadn't made love to her this morning even though she had brazenly left the bathroom door ajar when she took her shower.

"THIS IS A WASTE of time," Alex muttered once the plane was airborne and there was nothing to do but sit and wait.

"I know you'd rather travel by magic carpet and you'd rather spend your time doing something more interesting than riding in a plane for several hours, but we have to do this by conventional and traceable means," Chelsey told him for the fourth time. She suspected she sounded more stubborn than understanding.

Leaning forward, she rummaged in the seat pocket in front of her and withdrew a copy of the *Enquirer* that a previous passenger had left behind. She shook it open across her lap, the pages making a firm snap.

"Oh my God!" After reading the headlines a second time, she stared at the accompanying picture, then burst out laughing. "Look," she said when Alex turned to her with a raised eyebrow.

The headline read, Aliens Invade Fifth Avenue. There was a photograph of the bag lady, complete with shapeless hat and indignant feather.

Chelsey dropped her head into her hands and continued to laugh helplessly. "It's not just *my* life that you've turned upside down. You're having a weird effect on a lot of people's lives."

After he read the article, he gave her a sheepish grin. "I don't know what to say."

Chelsey leaned her head against the seat back and turned to face him. "Tell me why you're behaving so strangely," she said softly. "What's wrong between us?"

"Do we have to talk about this?"

"Believe me, this isn't easy. In the past, when I've sensed something amiss in a relationship, I haven't confronted it. I've stiffened my pride and walked away." She frowned. "But Alex, your rules won't let us walk away from each other. So let's talk. We agreed to communicate."

She hated it that she blushed so easily. Chelsey considered herself a brisk no-nonsense type of woman. That's how she conducted her classes; that's how she ran her life. But let a man enter the picture, and she turned vulnerable and squishy inside. Her emotions turned pink and flamed in her cheeks. It made her furious.

Alex looked past her at the clouds drifting beneath them. "All right," he agreed finally. Chelsey suspected that his acquiescence was a genie thing and had more to do with pleasing his mistress than his own preference.

"So, talk," she said quietly.

"Look, Chelsey. We made love because that was what both of us wanted." When he paused, Chelsey tried to think about pale cool cheeks and snowy throats, hoping the blush pulsing in her cheeks would recede. "But there's no future here. I must leave you after your next wish. I don't want you to get hurt."

She drew back, feeling stung and defensive. Obviously he thought she was becoming emotionally involved and he didn't return her feelings. If he had, he would have mentioned the possibility of getting hurt himself.

"Wait a minute. For your information, I'm not the type of woman who falls in love with someone I've only known for a few days. So if you think I'm going to be hurt when you hop on your magic carpet and fly back to never-never land, you can put that idea right out of your head."

Chelsey wasn't lying. She wouldn't be hurt—she was going to feel as though she'd lost a limb when he left her.

"I know our relationship is temporary," she went on, feigning courage. "I know it doesn't really mean anything except the chemistry is right. I'm not looking for happily-ever-after, Alex. Not this time—not with you. Happily-ever-after is impossible in our situation. All I'm doing is taking it a minute at a time and enjoying what we do have. I thought you were, too.''

"I'm starting to feel foolish," he said in a quiet voice. "I thought you were beginning to..."

She placed her hand on his arm. ''Even if I were becoming emotionally involved, don't you think I've figured out there is nothing but loss and hurt at the end of the ride?'' Stating it aloud darkened her eyes with anticipated pain. "If I ran away from every situation that might end badly, nothing good would ever happen, either. Look, Alex, I'm a big girl. I'm going into this with my eyes open. I care about you, yes. But it isn't love. This isn't the grand passion of my life.''

Pride was speaking, not truth. Chelsey knew there would never be another man in her life like Alex. And it wasn't just that he was a genie. What she felt for Alex reached beyond mere emotions. It was a primal passion that originated in a cellular recognition. This was the man who completed her. This was the man she needed in order to feel whole.

In a peculiar way it didn't matter if Alex returned her feelings. She could almost believe that it was enough just to experience an all-consuming passion once in her life. To know what it was like. To know that she would live her life having experienced the chaos and joy of a grand passion that transcended time and space. Not to have experienced this would have been a tragedy; she saw that clearly. And it could so easily have happened that way.

"So," she finished softly, gazing into his intent eyes, "don't pull away thinking you're doing what's best for me. I'll decide what's best for me. And I'll deal with the consequences. In the meantime, let's enjoy the time we have together. Let's enjoy each other to the fullest.''

His blue-green eyes seemed to bore into her brain. Chelsey suspected he sensed she was not being straight with him.

"All right," she admitted after a minute, turning her face away. "Forget what I said a minute ago." Her shoulders stiffened and her chin lifted. The hated pink flamed on her cheeks. "I will be hurt when you leave. Terribly. If you're pulling inside yourself in order to spare me from hurting when you leave...it's too late. I'm emotionally involved. The damage is done."

She felt his presence beside her, the hard warmth of his shoulder pressing against hers, the tension mounting in his silence.

"For God's sake, Alex. Say something."

His arms came around her and, none too gently, he turned her to face him again. The armrest gouged into Chelsey's side as he pulled her toward him. Then his mouth came down on hers, hot and passionate. His large hand cupped the back of her head, holding her mouth to his as he parted her lips with his tongue.

Chelsey was glad she had booked first-class tickets, glad there was no one sharing their row of seats.

When his palm slipped to her breasts, she reluctantly pushed him away. "Not here," she said weakly, managing a small smile. Her heart was pumping wildly. It was hard to remember what they had been talking about.

His hands slid upward to frame her face. "Listen to me. The last thing I want is to hurt you or cause you pain. But I forgot how brave you are and how clear-sighted. For that, I apologize."

He kissed her again, and all thought rushed out of her mind, replaced by rapturous sensation. His hands, tightening on her shoulders, his firm hard lips claiming hers. She heard her pulse pounding in her ears and felt the quickening breath lifting her breast.

Before the possibility of rational thought went up in flames, Chelsey eased back from him and let her head fall against the seat back. Lifting a hand, she pressed it against her thudding heart. Never before had she indulged in such a spectacle in public. Oddly, it didn't bother her as much as she would have thought. There was something wildly appealing about a man without inhibitions, a man who took what he wanted when he wanted it and the rest of the world be damned.

"Do we have this settled?" she asked, unable to speak above a whisper. His face was classically beautiful and perfect.

The back of his hand stroked down her cheek and throat. His eyes made love to her mouth. Finally he smiled, sending her nervous system into overdrive.

"Being together may end painfully, but consequences will be dealt with when they arise. In the meantime, we'll follow our inclinations. Would you agree that's an accurate statement of our situation?"

"I'd say so." Chelsey gazed at him with a soft expression. His dark hair curled on his collar. His eyes were the shining color of the Mediterranean. Needing to reassure herself that this splendid man was real, she raised trembling fingertips and touched his jaw.

"You need a shave," she murmured, smiling, trailing her fingertips across his cheek and chin.

"I do?" Surprise lifted his eyebrows, and he touched his face. "I do." A frown sobered his expression. "How odd."

"Don't you shave?" Now that she thought about it, Chelsey didn't recall seeing him shave. But that didn't mean anything. He could have disposed of his whiskers through magic.

"I'm sleeping longer. I haven't shaved since Selidim...."

Chelsey could almost see his mind working. She straightened in her seat. "Alex, why does this upset you? What does it mean?"

"I don't know." They stared into each other's eyes. He touched her hair. "Maybe . . . it means our time together is growing short."

The instant they stepped off the plane at La Guardia, Chelsey turned to him, speaking quietly. "The airport is crowded. Maybe no one will notice." Right now she didn't care if anyone saw them vanish. She was willing to throw caution to the winds because his suggestion about time growing short had shaken her badly. "Take us to the street outside the hotel. I don't want to waste another minute."

Alex pulled her into his arms and kissed her deeply, spreading hot fire through her veins. He didn't care that other passengers had to walk around them and neither did Chelsey. All she cared about was having Alex's arms around her. When Chelsey pulled back, feeling weak-kneed and shaky, they were standing on the sidewalk in front of the St. Moritz Hotel.

"Hurry," she whispered. They raced through registration, ran to their room and tore off each other's clothing.

In the back of their minds they were both aware that somewhere a clock was ticking, counting down their time together.

IN THE MORNING, happily tired from a night of enthusiastic lovemaking, Chelsey shifted in bed and drew a finger down Alex's naked muscular shoulder. "You know," she said, "the busts will keep. They aren't going anywhere. I could follow up later. We could just—"

He stopped her words with a kiss, then pulled her down on the pillow so he could look in her eyes.

"No. I want to be with you through as much of this as I can. Certainly it must have occurred to you that tracing the thief could be dangerous."

She smiled, seeing the eagerness behind his eyes. "The danger appeals to you, doesn't it?"

Naturally she had considered that tracing the thief might be dangerous, but she hadn't allowed herself to examine the possibility too closely. There had been Alex to think of, and their growing passion. Besides, if her quest turned dangerous or frightening, she could quit.

She must have spoken aloud, because Alex rose on an elbow to look down at her. "If you abandon the quest, then you will have wasted your first wish. Restoring your reputation is important to you, and we'll follow the trail to the end. Or as close to the end as time allows us."

So he was worried, too.

After propping up the pillows, Chelsey remained in bed and watched through the open bathroom door as Alex shaved with a strap and straight razor he produced out of thin air.

She didn't know how she was going to bear it when he left her. His departure would be like a hand crushing her heart and leaving it as withered as her leg.

The good news, and she tried to focus on the good news, was that she could exert some control over the situation. She would not make her third and final wish until Alex told her the time had come when she must.

"The sleeping and the shaving... are you becoming more—I'm not sure how to say this—more human the longer you stay in the reality plane?"

"I don't know." He frowned at his image in the mirror, and Chelsey realized he was wrestling with the same question. "I honestly don't think that is possible."

Chelsey sat up in bed. "Alex...will you know when you have to return to the dream state? I mean, you won't just vanish, will you?" Although she tried to keep any hint of panic out of her voice, the sudden panic was there. Surely there would be time for goodbyes and final words.

"I think I'll know when the time arrives," he said, speaking slowly, his frown deepening. He met her eyes in the mirror when she stepped up behind him. "It's tied to the third wish. I know you're delaying the last wish and I'm grateful. But there may come a moment when I tell you that you must make the last wish or lose it."

Chelsey wrapped her arms around his waist and rested her cheek against his smooth, satiny back. The smell of shaving soap and clean warm skin rose in her nostrils.

"We'll cross that bridge when we come to it," she said finally.

He put down the razor and spoke in a gruff voice. "What time is our appointment with the curator? Maybe you'd like some company in your shower?"

Laughing, Chelsey threw off her nightgown. She had a moment to think how strange and wonderful it was that she no longer felt embarrassed to stand naked in front of him.

Then he stepped into the shower and molded her against his rampant body. He groaned and ran his hands over her naked eagerness, soaping her body until she was covered with glistening bubbles and laughing at the designs he drew through the bubbles with his fingertip.

"Oh, Alex," she whispered, wrapping her arms around his neck. "I didn't know sex could be fun. I always thought it was so serious."

She had been wrong about so many things.

# Chapter Ten

"I assure you the provenances for the Lupberger's Marcellus busts are beyond reproach. The Lupberger would never traffic in stolen artifacts! The suggestion is preposterous!"

"Perhaps not knowingly," Chelsey agreed, watching Albert Petre, the curator at the Lupberger Athenaeum. He sat behind an ornate Louis XV desk, twisting his hands together. When Chelsey looked at him, she saw circles. A round face, round nostrils, round wire-rimmed spectacles and a round pursed mouth.

She drew a breath and leaned forward. "Mr. Petre, I've inspected the busts flanking the Roman room and I'll stake what remains of my reputation that you have two of the missing Marcellus busts." She kept her expression blank. "I'm sure you're aware that it's illegal to remove antiquities from Turkey."

Mr. Petre tugged at his collar. A glisten of perspiration appeared in the gray hair at his temples. "It is simply not possible that the Lupberger's Marcellus busts were stolen."

"Obviously the provenances are forgeries," Alex snapped.

Without having discussed it previously, Chelsey and Alex
fell into the good-cop/bad-cop routine. Chelsey kept her
voice and expression quiet and sympathetic. Alex stared at
Petre as if the man were a confessed ax murderer.

"Mr. Petre, if I can prove to you that your busts are the
same busts that vanished from the Caraki, will you tell us
where and how you acquired them?"

Mr. Petre mopped his brow with a snowy handkerchief.
He started to rise behind the desk. "I'm sorry, Dr. Mal-
lon, but I think I must terminate this appointment at once.
We have nothing further to say to one another."

"My colleague's request seems reasonable," Alex
growled. His eyes were glacial. "Dr. Mallon believes she
can prove to your satisfaction that your busts are stolen. If
Dr. Mallon is wrong, she will apologize and we will leave.
If she is correct—"

Chelsey interrupted. "Then naturally you'll want to return the busts to the Turkish authorities and correct an unfortunate error."

Petre's voice spiraled upward into a squeak. "Do you
know how much the Lupberger paid for those busts? The
trustees will..." He sat down heavily and rubbed his
handkerchief across his forehead. "Dr. Mallon, these cannot be the busts you helped discover."

"I'm certain you believed that when you acquired the
busts for the Lupberger," she said generously. "Surely you
want to know for certain."

"Of course he does," Alex said, standing. His posture
was vaguely threatening.

Petre also stood, and Chelsey suspected he hadn't done
so of his own volition, but was helped along by magical
prodding.

"Shall we go to the Roman room and allow Dr. Mallon
the opportunity to present her proof?" Alex continued.

"This will ruin me," Petre muttered as he led the way through the halls of the museum. "I don't know why I'm doing this. Our Marcellus busts are not the stolen Turkish busts. I would never purchase stolen antiquities."

Before approaching Petre, Chelsey and Alex had visited the Roman room to inspect the busts. They were magnificent, so beautiful that Chelsey couldn't view them without feeling the heat of appreciative tears behind her eyes. She didn't blame Alex for stroking his fingers over the marble faces—they seemed so real.

"I think it would be prudent to have other witnesses present," she suggested, casting a meaningful look at Alex. At once, two museum guards appeared, along with a woman who had been viewing the Roman exhibit.

Chelsey gazed at Petre, who wore an expression of deepening despair, then she studied the busts. "If you tip the busts to expose their bases, the bust on the right side of the archway will have a Roman numeral II carved into the underside. The bust on the left will have a Roman numeral IV carved on the base. These are original markings, and I can't imagine they were effaced. If these are the stolen busts, both will have a tiny *M* in a circle next to the Roman numerals. That is my own mark."

Under Alex's steady stare, Petre mopped his forehead, then nodded at the two guards. "Raise the bust on the right and tilt the base toward us." His instructions emerged in a whisper.

Chelsey didn't have to look; she knew what the base would reveal. "There's the Roman numeral II and there's the *M* within a circle."

Petre covered his face. Turning on his heel, he walked back to his office and collapsed into his chair. His eyes seemed to shrink behind the magnifying lens of his glasses.

"This is going to be terrible," he said quietly. "The Lup-berger's reputation will be destroyed."

"Not necessarily," Chelsey offered. "You might turn this to your advantage if you make a splash about returning the stolen items. The Lupberger's integrity and all that."

"Possibly," he murmured.

Chelsey drew a breath. "From whom did you purchase those busts, Mr. Petre?" When he hesitated, she added, "You might as well tell us. You must know the story is going to come out."

He sighed, then removed a file folder from the cabinet behind him. "I purchased the busts from the Burgeson Import House. This is the first time we've done business with them." He pushed the file across his desk toward her. "I've been with the Lupberger for twenty-eight years, Dr. Mallon." He spread his hands in a helpless gesture. "The Marcellus busts were just so beautiful."

Chelsey felt sorry for him. "I know," she said softly.


"I DON'T LIKE THIS," Alex said, frowning at the dilapi-dated warehouse in front of them. Harbor gulls dived overhead. The area smelled of decay and rotting garbage.

"It's not the location I would have expected for a repu-table import house," Chelsey agreed with an uneasy ex-pression, watching their cab depart. Speaking in under-statement was getting to be a habit. "But this is the address on the invoice Mr. Petre gave us." Unconsciously, she stepped closer to Alex and squared her shoulders. "I hope Mr. Burgeson is in. I'm not crazy about having to come here again."

Maurice Burgeson was in, and he granted them an au-dience, looking surprised that he did so. Chelsey followed his scowl into a shabbily furnished office above the warehouse, sliding a look of gratitude toward Alex. She almost stumbled when she saw him.

Alex's hair was slicked back in the wet look favored by Hollywood mobsters. His lightweight summer suit had vanished, replaced by dark silk, a crisp white shirt and a black tie. Only someone who knew him well could have identified the twinkle of enjoyment in his eyes. Anyone else would have seen an aggressively hostile man who projected a silent threat of physical force.

Maurice Burgeson hunched down behind his desk, puffing on a cigar while Chelsey explained the purpose of their visit. Occasionally he glanced at her. For the most part, he kept his cold gaze fixed on Alex.

"So?" he asked when she finished.

"So it appears you sold the Lupberger Athenaeum two stolen Marcellus busts," Chelsey repeated uncomfortably. Burgeson was a large man running toward fat. Diamond rings flashed on his fingers. Power and ruthlessness flattened his eyes. His stare made Chelsey's nerves jump, and she gripped the handle of her cane with shaking hands.

"How was I supposed to know the busts were stolen?" Burgeson offered in a bored voice, measuring Alex's unblinking stare.

"I'm sure you didn't," Chelsey said, not believing it for a minute. "We'd like to know where you acquired the busts. From whom."

"Are you cops?" Burgeson inquired, exhaling a stream of smoke in Chelsey's direction. Cigar smoke stacked in blue layers above the cardboard cartons surrounding his desk.

"It's a fair assumption that you'll be hearing from the NYPD in the next few days. But no, we're not with the police."

"What's it going to take to make you people go away and forget about this?"

Chelsey looked into his flat, icy eyes. She felt as if there wasn't enough air in the room. "Information. How did you acquire the Marcellus busts?"

The cigar glowed cherry red, then he grinned, exposing a gold tooth. "Nice try. But this interview is over, honey."

The blood rose in her cheeks. "All I'm asking is—"

"We can do this the easy way or the hard way. You walk your gorgeous butt out of here right now, or I'll sic my henchmen on your henchman." He inclined his head toward Alex, not looking away from her. "You're outnumbered, Doc." He dropped a hand under his desk. "Now what's it gonna be? Do I call my boys?"

She gave him her most scathing stare. "I'm not leaving until I discover who sold you the Marcellus busts." Her most scathing stare only amused him. Chelsey wasn't sure she would have been so courageous and foolhardy if she hadn't had a genie in her corner.

Burgeson's grin widened. "Forget it. Trust me on this one, babe. You don't want to know. We're talking some nasty people here. Real nasty. I'm doing you a favor to kick you out of here."

"Dr. Mallon asked you a question," Alex said, his voice a menacing rumble. Chelsey shifted to stare at him. His French accent had altered into something more rough and threatening. "Answer the lady."

Maurice Burgeson's heavy brow clamped into a frown as he leaned to inspect the button he was pushing without effect. A handful of thugs should have responded to his summons.

"Your pretty boy don't scare me, Doc." He smiled at the idea. "We'll see if you can say the same." Rising behind his desk, he looked expectantly toward the door of his office.

Invisible hands flung him against the middle of his office wall. His arms and legs spread in an X shape. He looked as if he were stuck to the wall with universal-strength Velcro. Burgeson's mouth fell open and the cigar dropped to the floor as Alex stalked forward. "Tell Dr. Mallon what she wants to know."

Chelsey gasped. She couldn't guess what this turn of events was doing to Maurice Burgeson's nervous system, but she knew what it was doing to hers. Her pulse raced at a million miles a minute. Her eyes were as wide as pie plates. This was a side of Alex that she hadn't seen before. All traces of playfulness had disappeared from his gaze, assuming any playfulness had existed to begin with. Chelsey wondered if she had only imagined it. She stared at him.

The man whose intent gaze pinned Burgeson to the office wall was the angry crusader, a man infuriated by humanity's baser side, a knight protecting his lady. Alex looked coldly furious. His hands opened and closed at his sides as if he wanted to do more than merely stick Burgeson to the wall.

"Jeez!" Burgeson breathed, looking down at himself in disbelief before he raised his head to stare at Alex. "Who the hell *are* you?" Sweat poured down his reddened face. He tried to pull his arms free but couldn't.

"Who sold you the Marcellus busts?" Alex demanded.

Burgeson studied Alex's face, then answered promptly. "Sami Kahd. The information you want is in the file cabinet. The key is in my desk."

They didn't need a key. The file drawers along the east wall burst open and files began pouring out onto the floor like a paper river. One of the files floated across the room and hovered in front of Chelsey until she grasped it in her shaking fingers.

"Thank you," she whispered, not certain if she was thanking Burgeson or Alex. She just wanted to get the hell out of there.

Burgeson was splayed against the wall like a grotesque doll, his weight beginning to sag. He stared at Alex. "Whatever she's paying you, I'll triple it."

"Do you have everything you need?" Alex asked.

"I think so," Chelsey answered, swiftly scanning the contents of the file. "I'll need copies for the police and for Eric Fry."

The copies instantly appeared. Her plan was to add this file to the file Petre had copied for her, scribble a note about locating two of the stolen busts, then send the package to Eric Fry, an Istanbul stringer for CNN who had spearheaded the story about the busts' discovery and their subsequent theft. Eric had been the first to report Julian Porozzi's innuendo that Chelsey was the thief. Chelsey didn't hold the revelations against Eric. He was only doing his job.

Once Eric received Chelsey's package, he would guess what she was doing. When the time came, Chelsey hoped she could count on him to devote as much space to clearing her name as he had devoted to besmirching it. She hoped she wasn't wrong about him.

"Let's get out of here," she said to Alex, stuffing the file into her oversize purse. She glanced at Maurice Burgeson. "I trust you won't mention our visit to your friend Sami Kahd."

"If you do," Alex snarled, "I'll have to pay you another visit. And I won't be in a good mood."

Burgeson just muttered, his eyes bulging as he watched the files pouring out of his cabinet, the papers piling on the floor.

Once they closed Burgeson's office door behind them, Chelsey bent forward at the waist and breathed deeply, trying to calm herself. "That got a little scary," she whispered when she could breathe. "How long will he stay stuck to the wall?"

Alex shrugged. When she looked at him again, he was dressed in faded jeans and a blue shirt, the sleeves rolled to the elbows. This was the Alex she knew.

"I think we'll leave him there for a while," he said, grinning down at her.

"You enjoyed every minute of that, didn't you!" Chelsey wished she knew if she was amused or furious. Her emotions swung somewhere in between.

Taking her arm, Alex led her out of the building and onto the street, where he turned her to face him. "I hope you've noticed that the people we're encountering on this quest are getting progressively nastier." His expression had sobered.

"Thank heaven I have a genie on my side." She didn't know how the interview with Burgeson would have ended it Alex hadn't been present. She suspected the outcome wouldn't have been good. Certainly she would not have obtained the information she needed.

"If I have to leave you before this is finished...I want you to promise that you'll end the quest at once. It stops that minute."

Chelsey considered his request. "I'm sorry, but I can't make that promise," she said finally.

He gave her a shake and his hands tightened on her arms until she winced. "Don't be a fool, Chelsey."

She eased out of his grasp, straightened her jacket, then leaned on her cane and eased the weight off of her leg. "Look, Burgeson scared the hell out of me, and this Sami Kahd sounds even worse."

"All right, then."

"But without my good name, I have no future. I have to go as far with this investigation as I can, Alex."

Alex thrust his hand through his hair and swore heatedly.

Leaning on her cane, Chelsey waited until he fell silent and glared at her. She straightened her shoulders and shoved her pride aside. "But I'm willing to do a little backpedaling." Willing? After Burgeson, she was ready to jump at the chance to reconsider. "I'm starting to believe archaeologists should restrict their sleuthing to the ancient past. What I'm saying is, maybe the procedure isn't important, after all. I've reconsidered and I'm willing to do this the easy way." She drew a breath. "So, okay. Let's use your magic to jump ahead to the end of the quest. Tell me who the thief is and we'll go confront him."

"Shazam."

Chelsey gasped and flung out her hand, steadying herself against the top of a chair. They were back in their suite at the St. Moritz. "Damn it, Alex. Do we really need more stories about aliens teleporting themselves around New York City?"

"I can't tell you the name of the person who stole the bust out of the Caraki Museum. I can't tap into that information without you spending another wish."

"The final wish," Chelsey whispered. They stared at each other across the bedroom suite. Turning abruptly, she took off her suit jacket and hung it in the closet, then fluffed out her hair and smoothed her palms over her slacks. "Well then, we'll proceed as we planned."

"That works as long as I'm with you. But suppose time runs out before the quest ends? I saw Burgeson's file, Chelsey. Sami Kahd, the next step in the chain, is in Munich, Germany. Since you insist on traveling by conventional means, we're talking about a twelve-hour flight, maybe a day or so to track down Kahd, then on to the next step. Time is passing. I don't know how much time I have left. I think we should discuss the advisability of using the final wish to end this quest and ensure your safety. We can structure the wish to expose the thief, reveal the remaining busts and restore your reputation.''

"Is that what you want?"

Their eyes held. "What I want is unimportant. I'm only making a suggestion."

"I'll decide what's best for me. And the answer is no, I'm not ready to spend my last wish." She could hardly bear to think about it.

"Sometimes you irritate the hell out of me," he said, striding forward to glare out the window at Central Park.

"And sometimes you irritate the hell out of me," she said, frowning at his profile. "I think that's called a relationship. Maybe it's a by-product of spending every waking hour with the same person." She thought about that a minute. Other than Alex, Chelsey couldn't think of a single person with whom she could have spent this much uninterrupted time without being bored silly or going crazy. But every minute with him was fresh and exciting and wonderful. And sometimes irritating.

"You're a practical woman. So why can't you be sensible now? Each step of this quest becomes more and more dangerous. If I wasn't here—"

"But you are here," Chelsey pointed out in a reasonable tone. She sat on the edge of the bed and opened Maurice Burgeson's file on Sami Kahd. Leaning forward, she studied the papers in the file.

"You know," she said, examining the information, "I think we've stumbled onto a smuggling ring. If the information in this file is correct, Burgeson has been buying stolen artifacts from Kahd for at least three years. He's sold them to museums all across the United States.''

Her gaze settled on the telephone. Her instinct was to give the files to the police and let them complete the investigation. But there were problems with that scenario.

First was time. An official investigation would eat up weeks. And how would she explain her role? The police would demand to know how she had learned the two Marcellus busts were in the Lupberger. Okay, she could claim an anonymous tip. But how could she hope to explain what had happened in Burgeson's office? A two-hundred-pound man stuck to the wall? Files magically pouring out of a file cabinet? And what if the police insisted that she produce Alex for questioning?

There was nothing to do but go forward. She would mail the files to the NYPD. By the time the police had deciphered the contents or Eric Fry broke the story, maybe she would think of some answers that sounded plausible.

"Does the file explain who Sami Kahd is?" Alex asked from his position beside the window.

It always surprised her to realize there were things Alex didn't know. "The paperwork involving Kahd shows the address of a Munich gallery. It's probably a clearing house of some kind for artifacts smuggled out of Turkey. And other parts of the world."

"We can speed this process by—"

"No, Alex. We still need that paper trail. Now more than ever. If you want to help, phone Lufthansa and make airline reservations for us." He glanced at the phone with an unhappy expression. "I'll make it up to you," Chelsey promised softly.

As she reached for the tiny pearl buttons running down her blouse, Chelsey kept remembering how he had jumped to her defense. She recalled the look on his face, and a tiny shiver traveled down her spine. There was something powerfully arousing about the image of a man leaping into battle for his lady, a subtle seduction within emotional fury.

"Come here, crusader," she said in a husky whisper.

THEY WALKED IN THE PARK and took a carriage ride, then explored Fifth Avenue, window-shopping until it was time to dress for dinner. Chelsey's leg throbbed with fatigue, and she would have preferred to order dinner in their suite, but she said nothing. Alex had made reservations in the Mirage Room. She suspected he was still trying to make up for the special dinner she had missed with Howard Webber.

Howard now seemed like an unpleasant memory from a different life. Whenever Chelsey thought about him, which wasn't often, she felt embarrassed and appalled. If it hadn't been for Alex, she would have made a hideous mistake. She might actually have gone to bed with Howard, an error of judgment she would have regretted for the rest of her days.

"I'm so glad you came into my life," she said softly, looking at Alex in the mirror as she spritzed perfume on her wrists and behind her ears.

"So am I," he said, coming up behind her. His arms wrapped around her waist, and he buried his face in her upswept curls. "You smell like apples."

Chelsey laughed. "Like apples?"

"And you look beautiful," he said, gazing at her in the mirror. She wore a silk slack suit, the color of which almost exactly matched Alex's eyes.

"So do you."

For a moment she gazed into the mirror and saw them as a couple. No wonder people stared. Alex was tall and handsome; his air of confidence and curiosity was commanding. As for her, it surprised Chelsey to recognize how pretty and happy she looked. There was a radiant vibrancy to her skin and features that she didn't recall noticing before. And tonight she didn't consider her cane ugly and detracting. She could almost convince herself that it was somewhat elegant and made her look interesting. Not quite, but almost.

Throughout a lavish candlelight dinner they leaned toward each other in the banquette and spoke of ordinary things. If they touched too often or gazed too deeply into each other's eyes, if observers smiled and recognized them as lovers, they didn't notice. They delighted in pretending they were an ordinary couple enjoying a special evening in an ordinary way.

It wasn't until the dessert cart had come and gone and the waiter had served coffee and brandy snifters that Chelsey returned the conversation to an earlier subject.

"Alex, did I understand you correctly?" she asked, discreetly massaging her left calf under the table. She had overdone it today. Her leg throbbed and ached and felt hot beneath the skin. "Are you suggesting that I use my final wish to conclude our quest?"

"That's one possibility," he said cautiously, watching the candlelight reflecting in her dark eyes. "I know how important restoring your reputation is to you. But it isn't my place to suggest how you use your wish."

"Without a good reputation, I might as well retire from archaeology and find a job checking groceries." She saw his grin, then laughed aloud. "I keep forgetting that I'm rich now. But you know what I mean. Archaeology is my passion. It's the only thing I've ever wanted to do. And in this field, reputation is all."

The music began.

Only now did Chelsey notice the raised stand at the front of the Mirage Room and the musicians who had assembled there. They began the evening's repertoire with a lively cha-cha. A half-dozen couples moved through the tables toward a small polished dance floor, facing each other with smiles before they floated into the rhythm.

Falling silent, her buoyant mood fading, Chelsey watched the dancers with longing in her eyes.

Over the years, and without really being aware of what she was doing, she had focused all the bitterness, disappointment and frustration about her withered leg on dancing. Dancing embodied all of her limitations. She would never be graceful. Would never be fluid or lithe. She would never move without thought, without considering her next step. She would never be symmetrical, would never be fully harmonious within herself.

Suddenly her image of herself as a radiantly desirable woman evaporated. It was nothing but self-deception. Had she approached the dance floor, everyone would have seen her as she really was.

"I'm tired," she said in a tight, thin voice. "I'd like to return to our room."

Alex followed her gaze from the dancers to the hands twisting in her lap. "Is it the dancing?"

She tried to see past the curve of the banquette. "Where's our waiter? We need our bill."

"Wait a minute." He stared at her. "Something just occurred to me."

"Please, Alex." She averted her face from the dancers, unable to glance at them without feeling the shame of white-hot envy. "It's time to leave."

"My God," he said softly. "You really don't know, do you?"

"Know what?" Something very like panic was squeezing her chest. She felt an irrational compulsion to rush out of the room, away from the music and away from the dancers flowing smoothly into something slow and achingly romantic.

"Chelsey." Leaning forward, he caught her hand and clasped it tightly between his. "Chelsey, I can fix your leg. I can make your left leg as strong and perfect as your right."

Her head snapped up and the blood drained from her cheeks. She stared at him as if she had never seen him before. "What?" The word was no louder than a breath.

"All you have to do is wish it."

She continued to stare at him, hardly daring to breathe. Her heart slammed around inside her chest, and she couldn't hear over the pounding in her ears. "That isn't possible," she whispered. "You couldn't cure Dr. Harding's Alzheimer's."

"Oh my God." Alex closed his eyes, then leaned toward her, cradling her hand against his chest. "Restoring your friend's health was not a direct benefit to you. Repairing your leg *is*. I thought you understood that."

"But history—you said you couldn't alter history."

"If I repair your leg, nothing in your past history will change. What changes is the future. It will be as if you had an operation at the time of the wish."

Chelsey wet her lips and clung to the edge of the table for support. She felt dizzy, almost sick to her stomach from the sudden surge of blinding hope. "The best doctors in the United States couldn't do anything for my leg. They tried."

"I can. If you wish it."

She released the table edge and clutched both of his hands. Hope exploded inside her chest and flamed into excitement so intense that she was on fire with it, hurting inside with it. She could hardly breathe. "Alex... is it really true? Please don't promise this unless you're very, very certain. Could you really...?"

"Yes."

"Oh God. Oh dear heaven!" She closed her eyes and fell backward against the banquette. "If you only knew how much I..." Tears sprang into her eyes, shining on her lashes when she opened her eyes and looked at him. "Oh, Alex, I could wear skirts! Short skirts! Skirts that split up the side. I could run if I wanted to! Kneel for hours on a dig like everyone else. I could swim or ski without being afraid I was making a fool of myself. And Alex! Oh, Alex." She turned shining, wet eyes toward the dance floor. "I could dance!"

Alex held her hand so tightly against his chest that she could feel his heartbeat. "I know you won't believe this," he said quietly, "but I love it when you forget your special shoes. You have a slightly rolling gait that is wildly seductive and provocative."

"A rolling gait," she repeated with a shudder of revulsion. She hunched her shoulders as if hiding from the image. Then she grabbed his hands again. "Oh, Alex. Thank you, thank you, thank you! You can't possibly know what this means to me! It's a miracle! A miracle!" Tears ran down her cheeks, but her eyes were radiant and blazing. "I don't know what to say. There aren't enough words to express my gratitude. This will change my life! I'll be a whole person again!"

He straightened beside her. His voice was low and somber. "Is this your wish, mistress?"

"Yes. Yes!" She didn't understand the sadness in his eyes. He raised his hand to her face, and she felt a tremble in his fingertips. Grasping his hand, she pressed it against her cheek. "Be happy for me. Please, Alex, be happy for me. I've dreamed of this, ached for this! But I never imagined it could really happen. Will I feel anything? Will it

hurt? No, don't tell me. I don't care. Just do it,
Alex, right now! I wish . . .''

The last gold coin appeared in her hand, caught the glow
of the candlelight and grew warm against her palm.

"I wish . . .''

## Chapter Eleven

"Oh my God!"

Chelsey snatched her hands back, horror darkening her eyes. Not breathing, she watched the gold coin fall to the tablecloth and wobble to a stop against the base of her brandy snifter.

She raised large, stunned eyes to Alex. A tremor began in the pit of her stomach and rocked through her body, leaving her trembling as if she'd been gripped by a violent seizure.

Collapsing against the banquette, she buried her face in her hands. "Oh my God," she whispered again. "I almost...I... It was so close!"

Turning blindly, she pressed against Alex's chest, wishing she could crawl inside of him. His arms came around her. He stroked her hair, caressed her shaking back. Soothing murmurs rumbled deep in his throat.

When she could breathe again, Chelsey lifted wet eyes to his face. "Why didn't you stop me?"

"The rules state—"

"Your stupid damned rules!" Anger fueled by the deep fear of almost losing him shot through her body. "One blindingly selfish minute almost sent you back to oblivion! And you couldn't say anything? Not a word? Not 'Do we have to do this now?' Not 'Goodbye'? Or 'Hey, it's been fun'?'' She couldn't stop shaking.

Alex gripped her shoulders and lowered his face close to hers. ''Listen to me. There is nothing wrong with wanting a perfect leg! You never complain, but I know your leg hurts sometimes and pains you. I don't agree with the way you see yourself, but I know nothing I say will change your opinion. Your image is valid for you. But is it selfish to want something for yourself? Is it selfish to wish for a dream come true? No. Chelsey, Selidim forced the wishes to be selfish. They can't be anything else. So don't flog yourself for wanting something wonderful that you can have simply by wishing it.''

''But not now, not yet!'' Accepting his handkerchief, she wiped her eyes, then blinked at the smudges of mascara. She felt like someone who had leaned too far over the edge of an abyss and was snatched back a split second before plunging down. She couldn't breathe and her nerves continued to jump and twitch. Her stomach rolled in long, slow loops. She didn't start to feel better until the gold coin shimmered briefly, then disappeared.

A waiter appeared to refill their coffee cups, sliding a quick, curious glance toward Chelsey.

''I can't believe that you couldn't have said something,'' Chelsey snapped after the waiter had moved to the next table. ''Don't you care?'' She stared into Alex's steady blue-green eyes, trying to read his expression. ''Are you ready to return? Is that it? Are you tired of me, Alex?''

His fingers tightened on her shoulders so powerfully that she winced. ''If I thought it would make a difference, I'd cut off my right arm to stay here with you. Every little thing you say or do delights me. You fascinate, irritate and excite me. I couldn't grow tired of you if we had a thousand years together.''

"But..." Confusion drained the color from her face.

"Chelsey, listen to me. The third wish must come. It will happen. I won't allow you to forfeit your wish. I want you to have it, to have your reputation restored or a perfect leg or whatever you decide. Then I must leave you. We've both known from the beginning that's how it will end. Nothing can change that. Your final wish may come tonight or two weeks from now. But it *will* happen. We can delay it, but the moment will come."

"Alex—"

"There may not be time to say goodbye or to tell you how much it has meant to me being with you in the reality plane. The wish could overwhelm you again as it nearly did tonight. Swiftly, emotionally, joyfully. If that should happen, then I want you never, never to look back with regret. You know I care about you, and I know you care about me. And we both know our time together is measured. Enjoy your wish. Exalt in it. Don't castigate yourself that you claimed your wish at my expense. You have no choice. And please, my dearest, dearest mistress, please know that wherever I am, I'll be sharing your joy."

Chelsey dissolved in tears. "Use your magic and take us out of here. Right now I don't care if anyone sees. Hold me, Alex. I need you."

Standing he threw some bills on the table, then swept her into his arms.

And they vanished.

THEY MADE LOVE frantically, hurriedly, straining to get closer, closer. Their hands flew over each other's bodies, stroking, caressing, reassuring. They rolled off the bed to the floor but neither of them noticed or cared. All that mattered was melting into one another, becoming one entity, one being. All that mattered was the urgency of finding each other and, in the discovery, finding themselves.

Later, lying side by side in blissful exhaustion, they sipped chilled wine from crystal goblets and murmured words lovers have murmured since man first stood upright. And because it was their words and their moment, the sentiments seemed fresh and new and wonderfully unique to them. Only gradually did their whispers bend toward more ordinary conversation.

Alex cushioned her head on his shoulder and brushed his fingertips over the wet tendrils clinging to her forehead and cheeks.

"It isn't fair," Chelsey said softly, feeling a prick of tears. "I've looked for you all of my life. I thought you didn't exist. Now I find you, but only for a brief moment."

Alex's arms tightened around her in a gesture of possessiveness that was a mockery given their circumstances. "I thank the powers that be that I've had this time with you," he said gruffly. "Never to have had this, never to have known you..."

Turning her in his arms, he kissed her, long and deep, trying to tell her with his mouth and hands what he could not put into words.

This time when they made love, the frantic urgency had abated. They touched each other with tenderness and gentle delight, marveling in the differences between them. His hardness; her softness. The silkiness of her hair; the scratchy coarseness of his whiskers. The golden bronze of his skin; the milky whiteness of hers. The jigsaw compatibility of male and female.

And when he kissed her withered leg, tears of love, gratitude and excruciating loss slipped from the corners of her eyes.

ALTHOUGH ALEX FIDGETED, the twelve-hour flight to Munich passed in the blink of an eye for Chelsey. She dozed once or twice, but her mind was too active to permit a deep sleep. She couldn't concentrate on the new Anne Tyler novel.

Finally she gave up and let her mind wander freely among the possibilities offered by the final wish.

Alex was right. The time would come when the final wish could be delayed no longer. She needed to push her mind beyond the devastation of losing him and decide what she would wish for so she would be ready when the moment came.

Last night she would have stated emphatically that her final wish would be for a perfect left leg. There was no real choice to make.

But upon reflection, Chelsey experienced a disturbing nibble of doubt even though her idea of herself was linked intrinsically with her leg, her cane and her limitations. To a large extent her personality had been shaped by these things. But at the same time her idea of herself was also tightly bound to her profession. Archaeology was how she defined herself, her accomplishments, how she measured herself.

But unless the timing worked out exactly right, she would have to choose between restoring her professional reputation, thus preserving her identity as an archaeologist, or repairing her leg and that part of her psyche that was as damaged as her withered muscles.

It was a terrible, impossible choice. Like trying to decide whether to relinquish her heart or her soul.

Shifting, Chelsey turned to gaze at Alex, who was trying unsuccessfully to doze. Long, curling lashes rested on his cheeks. His arms were crossed over his chest in an effort to squeeze himself into a seat too small for a man his size.

A dark hint shadowed his jaw and upper lip; already he needed to shave again. She decided he could also use a haircut. Last night he had slept a full two hours. And he had perspired during their lovemaking, which had surprised him. She wondered if Alex had realized yet that he'd stopped eating anything and everything for the taste and tactile pleasure and had become selective in his choices, stopping at almost the same point at which an ordinary man would. This change indicated he was experiencing hunger and satiation.

Chelsey didn't fool herself that these physical changes meant Alex was becoming less of a genie and more of an ordinary man. They had discussed the possibility several times and had reluctantly dismissed it as wishful thinking. His magic was as strong and effective as it had ever been and as readily available. Had he been undergoing a transformation from genie to man, the magic would have diminished correspondingly.

The physical changes were a result of his prolonged sojourn in the reality plane. An indication that his time here was growing short.

"A penny for your thoughts," he said softly, and she realized he was watching her.

"I was thinking about whiskers and perspiration and haircuts," she said, looking down at her hands. "Selfish things."

He understood as she had known he would. "You're worrying that I'll have to return before we conclude the quest."

And worrying about terrible choices. "How will it happen, Alex? How will you know it's time to return?"

The dream state had assumed an aura of horror for her. Chelsey couldn't imagine the unthinkable frustration of drifting through time in a dream, unable to touch or feel, unable to reach out and experience.

"I think the process has already begun," Alex admitted quietly, rubbing his fingers across his jaw. "The physical changes are a signal."

She closed her eyes and lowered her head, swallowing a cry of the heart. "What happens next?"

"I don't know. I've never stayed in the reality plane this long before." He frowned and looked past her shoulder at the wing of the plane. "I think a pressure will begin to build. And continue building until it becomes almost unbearable. Something like what happens when I wander too far from your voice, only a hundred times more intense. The knowing will come. I'll know you must make your final wish immediately or agree to forfeit."

"Has it begun?" she whispered. "Do you feel the pressure?"

His hand dropped to his chest, the movement involuntary. "Not yet. But it's there, Chelsey. I sense it gathering."

Heaven help her, so did she. She felt like a person trapped in the bottom of an hourglass, watching helplessly as the unstoppable grains of sand poured down on her. Burying her, choking her.

"I don't want you to forfeit your final wish."

She made a helpless gesture with her hands. "Without a reputation for integrity, I might as well give up my profession. And that would be like giving up breathing. But I want a perfect leg, too. I've dreamed that impossible dream for over a decade."

He took her hand. "Maybe you won't have to make that choice."

But the pace had accelerated in their race against time.

THE HILTON INTERNATIONAL was located on Am Tuckerpark, a scenic avenue between the Isar River and the Englischer Garten. As their suite wasn't made up yet, they walked in the Englischer Garten, passing beneath ancient oaks and elms, birches and fir.

The long flight had left her leg feeling cramped and tight, and Chelsey relied heavily on her cane.

"There's a bench. Would you like to rest a minute?"

Chelsey hesitated, pride warring against fatigue, then she nodded gratefully. Ordinarily she would have vigorously denied an urge to rest her throbbing leg. But knowing that very soon she would be able to walk for miles and miles without tiring made it acceptable to give in now.

"It's beautiful here," she said, admiring the banks of summer flowers surrounding the bench. A hundred yards to Chelsey's left, a naked couple reclined in the grass, casually embracing. She smiled, wondering if Americans would ever be comfortable with the less inhibited mores of an older culture.

Alex offered her a frosty stein of strong German ale, and she accepted it with pleasure. They sipped ale and listened to music drifting toward them from a nearby beer garden.

"Does the music upset you?" Alex asked.

"Why would you ask that? Oh. No, music has never upset me. I love music, all kinds except jazz. I don't understand jazz—it sounds like noise to me." She smiled, then fingered the handle of her cane. "It's dancing that upsets me."

But not for much longer. Tilting her head back, she gazed at a leafy overhang of thick branches and leaves so dense they smothered the morning sunshine.

The one man in the universe with whom she longed to float around and around a dance floor would be gone. She and Alex would never dance together.

"While you were freshening up, I phoned Kahd's gallery," Alex informed her. "It's located on Prannerstrasse, a few blocks from the National Theater. Are you familiar with the area?"

Chelsey frowned, trying to remember. "I haven't been in Munich since the year after I graduated from college, and then it was only for a few days. But I think that's a good area." Which surprised her. She had expected Sami Kahd to have located his gallery and/or clearing house for stolen antiquities in a spot as seedy and out of the way as that chosen by Maurice Burgeson. She gazed at Alex over the foam capping her stein. "Did you make an appointment for us?"

"Kahd wasn't in. But his secretary recognized our names. She said Sami Kahd would see us at four-thirty this afternoon. Is that too soon? Would tomorrow have been better for you?"

Chelsey met his eyes. In the back of her mind she listened to a clock ticking. "The sooner the better." A full minute elapsed before she spoke again. "What does it mean that Kahd expected our call and granted us an immediate appointment?"

Alex stretched his arms across the back of the bench and gazed forward. "It means our friend Maurice phoned ahead."

"Then why did Kahd agree to see us? Did you use your magic to make him agree?"

Alex shrugged and shook his head. "Who knows? Maybe Kahd's curious to meet the people who stuck Burgeson to his office wall. Maybe he wants to discover how much we know about his operation. Or maybe he thinks we're Tupperware salespeople and he's in the market for a lettuce crisper."

His last remark was so unexpected that Chelsey burst into laughter, spilling foam and ale across her slacks. "Sometimes you know things that I'd never imagine you would know. Other times you don't know things that any self-respecting genie ought to know. Where did you learn about Tupperware? No woman worthy of the name can run a kitchen without it."

"What do you do with all those little plastic bowls?" he asked, offering his arm. They headed back toward the Hilton.

"Contrary to the genie method, most women can't consign leftovers to a cosmic black hole. We save them in airtight plastic bowls."

"Why?"

"Because we can't bear to throw food away until it's green and fuzzy." She started laughing again. "The longer the period between usable and green and fuzzy, the better we feel."

By the time they reached the Hilton, tears of laughter rolled down their faces. Part of the silliness was due to the fatigue of jet lag, but part was a release of the tension they felt about meeting Sami Kahd in a few short hours. The mention of Kahd's name had caused Maurice Burgeson's lips to pale. It wasn't going to be a pleasant experience.

THEY ASKED THE CAB DRIVER to circle the block so they could examine Sami Kahd's gallery and the building that housed it. Although the building was large, the gallery portion appeared unusually small. A glimpse of the alleyway revealed unmarked trucks unloading crates into the building's warehouse entrance.

"My guess is the gallery is mainly a cover," Chelsey suggested, leaning from the cab window to peer up. Even the windows on the third and fourth floors were protected by thick iron bars. "I'll bet most of Kahd's pieces are moved in and out of the back without ever appearing in the gallery."

They entered the deserted gallery and confirmed Chelsey's guess. Inside were two rooms crammed with indifferent items of little interest or value. An overlay of fine dust coated pieces that would have disappointed even a novice collector.

At the sound of their footsteps against the hardwood floor, an unsmiling older woman appeared from the gloom shadowing the end wall of the second room. After inspecting Chelsey's cane, then sweeping a glance over Alex, she gave them a short nod. "Follow me, *bitte.*" Turning sharply, she led them through a door at the back of the gallery, locked it behind them, then indicated an elevator at the end of a dim hallway.

After giving each other a glance, Chelsey and Alex rode the elevator upward in silence, stepping off on the fourth floor. Here the corridors were carpeted in thick, rich plush. The walls were a deep plum color. Here and there urns and marble busts rested on ornate pedestals. Skillfully lit paintings lined the hallways.

"Good Lord," Chelsey breathed. "That's a Rubens! And there's a Titian!" She tried to calculate what the paintings in this corridor were worth. So many zeros made her eyes glaze.

The woman led them to carved double doors at the end of the corridor. Without a word, she turned and departed the way they had come. Alex waited until they heard the hum of the elevator, then he raised an eyebrow at Chelsey and pushed open the doors.

Inside was a lavishly appointed reception area. The antique chairs and settees were worth a king's ransom. Many of the paintings and artifacts were simply priceless. Chelsey recognized a magnificent jeweled cross that had vanished four years ago in a bold daylight theft from a museum in Seville.

Two secretary desks faced the doors, both deserted. Directly ahead was a second set of double doors. These doors were open and a massive, custom-made desk faced them from inside the room beyond. The man behind the desk, Sami Kahd, examined them with eyes the color of black ink.

His hair was black; his Italian silk suit was black. A hawk nose jutted from the middle of a swarthy complexion. If it were true that a man's eyes offered windows to his soul, then this man had no soul. Not a flicker of emotion stirred behind Kahd's icy black stare.

"Oh boy," Chelsey murmured. Her heart flip-flopped in her chest, then sank. She thanked God that Alex was beside her. Placing each reluctant step with care, she summoned a whisper of courage and walked into Kahd's office.

Before she could sort out what was occurring, five men sprang from behind the doors and jerked her away from Alex. Rough hands pinned her arms behind her; a huge man stood in front of her, aiming a gun at her breast. On the other side of the door two men subdued Alex. A third thrust a gun against his jaw. It all happened in less than a minute.

Sami Kahd walked around his desk. "We're going to discover why you're so interested in the Marcellus busts. Then we're going to kill you." He spoke in a bored voice, neither pleasant nor unpleasant, glancing at a medieval clock as if he resented time lost on interrogation, torture and killing.

A gathering noise rumbled across the room like an angry wind.

The guns flew out of the hands of Kahd's men, burst from shoulder and leg holsters, out of a desk drawer and a wall safe that banged open. Two or three knives ripped up out of jackets or pants. The weapons whirled in the air near the high ceiling like strange blue-black birds, then vanished.

The men stared, their jaws slack. One of them swore. "You said Burgeson was lying!"

Lengths of rope and thin chain poured out of the ceiling. It happened so swiftly there was no time to react. The rope and chain sought Kahd's thugs and wound around them with a faint hissing sound. Once they were bound, a giant invisible hand hurled them across the room against the back wall. They slid to the floor like limp rag dolls. Dark hoods materialized in the air above them and dropped over their heads. Aside from a single moan, no one made a sound. None dared move a muscle.

"Did the bastards hurt you?" Alex gripped Chelsey's shoulders and scowled into her face.

"No," she whispered, dragging her gaze from the pile of bound men. Her heart was galloping a mile a minute and her nerves were raw, but she wasn't harmed. Only frightened and more than a little awestruck. She wasn't sure she had the nerves for this kind of thing. Pressing a hand to her forehead, Chelsey leaned against the wall and fought to compose herself.

When she opened her eyes, she noticed a tiny kernel of interest growing across Kahd's bored expression. "It seems I erred. I didn't believe Burgeson." Ignoring his men, he studied Alex. "Who are you and what do you want?"

"Dr. Mallon wishes to know who sold you the Marcellus busts."

Kahd's dead eyes shifted to Chelsey. His accent was faint, but suggested Turkish origin. "I'd think you would know, Dr. Mallon, as you stole the busts in the first place."

"No," Chelsey said, her face hot.

"Oh?" A thin smile made his face look grotesque. His eyes remained removed and empty. "Whatever your motivation, the trail ends here." His smile held. "You—or any officials you may think to involve—will find nothing here to suggest stolen artifacts. No evidence leads to this gallery."

Chelsey leaned forward. "Maurice Burgeson—"

"It seems Mr. Burgeson has vanished. I doubt he will reappear. Last night his warehouse and all his records burned to the ground." His gaze returned to Alex. "None of your theatrics impress me, Mr. Duport. Nor would a further display induce me to jeopardize a lucrative venture. So, I'll wish you good day and advise you to forget the Marcellus busts." His smile tightened. "Perhaps we'll meet again."

He started to turn away, but the invisible hand returned and slammed him into a straight-backed chair that appeared in the center of the room. After a brief struggle to rise, Kahd relaxed and lifted an eyebrow at Alex.

"An interesting parlor trick. I confess a curiosity as to how you accomplish these feats. But you're wasting your time. Perhaps I should mention that I once spent two years in a Turkish prison. Are you familiar with Turkish prisons, Mr. Duport?" The glacial smile returned. "Turkish prisons are the most brutal in the world. There is nothing you can do that has not been done to me before. I did not speak then, either."

"Chelsey, I want you to leave the room." Alex walked around Kahd's chair, watching and circling. The muscle and tendon stood out on his arms like cords of cable.

"Leave the doors open so I can hear if you call. Under no circumstances are you to look inside this room. No matter what you hear or think you hear, you are not to enter this room or look inside it."

"Alex...I don't know about this." Chelsey wet her lips. She glanced at the bound and hooded men lying against the back wall, then back at Sami Kahd, stuck to a chair in the center of his lavish office. Although Kahd's complexion had paled and his darting eyes no longer seemed as lifeless, he effected a relaxed and arrogantly confident posture. Actually it was Alex who worried her most. Chelsey no longer knew him. He looked large and ruthlessly powerful. Icily furious and frightening.

"Go."

There was no room for argument in that growled command. No mercy. No yielding. Chelsey picked up her cane and went.

Standing well outside Kahd's office doors, Chelsey pressed her back flat against the paneling and wondered what in the hell she had gotten them into. It frightened and appalled her to think of the destruction that had followed the discovery of the Marcellus busts. Lives had been altered. Reputations had been destroyed. Now someone had died.

If Alex hadn't employed his magical powers, he and Chelsey might also have been dead by now.

She shuddered, straining to hear the murmur of voices from the room behind her, unable to decipher more than a few isolated words. The voices rose to shouts, followed by a period of thick taut silence.

Then Sami Kahd began to scream.

There were words within the screams, and pleas, but Chelsey didn't hear them. She heard only the shocking sound of a man's screams. The screams clawed across her nerve endings. Rocking mindlessly, she clapped her hands over her ears and chewed her lips until they bled. She reminded herself that Sami Kahd had intended to have her and Alex murdered. It didn't help. The horror and pain in Kahd's screams made Chelsey sick to her stomach. She had never heard anything like this and prayed she never would again.

She spun toward the doors, hoping she wouldn't vomit or faint before she stopped the torture in the other room, but she had to stop it or go insane herself. She took two steps before Alex appeared, closing the doors firmly behind him.

"We're leaving now," he said calmly. He opened a humidor on one of the secretary's desks, removed a thin dark cigar and lit it, sucking the smoke deep into his lungs.

"I didn't know you smoked," Chelsey whispered inanely. Her nerves jangled. Her body shook and her skin twitched. She thought it possible that she was about to throw up.

"I need to cut the taste in my mouth." After drawing deeply on the cigar, he tossed it aside, then led Chelsey out of the reception area.

Kahd's screams followed them into the corridor.

The screams didn't end until Alex dropped his arm around her waist and said, "Shazam." They materialized in their suite at the Hilton.

Chelsey collapsed into the chair near the window, pitched forward and covered her face in her hands. "Oh my God, Alex! What did you do to him?"

"One of Kahd's men put his hands on you."

"You tortured him, didn't you?"

"In a manner of speaking." Anticipating her needs, he materialized a frosty pitcher of ice water and poured a glass. He also produced a cold wet cloth which Chelsey accepted and pressed against her forehead.

When she had stopped shaking enough to speak again, Chelsey looked up at him with a white face. "What exactly did you do? Please, Alex. I have to know."

Alex sat on the edge of the bed, watching her. "Every man has secret fears, his own brand of terror and hellish nightmares. I showed Kahd his fears and nightmares in a hologram much as I used to show you the location of the Marcellus busts. But I let his terrors and his nightmares escape the hologram. They crawled over his body and into his eyes. They entered his mind."

Chelsey tried to imagine the horror of what he was describing. She couldn't. "What were Kahd's nightmares?"

"No," he said quietly, looking away from her. Now she noticed how pale his lips were. "That I won't tell you."

Standing abruptly, Chelsey wordlessly threw off her clothing. When she was naked, she walked into the bathroom and stood under as hot a shower as she could stand. It was a long time before she felt clean and safe again.

THEY ORDERED DINNER in their suite, but neither had an appetite. After making a pretense of eating, Chelsey gave it up. She carried a china cup of rich dark coffee out onto their small balcony. Her hair was still damp from her shower and she wore the thick, plush bathrobe provided by the hotel.

She pushed back the terry sleeves and leaned on the balcony railing, gazing out at the dark Englischer Garten. Somewhere far below, an oompah band played German drinking songs. The night air was pleasantly cool. Clouds obscured the stars.

When Alex joined her, leaning his elbows on the railing beside her, she rested her head against his shoulder, suddenly so tired she thought she might collapse.

"Kahd ordered Burgeson killed, didn't he?" she murmured, closing her eyes.

"Yes."

"I wish I'd never started this." She glanced at the gold coin that appeared in her fingers, then tossed it off the balcony. "I want to set the record straight and restore my reputation, but..." It occurred to her that even Sami Kahd had believed she was responsible for the theft of the busts. Maybe Albert Petre had believed so, too. And Maurice Burgeson. People all over the world believed Dr. Chelsey Mallon was a thief. "Did you learn anything from Sami Kahd?"

"Kahd masterminds a very large, very profitable operation dealing in priceless antiques and artifacts." Alex moved behind her. His large hands massaged the tight knots that had turned her shoulders to stone. "These items, all stolen, are smuggled into Munich from Europe, the Middle East, and the Orient. Kahd's organization creates new provenances for the antiquities and notifies a hundred outlets like Maurice Burgeson's. It doesn't take long to locate a buyer, even for items known to be stolen. The highest bidder is selected, then the items are shipped from Kahd's gallery to a middleman like Burgeson."

"You make it sound simple," Chelsey murmured, closing her eyes and leaning into his hands.

"The Marcellus busts came to Munich through Bulgaria. Kahd's deal was with two shopkeepers in Istanbul, two brothers named Achmed and Ish Hamish. I have their shop address."

"So," Chelsey whispered, looking at the dark sky, "Istanbul is next." They had been moving toward Istanbul from the beginning.

"There's something else. Kahd purchased three of the Marcellus busts. Not four. Two went to the Lupberger Athenaeum, one to the London Museum of Roman Antiquities. He knew nothing of the whereabouts of the fourth bust."

"The bust in the storeroom," Chelsey remembered, frowning. "I thought about that on the plane. I think the thief still has the fourth bust. Maybe he can't bear to part with it. Or maybe he's waiting for the price to rise. If we find that bust, we'll find the person who stole them all."

"I phoned Pan Am while you were in the shower. We have reservations on the morning flight to Istanbul."

That's where Chelsey's nightmare had begun. That's where it would end. Along with the greatest joy she had ever experienced.

She had wanted events to move rapidly so she wouldn't have to choose between restoring her reputation or her leg. Now that the end was in sight and speeding toward her more swiftly than she had dreamed possible, she wanted to throw up a barrier and hold back time.

That Alex had phoned Pan Am without any prodding from her told Chelsey the dream state was stirring. Alex had begun to feel not a vague sense of impending pressure, but the pressure itself.

Blindly she turned toward him. "Hold me, Alex. Hold me like none of this is happening, like you'll never let me go."

He caught her in his arms and buried his face in her damp curls.

# Chapter Twelve

Chelsey and Alex flew into Yesilköy Airport, then took a cab to Pera Heights, crossing the Golden Horn to reach Beyoglu north of Stamboul, the old walled city. Although still referred to as the "new" city, Beyoglu had housed foreigners since the tenth century. Now the hills of old were flattened, crowned by luxury hotels and restaurants, theaters and consulates.

"Is this where you stayed last summer?" Alex asked as they registered into the Topkapi Hotel, which was almost as ornate as Topkapi Palace but nowhere near it. The palace commanded the tip of the promontory fortifying the old city.

Chelsey laughed. "Not hardly. I spent a few days in a run-down place outside Kanlica. Then weeks camping in the desert."

While the bellman explained their water supply would be erratic because the rivers were running dry earlier this year than last, Chelsey wandered outside onto a tiny balcony.

What she loved most about Istanbul were the domes, minarets and fountains. The multitude of minarets reminded her of spears challenging the sky. And, of course, she couldn't think of Istanbul without the Bosporus, an incredibly crowded waterway that sustained the city like a brown artery. Docks and wharves jutted from every available piece of waterfront.

Today the wind was from the southwest, blowing the exotic scents of the old walled city to the heights. The pungent smell of packed humanity invaded every breath, as did the stench of burning rubbish and automobile emissions. Riding atop the breeze was the sweet smoke of a hundred different varieties of incense. No city smelled quite like Istanbul, Chelsey thought. It smelled of people and food and religion and history.

There was also a dark side to the city's beauty. Secrets flourished here. Every imaginable vice had a price tag and a vendor. Human life was cheap. Nothing was quite what it seemed on the surface.

"Have you been here before?" Chelsey murmured as Alex came up behind her and wrapped his arms around her waist.

"I've dreamed of Constantinople. I watched the armies of the Fourth Crusade sack the old city."

"A disgrace, if I remember correctly. The gentlemen, and I use the term loosely, of the Fourth Crusade behaved abominably."

They stood close, gazing out at the sun-bright domes and minarets. Wistfully, Chelsey wished they were visiting as tourists with nothing more pressing to do but enjoy historical tours and pleasure excursions.

"Do we have a plan?" Alex murmured against her ear. His large hands slid up to gently cup her breasts and pull her back against his chest.

"Only to find Achmed and Ish," she said, closing her eyes.

The realization that their time together had dwindled to a matter of days increased their hunger for each other. They had to compress a lifetime of memories into a few spare hours.

"The Hamish brothers can wait," Alex said hoarsely, turning her in his arms. His eyes smoldered down into hers.

Chelsey unbuttoned his shirt and ran her palms over his powerful chest, anticipating the timeless delirium of his hands on her thighs, her belly, her breasts.

Truly he was magic.

THE CAB LET THEM OUT on Mevlanakapi Street near a side street that veered into a labyrinth of twisting alleyways. From here they proceeded on foot through unpaved alleys overhung by dilapidated wooden houses and laundry lines. The smells were strong and unpleasant. The heat trapped in the alleyways was intense, but no sunlight penetrated the overhang. The residents of this dismal section lived in perpetual gloom.

Chelsey blotted perspiration from her forehead, then edged closer to Alex and took his arm, aware that hidden eyes watched. Few tourists ventured into these mean streets.

"There are moments when I'm damned glad you're a genie," Chelsey whispered, sensing hostility from the dark forms who slid past them in the alleyway.

"Only moments?" he asked. His arm beneath her fingertips was taut and tense. He scanned the alleyway in front of them.

"This is one of them."

At length the gloom opened into a noisy square that housed a local bazaar. Chelsey eyed the rabbit warren of aisles that twisted and turned in a confusing maze. The sound of animal bleatings and human haggling pounded against her skull, as did the high whine of Turkish music, which she had never learned to appreciate. A biting blend of incense, roasting lamb and other less pleasant smells assaulted her nostrils.

"Is this where we'll find the Hamish brothers?" she asked in a faint voice.

"Over there."

Following Alex's gaze, Chelsey was relieved to see they would not have to plunge into the chaos of the bazaar. Achmed and Ish's shop was a permanent structure located on the corner of one of the alleyways spilling people into the bazaar.

"Good God!" Chelsey breathed, gripping Alex's arm. "Do you see that man entering the Hamish brothers' shop? He's carrying a bronze amphora that must have come from Gilmach! I read in the trade journals that Dr. Robinson uncovered a stunning cache." Shock darkened her eyes almost to black. "He isn't even trying to conceal it! The Hamish brothers are so damned brazen they're trafficking in stolen antiquities in broad daylight in front of a thousand people!"

"Do we confront them or not?" Alex inquired, watching her face, protecting her from the jostling of the crowds.

She hesitated. "We need to think about this."

It occurred to Chelsey that Achmed and Ish Hamish were not likely to be any more forthcoming than Burgeson or Sami Kahd. Alex would again have to intervene. But in this instance, Alex's persuasion would be conducted in an open-front shop before hundreds of people. Chelsey doubted that performing before an audience would inhibit Alex, but the idea horrified her.

"We're so close," she said, thinking aloud. Sliding a look toward Alex, she added, "Maybe it's time to involve the authorities."

"It's your call," Alex said reluctantly. He cast a final glance at the Hamish brothers' shop, impatience hardening his eyes, then he led her back through the maze of alleyways.

They returned to the Topkapi Hotel and ordered a late lunch in their suite. While Chelsey made one frustrating telephone call after another, Alex expanded the room and replicated a Roman ruin. The carpet disappeared beneath packed sand and tufts of salt grass. Patiently, Alex applied himself to excavating the cornerstone of what he told her was a Roman temple.

"I want to understand what you do," he explained.

Trying to ignore the sand dunes behind her, Chelsey telephoned the official who had investigated the theft of the Marcellus busts from the Caraki Museum. After several attempts, it became clear he would not accept her calls.

"All right, we'll do this the hard way," she muttered with a sigh. She began the tedious process of wending her way through the leviathan bureaucracy of the Turkish government.

IT WASN'T UNTIL the next morning that she discovered Harry Sahok and convinced Sahok to give her and Alex an appointment.

On the positive side, Harry Sahok headed a department whose purpose it was to stem the flood tide of antiquities leaving Turkey. Chelsey hadn't realized there was such a department. The bad news was that Sahok's department was ridiculously understaffed and underfunded.

When Chelsey finished explaining the route of the stolen Marcellus busts, Sahok leaned back in his desk chair and studied her with sympathetic dark eyes. He was a handsome man approaching forty, Chelsey guessed, but his eyes were much older. Lines of fatigue bracketed his mouth and carved railroad tracks across a broad forehead. His office was no larger than a cubicle. His cluttered desk was made of scarred metal.

"The Hamish brothers buy stolen antiquities and smuggle them out of the country almost before we know about the theft." Sahok leaned forward and folded his hands on his desk top. "Their father ran the operation before them, their grandfather before that. But prove it?" He shrugged, glancing at an overhead fan that wheezed, then coughed to a stop.

"The Hamish brothers aren't making any effort to hide what they're doing," Chelsey insisted. "A thousand people must know they're trafficking in stolen antiquities."

"But will any of those thousands of people testify?" Sahok passed a hand over his eyes. "People who threaten the Hamish brothers have a nasty way of disappearing. If I could help you, I would. But unless I can catch Achmed and Ish in the act...my hands are tied."

"But you *know* they're shipping stolen antiquities to Sami Kahd in Munich!"

"I know it but I can't prove it, and I don't have the resources to protect witnesses if I had any. I don't have the manpower or the finances to conduct a full-scale investigation." He spread his hands, indicating his cubicle and shabby furnishings. "Turkey has problems more pressing than preserving antiquities, Dr. Mallon. Here, Roman ruins are as ubiquitous as mosques. If a few artifacts get smuggled out of the country, there are more where those came from."

Chelsey stared. "Do you believe that, Mr. Sahok?"

"That's the official attitude. Every country has priorities. Maybe someday...but for the present my department is near the bottom of the funding list." He studied her. "I'm sorry about what happened to you. For what it's worth, I never believed you stole the Marcellus busts. I figured the curator, maybe Porozzi.''

Chelsey spread her hands in frustration. ''Is there anything I can say to—''

''I'm sorry. There's nothing I can do.''

Desperate, she searched her mind. ''Will you agree to this much? If I can set up a sting, will you put some official weight behind it? Will you arrest Achmed and Ish? And cooperate on an international level to shut down Sami Kahd's operation?''

Harry Sahok glanced at Alex.

''This is Dr. Mallon's show,'' Alex said. ''I support however she wants to handle the situation.''

Sahok nodded and looked back at Chelsey. ''If you can arrange something where I can catch Achmed and Ish redhanded, I'll slap the handcuffs on. But I don't have the hours or the manpower to get involved before your sting is about to unfold.''

''Fair enough. I'll let you know when we're ready.'' She shook his hand. ''It'll be very soon.''

''A sting?'' Alex asked, raising an eyebrow when they were back on the hot, teeming street.

''I'm so frustrated I could scream,'' Chelsey said, banging the tip of her cane against the pavement. ''We're this close, but time is speeding by and no one gives a damn!''

Alex took her arm and flagged a cab. ''Sahok's a good man, but tired and overworked. He'll be there when the time comes.''

''The problem is, I don't know when that will be.'' Chelsey slid into an air-conditioned cab with a sigh of relief. She leaned forward to massage her throbbing leg. ''I don't have a plan, worse luck. Can you think of something?''

"Suppose we make Achmed and Ish an offer," Alex suggested after a minute, his blue-green eyes twinkling. "Suppose we offer to buy the fourth bust..."

"Wait a minute. Yes!" Chelsey sat bolt upright and stared at him, excitement building in her chest. "Achmed and Ish will have to contact the thief to relay our offer. We follow and—bingo—we discover the thief's identity! We'll phone the Hamish brothers first thing in the morning and set it up"

"Or maybe we arrange to meet the thief and make the buy on our terms. But let's phone the Hamish brothers now, Chelsey. Perhaps we can arrange a meeting for tonight."

"So soon?"

Chelsey met his gaze, and her expression instantly sobered. She caught a ragged breath and held it, wishing she could hold time as easily. Suddenly there were a million things she wanted to say to him. A million questions she needed to ask.

But all she said was "There's a pay phone at the university. It's not far from here."

THE FORCES GATHERING around Alex began as a vague sense of unease and gradually deepened toward discomfort. The mounting pressure made him restless and irritable. He found himself particularly impatient with delays. Chelsey's insistence on rail and cabs drove him wild. Magic could have lessened the time required to resolve their quest, time he didn't have to spare.

The physical changes were the most worrisome. Last night he had slept three hours. When he woke, he left Chelsey in their bed and slipped into the bathroom where he trimmed his hair, shaved, and clipped his finger- and toenails, frowning while he did so. He had not performed these ablutions in centuries.

There were other signs. His physical acuity was not as intense as it had been when he had first arrived in the reality plane. It was as different as stroking a red-hot stove top or one that was merely warm. During his first hour in the reality plane, he could feel print on a page. Now it felt as if his genie's body were going numb. He perceived the world more as he imagined an ordinary man would. The change was not unpleasant, merely different. But the implications alarmed him.

Time was his enemy.

Leaving Chelsey waiting in the cab, he hurried into the administration building at the university of Istanbul and found a pay phone. Achmed Hamish answered on the eighth ring.

"What happened?" Chelsey asked anxiously when Alex returned a few moments later and slid onto the seat beside her.

"The Hamish brothers agreed to see us tonight at nine o'clock. They'll phone our hotel at eight-thirty and tell us where to meet them."

Chelsey nodded, her eyes large. "What did you say to them?"

"They recognized our names. Achmed had spoken to Sami Kahd."

"And he still agreed to meet with us?" Amazement shot her eyebrows toward her heart-shaped hairline.

"I suggested it would be worth his while."

"Magic?"

"They sniff money." Leaning forward, he signaled the cabby. "Take us to the Hagia Sophia. We may as well do a little sightseeing." The restlessness building inside him required movement.

THE HAMISH BROTHERS chose a small, smoky coffee-house located near Mavlana Gate. The coffeehouse was reasonably accessible, being near the old-city walls and the railway that ran along the far side of an ancient moat. But it was in an area that only a very brave and very foolish foreigner would enter.

Alex swept aside Chelsey's objections and arrived at the coffeehouse by uttering "shazam." Even at nine o'clock, the unpaved alley was stiflingly hot and jammed with thick crowds. Chelsey glanced around, then pressed next to his body as they entered the coffee shop.

Inside, the dense air was gray with cigar and cigarette smoke and sickening sweet clouds of opium. A sharp-faced boy caught the end of Chelsey's cane and tugged them to a small banquette almost hidden at the back of the room. A double string of beads provided a thin curtain of privacy.

At first glance Achmed Hamish reminded Alex of Mehmed, Selidim's vizier. He was small and wizened, blackened by the sun. Mehmed's ancient, cunning eyes darted about Achmed's swarthy face. Ish appeared simple by comparison, but it would have been a mistake to disregard him. Ish Hamish was not cunning or shrewd like his brother, but he was the more impulsively dangerous of the two. Alex examined Ish's face and sensed the man preferred to kill first and consider later. Ruthless violence was his talent and his pleasure.

"Dr. Mallon and I own three of the Marcellus busts," Alex began.

The Hamish brothers flicked expressionless eyes across Chelsey, sweeping her ginger curls, her anxious face, the wedge of pale skin at her collar. They returned to Alex.

"It is our understanding that you can help us obtain the fourth bust."

"Perhaps. What's in it for us?" Achmed asked. He spoke perfect English with the merest trace of an accent.

"Nothing. Unless you have access to the fourth bust."

Ish made a grunting sound, rolled a dark, pungent-smelling Turkish cigarette between his thumb and forefinger. "Kahd didn't mention anything about you being buyers."

Alex's gaze narrowed. He felt Chelsey's fingers gripping his thigh beneath the table. "We prefer to deal direct. We're not willing to pay a dozen middlemen. Can you produce the bust or not?"

Achmed considered the surface of his coffee. He offered none to Chelsey or Alex. No waiter disturbed them. "Let us suppose for a moment that we know how and where to obtain the fourth bust...." One thick eyebrow lifted. Waiting.

"Naturally we would pay a commission for your assistance in arranging a sale." Alex dropped his hand beside the beads and lifted a suitcase which he placed on the table. He opened it to reveal stacks of banded hundred-dollar bills. The Hamish brothers stared at the cash, their black eyes glittering until Alex closed the lid and replaced the suitcase at his side.

"There's a condition," Chelsey said quietly. She continued to grip Alex's thigh under the table as if anchoring herself to reality. "We wish to purchase the bust directly from the present owner. If he won't meet with us, the deal is off."

"That is not possible," Achmed said flatly.

"I'm sorry we wasted your time," Alex said, gripping the suitcase. The bead curtain rattled like old bones as he parted it, and he and Chelsey started to rise.

"Is this point negotiable?" Achmed asked, making a motion with his hands.

"No," Alex said coldly. Beside him, Chelsey shook her head.

Achmed studied his coffee again. In the dim, filtered light it looked like mud. "How much are you willing to pay for the bust?"

Alex and Chelsey sat back down. "Name a price."

A silent dialogue ensued between the Hamish brothers. "Seven hundred thousand dollars American," Achmed said finally. Ish nodded. "Our commission for setting it up is ten percent."

"Agreed."

A tiny flutter of surprise disturbed Achmed's eyelids. Greed spun in his brain. Since the foreigners had not protested, he grasped that he should have named a higher price. Ish saw it, too, and was irritated. Alex read Achmed's thoughts as easily as if they were printed on his forehead.

"How soon can you set up the buy?"

A shrug. A swift glance at Ish. "A week from tonight."

"Make it two days—no longer," Alex said firmly. "We're leaving Friday morning with or without the bust."

"We'll decide where the exchange will take place," Chelsey interjected. When the Hamish brothers balked, she continued. "The spot will offer no advantage to either side."

A long silence ensued before another invisible signal passed between the two brothers. Achmed glanced toward the suitcase beside Alex. "We will phone you"

"We're staying at—"

"We know where you're staying." Ish produced an ornately handled knife and ran the blade across his thumb.

Alex laughed aloud. Grinning at Ish's murderous scowl, he took Chelsey's arm and led her out of the coffeehouse.

WHILE CHELSEY SLEPT, Alex stepped out onto the balcony and inspected the night sky. There were no stars overhead, at least none that he could see. The French couple next door had finally stopped arguing and now the night was silent except for distant city noises.

The pressure inside his chest continued to build.

He experienced a compelling urge to wake Chelsey and tell her that she must make her final wish. It was this urgency that had propelled him to the balcony and away from her. The push toward the final wish originated outside himself, it was not something Alex wanted. Right now he could still control whether or not he acted on the pressure filling his chest. He didn't know how much longer his control would hold.

The unwanted possibility of leaving her now, as events were coming together, flooded his mouth with a dark, brackish taste. He knew Achmed and Ish. He had dreamed their kind throughout the centuries. The Hamish brothers were masters of the double cross. And he had seen their eyes on Chelsey. He knew what they were capable of doing to her. She would beg them to kill her long before they did.

It was imperative that he remain in the reality plane until the sting was over. He wanted Chelsey to have her perfect leg without the anguish of having to choose between it and her reputation and future.

Until she had her perfect leg, she would not allow a man to fully love her. He had understood this from the beginning.

He wanted her last wish to bring her joy and fulfillment. That would be his gift to her.

Returning to the hot, darkened bedroom, he stood at the foot of the bed, listening to the drone of the overhead fan and watching Chelsey sleep. Leaving her would be the worst punishment of his life. If ghosts could laugh, Selidim was enjoying his revenge.

She loved him.

The knowledge of Chelsey's love sliced through Alex like the blade of Ish's knife, leaving a wound that almost doubled him over. He saw her love in her clear, shining eyes, felt it in her caress and in her touch. He heard her love in the softness of her voice, read it in the morning smile that was for him alone.

He clenched his fists, wanting to rage and shout and bellow at the injustice, at the sweet cruel pain of being loved.

He had never expected to find love again. Nor had he tortured himself by hoping for, or even thinking about, love. He had thrust such thoughts out of his mind, believing that that part of his humanity was long dead.

But along with his growing hair and beard, along with his increased need for sleep and diminished sensitivity to objects, his humanity had returned with human needs and desires. He needed Chelsey Mallon, needed her deep in his spirit. He needed her more than he needed reality, more than he needed life itself. His need for her roared through his blood and brain.

This was Selidim's cruelest revenge, not the lonely centuries that had preceded this moment. Selidim's revenge lay in obstructing the miracle of being loved, the intense wonder and joy of it. Selidim's revenge lay in the hopeless anguish of Alex's knowledge that he would betray Chelsey's love by abandoning her. To allow Alex to find love, then force him to betray it—that was Selidim's greatest revenge.

WHEN THE CALL CAME, Chelsey handed the telephone to Alex and listened to his side of the conversation with a worried expression. His manner was strange and erratic.

One moment he couldn't keep from touching her, holding her. The next moment he seemed almost hostile, striding away from her with a moody expression. He couldn't sit still. He'd started stroking things again, but this time with a frown, as if his fingertips no longer provided the sensation he sought. She thought he was trying to store physical impressions in his memory but the physical impressions disappointed him somehow.

Except for their lovemaking. Their lovemaking remained magical and wonderful, something Chelsey would never forget. A tiny shiver passed through her body. No man had ever made love to her so deliberately or so thoroughly. No man had ever made her feel so desirable and cherished. Their lovemaking truly was magical—enchanted moments they had created for themselves.

"No," Alex said sharply, speaking into the telephone. He paced the length of the cord to look out the balcony doors. "Not tomorrow. It has to be tonight."

Chelsey's heart lurched, and she swallowed hard, then looked away from him. Tonight was too soon. But she had only to glance at him to know further delay was perilous. Alex looked like a man in physical pain, a man with something dark consuming him from the inside.

"If that's what it takes, then tell your man we'll pay a million." He stared toward the waterfront. "In cash. But only if the exchange takes place tonight. For a million dollars, your seller can rearrange his schedule and be there." Finally he looked at Chelsey, his eyes almost translucent in the sunshine streaming past the balcony doors. "Tell your seller to bring the Marcellus bust to the Ballan dig site at nine o'clock. You know where it is." A hint of a smile brushed his lips. "Naturally we'll expect you and your brother to be present, as well."

After he broke the connection, Alex handed the telephone to Chelsey. "We're on for tonight," he said. "Whoever has the bust didn't want to meet in person, but he finally agreed. Achmed believes upping the ante will make our thief happier about exposing himself. It's time to call Harry Sahok and arrange the big finish."

"And Eric Fry, the CNN stringer," Chelsey added, taking the phone. "Alex...are you all right? Are you in pain?"

She could swear he had lost weight even since yesterday. His face was pale and drawn. There were new lines beside his mouth. He paced the hotel room as if he had to keep moving or explode.

"I'm fine," he snapped.

"No you're not."

"Please, Chelsey. Just make your calls."

Harry Sahok eagerly agreed to meet them at the Ballan dig site and to bring Eric Fry with him.

"If this works," Sahok said into the phone, "it will be a career capper. I'll owe you a big one, Dr. Mallon."

"All I ask is that you help me clear my name, Mr. Sahok."

"Count on it. You hand me the thief and the Hamish brothers, and I'll sing your praises to the skies!"

Eric Fry expected her call. "Where have you been?" he demanded, his voice crackling in her ear. "I've received your package of information and I have a million questions! But first, did you know that Burgeson's warehouse was torched? Yesterday Burgeson himself washed up in the East River. You don't want to know what was done to him. Dr. Mallon, I never believed you stole the Marcellus busts. I was just doing my job, you know?"

"I know," Chelsey said, covering her eyes with her hand. She sat down and nodded gratefully to Alex when a pot of café au lait appeared on the table in front of her. "I want you to do your job again, Mr. Fry. I want you to clear my name."

"Where are you and what have you got?"

"I'm here in Istanbul. With a colleague." Chelsey drew a breath and told him almost everything, editing out the genie parts. "That's the story. Can you be there tonight?"

"Are you kidding? Murder? An international smuggling ring? The recovery of the Marcellus busts?" A short bark of laughter came over the phone line. "I'd be there if I had to crawl on bleeding stumps! Can I bring a photographer?"

"You can ride out to the site with Harry Sahok. He'll fill you in on the back story. But bring your own camera instead of a photographer. It's going to be difficult enough to hide you and Sahok's men while we're waiting to spring the trap. We don't need another person to worry about."

After Chelsey hung up the phone, she studied Alex's expression, then dropped her head in her hands and quietly wept.

It was almost over.

How did one say goodbye to a genie? To one's own heart?

Always before, Chelsey had held something back in relationships. Maybe her wait-and-see attitude had contributed to the relationships falling apart. But not this time. This time she had held nothing back. She had given all she had to give and had taken all that Alex offered. Consequently, she was now dying inside at the thought of losing him.

And his urgency communicated itself to her. "It's time, isn't it?" she whispered in despair, wiping at hot tears. "Do I have to make the wish now?" No, she couldn't do it. She would rather forfeit the wish than have him vanish from her life. Thinking about a future without Alex caused a physical pain behind her heart.

"Not yet." Kneeling in front of her, Alex smoothed his hand down her white face. She could see the effort it cost him to smile. "You need me there tonight. Unless you have a suitcase full of cash that I don't know about."

She hurt too much to return his smile. "Alex ... will you be here when I wake up tomorrow morning?"

Gently he guided her into his arms and held her so close that she could feel his heart beating against her breast. Her tears ran into his collar.

"I don't think so, Chelsey." He buried his face in her hair. "You need to decide on your final wish. I'll ask you for it the instant tonight's business is finished."

"Oh God! Alex—" Her pain and frustration were so great that she wanted to scream and shout and hit something over and over.

"No, my darling mistress, don't cry. Smile for me. Tomorrow you'll have your perfect leg. Be happy, Chelsey. I beg you. Be happy." He caught her hands and held them tightly. "Please be happy."

"I am," she whispered. But she cried even harder.

# Chapter Thirteen

Although the night air was warm, a chill of dread and anticipation passed through Chelsey's body. She leaned against Alex's warmth. The Ballan site was as she remembered it, a windswept grid of crumbling stone foundations stretching away from her in the moonlight. Once these ruins had teemed with life. And someone had concealed four busts in an underground storeroom.

Chelsey turned away from the shadowy ruins. Twenty miles to the west she could see the glow of Istanbul against the sky. Two solitary headlights approached across the desert.

"That will be Achmed and Ish," she said. She didn't speculate on the identity of the seller. She was too preoccupied with Alex. Their time together was nearly over. It was all she could think about. She clasped his hand so hard that she was afraid the bones in her fingers would crack.

Stepping up beside Chelsey and Alex, Harry Sahok watched the headlights approaching in the distance. "Malmud and I will be behind that low wall," he said, nodding toward the ruins. He patted his shoulder holster, the gesture unconscious. "We've planted microphones there and there," he continued, pointing. "The instant they accept the suitcase and you get the marble bust, it's over. All you do is get out of the way. Understand?''

Chelsey blinked back the tears in her eyes and tried to concentrate on what Sahok was saying. She was shocked that he had only brought one man to assist. Although both Sahok and Malmud were professionals, hard and capable, she would have preferred a squadron.

Eric Fry, the journalist, crushed a cigarette under his heel and fiddled with his camera. ''Early tomorrow morning we sit down for a full exclusive interview, right?''

''Right,'' she agreed, wetting her lips. The headlights were almost upon them. Sahok prodded Malmud and Fry to the Roman wall. They ducked out of sight. Alex scanned the sand dunes that flowed away from the site like tall, moon-washed waves.

He pressed her arm against his side and examined her face. ''Are you all right?''

''None of this is important,'' she whispered. ''I thought it was, but it isn't. Oh, Alex. I can't stand knowing it's almost over.'' Raising her hands, she pressed the heels of her palms against her eyes.

''I know,'' he said in a strained voice. He hugged her close to him. There were no words of comfort, nothing either of them could say.

Headlights swept the ruins, then flashed off. An engine died and car doors opened. Achmed and Ish emerged. And Dr. Julian Porozzi, struggling with the weight of the fourth Marcellus bust.

Sadness filled Chelsey's dark eyes. ''I hoped I was wrong,'' she said softly, mourning the loss of heroes.

She hadn't remembered how defeated Julian Porozzi looked, or how stooped and small. Once she had believed that he stood as a giant among mortals.

Porozzi followed Achmed and Ish to where she and Alex waited. "You're young, Chelsey, and full of ideals. You don't know what it feels like to watch others make the big finds and garner the fame and the accolades. And the money." He passed a hand over his eyes. "I deserve something for thirty years of being an also-ran."

She stared at him. Moonlight fingered his white hair, deepened the wrinkles drawing his cheeks. "Why did you make everyone think it was me? I didn't deserve that, Julian. You ruined my reputation! Archaeology is the only career I ever wanted and you took it away—or tried to."

"Let's get on with this," Ish snapped. "Where's the money?"

"Aren't you afraid I'll expose you?" Chelsey asked Porozzi while Alex knelt to open the suitcase on the sand.

"My security rests on the fact that we're all at risk. Expose me and you expose yourself. I may be selling a stolen artifact, but you're buying one." His eyes flicked up to Chelsey, then returned to the suitcase. "May I inquire where you got this much money?"

"Hold it," Sahok's voice shouted. He and Malmud popped up behind the low wall, then stepped over it. "You're under arrest. Don't anybody move." Eric Fry ran up to the group standing around the suitcase. A flashbulb exploded.

The flashbulb momentarily blinded Chelsey. Gripping Alex's arm in confusion, she blinked hard and strained to identify a sudden burst of unexpected sounds. There were shouts, and the sound of hoofbeats. Then rifle shots.

Alex shoved her to the ground, and she heard him run forward.

Blinking frantically, Chelsey pushed up on her elbows. Her vision cleared in time to see a half-dozen men circling them on horseback. She screamed as blossoms of fire exploded from the men's rifles.

Horrified, she watched Harry Sahok, Malmud, Eric Fry and Julian Porozzi reel backward, then fall sprawling in the sand.

And Alex.

It seemed to happen in slow motion. Staring in shock and disbelief, Chelsey watched Alex grab his chest and fall.

"Oh God, no!"

No one was left standing except Achmed and Ish. They rushed through the milling horses and men toward the cash and the Marcellus bust.

"No!" Chelsey screamed. Blinded by tears, frantic, she crawled on hands and knees toward Alex. "No, this can't be happening!" He couldn't be dead. Not Alex! No! Desperately, she searched for a pulse beneath his ear.

"I want the woman," Achmed shouted.

One of the horsemen leaned from his mount and grabbed Chelsey, flinging her facedown across the front of his saddle before he galloped back toward the sand dunes. In a frenzy of grief and despair, Chelsey dashed the tears from her eyes and strained for a final glimpse of Alex. He lay sprawled and lifeless in the moonlight near the others.

Alex was dead. The only man she would ever love was dead.

Chelsey went limp, her head dropping. It didn't matter what they did to her, she thought dully. Alex was dead. As she might as well be. Without Alex, she had no life. Sobbing, she surrendered to a black hell of devastating grief.

THE IMPACT OF A DIRECT hit dazed Alex and knocked him to the ground. But, of course, no mortal can kill a genie. Mortals can, however, irritate genies and make them dangerously furious. Enraged, Alex jumped to his feet.

One by one the other men slowly sat up and gingerly touched their chests. Disbelief and amazement stunned their expressions.

Sahok exchanged a blank look with Malmud. "I don't remember putting on a bulletproof vest. Do you?"

Jerking open his blasted shirt, Eric Fry stared down at himself with huge, frightened eyes. "I don't even own one. But I'm wearing one. What the hell is going on here?"

When Alex roared "Shazam," they all swiveled to look up at him. Their mouths dropped open.

Alex stood wide-legged and raging. Heat lightning crackled around his body. His dark silhouette impressed the others as enormous and terrifying.

Flinging out a hand, he pointed to a spot on the sand, his eyes blazing. A white Arabian stallion caparisoned with silver fittings appeared before their astonished eyes, snorting and pawing the earth.

"Shazam!" Alex's jeans and white shirt vanished. He swelled before his stunned audience, garbed in the flowing black robes of a desert sheik, swinging a scimitar in his large hand.

"My God," Harry Sahok breathed. His eyes bulged.

Alex glanced at him, almost smiling for an instant. "I'm going to miss this," he said, giving Sahok a wink. Then he ran toward the prancing white stallion.

He leapt on the stallion's back and raised the scimitar against the starlit sky as the animal reared. Then his robes flew out behind him as he galloped across the dunes in pursuit of his lady.

Eric Fry fainted.

THE SADDLE DUG INTO Chelsey's stomach and her head banged against the man's rifle butt. Sand flew up in her face.

It didn't matter; with Alex dead, nothing mattered. She didn't feel the pain of her jolting body. The pain in her mind was so much worse. Each time she remembered Alex lying dead on the sand, her breath felt like hot razors in her throat. She was sick to her stomach. Her grief was so intense she didn't think she could bear it.

The blackness clawing at her mind parted enough to allow a dim awareness of something soft and wispy blowing against her wet cheeks.

Soft and wispy? Chelsey opened her eyes and dashed at the tears. Then she blinked uncomprehendingly at a length of scarlet chiffon flapping against her face. *Scarlet chiffon?*

Confused, she raised a hand and tracked the chiffon to her head. She was wearing a filmy headdress. A contorted glance over her shoulder, then down at her breasts, revealed she was also wearing a wildly imaginative harem outfit. A gold sequined bikini top covered her breasts. Gold sequins flew past her face, torn from where the saddle rubbed against her hips. Her arms were heavy with gold slave bracelets. More chiffon fluttered against her legs.

Alex? Alex!

Grabbing her abductor's knee, she used it as a lever and pulled upward to peer behind the horsemen, slapping the streaming chiffon out of her face. Hope flared in her wet eyes. It had to be Alex. It had to be.

A white stallion flew over the dunes. On the stallion's back, a dark rider bent forward, his desert robes billowing behind him. Moonlight flashed across the blade of the biggest scimitar Chelsey had ever seen.

Thank God, thank God! He was alive! Fresh tears of elation flooded her eyes, and relief drained the strength from her bones. She flopped limp across the bouncing saddle, then pulled herself up again. A strangled sound rasped her throat, partly a sob, partly a laugh, a combination of joy, fear and exasperation. Chelsey Mallon roared back to life.

"Alex," she screamed, cupping her hands around her mouth, slapping at the clingy chiffon. "Damn it, Alex, stop screwing around! These men are killers. Use your magic!"

But no. Magic would have been too easy. He was too furious and he was enjoying himself too much to use magic. He had to do this the hard way. Chelsey threw up a hand and swore. She jerked on the sleeve of her abductor and pointed back at Alex.

"You can't kill him, you oaf. He's a genie, understand? And he's coming after you!"

The horsemen had already spotted him. Their leader shouted, and they all twisted in their saddles and raised their rifles. Except their rifles had turned into scimitars. They stared at the scimitars in fear and horror. Chelsey understood just enough dialect to identify a few excited words. Demon. Magic. Something from the bowels of hell.

The men reined abruptly, milling in frightened confusion as they watched the fury bearing down on them. The man carrying Chelsey drew back from her, pointing to her harem costume, speaking in a rapid terrified voice.

The leader shouted, and Chelsey's abductor threw her off his horse as if he had discovered a viper in his lap. Screaming, the men dug their heels into their horse's flanks and galloped hard across the dunes, riding as if Satan pursued them.

The ground thundered beneath Chelsey's palms as she pushed to her feet and shook sand out of her hair. As the white stallion swept past her, a powerful arm scooped her up. Suddenly she was part of the man and the horse flying across the moonlit dunes. Alex held her tightly against him, his robes billowing around her harem costume.

Chelsey flung her arms around his neck. "Stop!" she shouted. "Let them go!"

Gradually the fury drained from his glittering eyes. Chelsey felt his thighs tense as he pulled back on the reins and brought the racing stallion to a walk. Dropping the reins, he slid his hands over her arms and shoulders. "Did the bastards harm you?" he demanded. "If they did..."

"Oh, Alex, I thought you were dead!" She buried her face against his neck. "I saw them shoot you and you fell and I thought, oh God, I was so sure that—"

"Shh." His mouth whispered against her temple as his hands moved over her body, reassuring himself that she was not injured. "Everyone is safe and unharmed." Responding to the pressure of his thighs, the stallion turned toward the Roman ruins.

"I don't want to go back," Chelsey murmured against his skin. She wished they could stay like this forever, close in each other's arms, sheltered by the night and Alex's warm robes. She wished they could ride like the wind over the sand dunes and emerge into a world where they could be together always.

"We have to go back," he said as if he had read her mind. She heard pain equal to her own in his strained voice. Their time together was drawing to an end.

Alex rode with his arms tightly cradling her. Chelsey rested her head on his shoulder. Tears slipped from beneath her closed eyes.

Harry Sahok walked forward as the white stallion pranced toward the low Roman wall. He stroked a hand down the stallion's arched neck, as if to prove to himself that the horse was real. He inspected Chelsey's chiffon and sequins.

"I don't understand one damned bit of this. Who the hell are you?" Sahok asked softly, staring hard at Alex.

"Not now," Chelsey interjected. "I'll explain everything tomorrow." Sahok deserved the truth. Maybe he would even believe it.

Sahok nodded slowly. "Porozzi, Achmed and Ish are in cuffs. We've got everything on tape."

Alex looked down at Sahok. "Go now. You have what you came for."

Harry Sahok hesitated, then raised his hand and gripped Alex's fingers in a hard shake. "We're going to need your rental car to help transport these people."

"Take the rental car," Alex said. Chelsey sensed the tension building where she leaned against his chest. His body was as hard as steel. She could almost feel the explosive forces working inside of him. She swallowed a sob and tightened her fingers on top of his hands, felt the horse shift beneath them. "Send a car back for Dr. Mallon," Alex said to Sahok.

Not for *us*. For *Dr. Mallon*. Chelsey ducked her head and closed her eyes. She was trembling all over. The time left to them had narrowed to minutes.

A dozen questions disturbed Harry Sahok's dark eyes. But he understood this was not the time. Chelsey waited atop the stallion, shaking in Alex's strong arms, watching as the cars departed.

The desert was never entirely silent. The earth whispered. Moonlight nested atop the Roman ruins and tinted the rustling sand silver. A warm, dry breeze caught the ends of the chiffon headdress and fluttered it across Chelsey's bare arms.

She wanted to scream and cry and hurl herself against onrushing time, wanted to hold it back. Pressing herself against Alex's warm, strong chest, Chelsey bit her lips and listened to her own mindless whisper. "No, no, no, no. Please no. Not yet. No."

When she opened her eyes, she saw a silken tent through her tears, lit by perfumed lamps. Inside, Chelsey could see gold pitchers and platters of figs and pears. Piles of silk cushions beckoned.

Alex dropped from the back of the stallion and lifted his hands to her. She slipped into his arms and clung to him. They stood together in a fierce embrace. "This is the end, isn't it?" she whispered.

"We have until dawn," he murmured against her hair, molding her body against his arousal. "No longer. Then you must use your wish or forfeit."

"I don't care about the last wish! I would forfeit it gladly if I could keep you here!"

He tilted her face up to him and gazed at her as if he strove to engrave her image on his memory. "You know I have to leave you," he whispered in a thick voice.

Chelsey leaned back in his arms, letting him support her weight. Her left leg was trembling and throbbing. She had landed hard when she was thrown from her abductor's horse. Her leg ached and burned deep within. She had no idea what had happened to her cane.

For the first time since she had been stricken by polio Chelsey realized that having one leg shorter than the other was not important. For over a decade she had fantasized about having two perfect legs, about having a body she could be proud of. She had fantasized about something that wasn't important. Loving and being loved—that was important. Her leg was not.

Clinging to Alex, holding him in silence, she wondered who she would have become if there had been no polio, if she had had two healthy, well-shaped legs of the same length? Would she have been a different person? Less strong and self-reliant? Less ambitious? Less driven to prove herself? Would she have been less sensitive to the pain of others?

"Come with me," Alex whispered against her hair. "Let me carry you to the tent and love you one last time." He bent to take her into his arms, but she flattened her palm on his chest and gently shook her head. A rush of tears blurred the outline of the silken tent.

"No," she said quietly. "It's time for the last wish."

Surprise flared in his eyes, followed by regret and the pain of rejection. Alex gazed deeply into her clear, steady eyes, then he stroked her hair, caressed her cheek with the back of his hand. He kissed her softly, tenderly—so tenderly that Chelsey's body ached with the bittersweetness of his mouth on hers.

Then his demeanor changed. He stepped backward and bowed deeply before her. "I am yours to command, mistress. I await your final wish."

"Goodbye," Chelsey whispered, closing her eyes. She fought to swallow the lump rising in her throat. "It was a lovely dream. For a while it seemed possible, and that was wonderful. I will always be grateful."

"Goodbye, my dearest. I'll never forget you, Chelsey. Never!"

"What?" She opened her eyes and clutched the front of his robe, afraid that he was leaving her. "Alex, I'm not saying goodbye to you. I'm saying goodbye to a fantasy that I've clung to for far, far too long. I'm letting it go."

"I don't understand," he said, frowning.

Chelsey almost laughed, feeling the excitement build deep inside and rush into her eyes. She was trembling all over. This had to work. Life would not be worth living if it didn't.

"I wish ..."

The gold coin appeared in her fingers. Moonlight gleamed along the rim as it warmed against her skin.

Alex gazed deeply into her eyes and spoke rapidly. "Thank you for this time. Thank you for restoring my belief in the goodness of humanity, and thank you for sharing yourself with me," he said softly. "I will never forget you, Chelsey Mallon. I will dream you." His eyes flew over her face, memorizing her, making love to her.

"I wish..." She gulped a deep breath and hoped to heaven that she phrased this correctly. "I wish that Alexandre Duport be released from his sentence as a genie and that he be restored as a real man in the real world. I wish this to happen now."

"Chelsey, no." Alex stared. "Your leg!"

"I choose you," she said softly, loving him so much that she ached with the force and depth of it. "You told me once that given a choice between self-interest and love, I would choose self-interest. My dearest Alex, you were wrong."

For an instant Isabel's image wavered between them and then faded forever. True love was not selfish. A love that was strong and true soared beyond self. True love transcended flesh and bone.

"My leg is part of who and what I am, it's all tangled together. We're uneasy friends, my leg and I, but we can live together. But dearest Alex, I cannot live without you."

A low groan rumbled up from his chest. He closed his eyes and clenched his fists. "With all my heart, I thank you for your generosity and your unselfishness. But, my noble mistress, I cannot grant your wish. Your wish must benefit you directly." The moonlight played tricks, making it seem that tears moistened his eyes. "That is the rule."

She held out the coin. "I love you, Alex. I'll never love another man but you. If you love me, too, and if you want to share my life and make it whole, then granting this wish will benefit me more than anything else in this world. Otherwise I will live my life alone and lonely." She held the coin between them and gazed directly into his damp, glistening eyes. "Whether you grant my wish or not depends on this. Do you love me, Alex? If you don't love me, then you're right. This wish brings no direct benefit to me and you cannot grant it. But if you love me, oh Alex, if you love me...then you must grant my wish and make my life complete."

"Oh my God," he whispered, staring at her face. "Do I love you? I love you with all my heart and mind and soul! I love your generosity of spirit, your quiet courage. I love your honesty and your laughter. I love the apple fragrance of you, the feel of your skin against mine. I love the way your eyes light and shine when you look at me and say my name. I love your goodness and integrity. I love you more than life itself!"

The coin sprang from Chelsey's fingers and shot upward above their heads where it burst into a white column of flame. Shimmers of strange color streaked the sudden wind that swirled around them, billowing Alex's robes and tearing at Chelsey's chiffon. The sand sang in their ears. Chelsey clung to him, staring in awe and fright at the flashing colors, listening to the clash of destiny within the wind and whirling sand.

When it finally ended, the abrupt silence was as shocking as the colored wind and the singing sands had been.

Slowly, holding on to each other, they raised their heads and stared around them. The stallion and the silken tent were gone. They were dressed in jeans and light jackets as they had been earlier in the evening.

Chelsey lifted shining eyes. She raised a trembling hand to his beloved face. "You love me," she whispered.

His hands tightened on her arms. "You gave me back my life!" Tears glittered in his eyes. Grabbing her by the waist, he lifted her and swung her in a circle. "I'm real, Chelsey! I'm alive! You did this, my darling, darling woman, my dearest love!"

When he set her on her feet, he kissed her, deeply and hungrily, pledging forever, promising with lips and hands what words could only hint. It was not until much later that they gazed toward the distant glow of Istanbul, impatient to return to their hotel and the passion of celebration.

"Do you suppose Harry forgot to send a car for us?" Chelsey asked, sitting on the low Roman wall. She didn't care. As long as she was with Alex, nothing else mattered. She couldn't take her eyes off him, couldn't stop touching him, reassuring herself that he was real and they were together.

"Shazam." A startled look lifted his eyebrows. He gave her a sheepish grin. "I forgot. The magic is gone." Sitting beside her, he took her hand. "We'll have to wait until Sahok remembers us."

"Alex," she said, turning to face him in the moonlight. A blush heated her cheeks, and she pressed her forehead against his shoulder, hiding her expression. "Will you do something for me?"

"I will move the earth for you, my beloved." He kissed the top of her head and drew her into his arms. "But remember," he added gently, "I'm no longer magic."

"Will you...will you teach me to dance?"

He lifted her face and gazed into her eyes. Then he stood and bowed before her. "Would the most beautiful woman in creation honor me with this waltz?"

Shyly, she placed her hand in his and stood with a nervous wobble. She bit her lip. "Maybe..."

But his strong arm came around her waist. He held her close for a long moment, smiling into her eyes. Then he stepped forward on the sand. Chelsey stumbled and felt the heat flame in her cheeks. He paused, kissed her forehead, then stepped forward again. This time she followed and didn't stumble.

And suddenly she was dancing! Twirling around and around on the moonlit sand, floating to the strains of the waltz filling her imagination.

And it was fabulous, lovely, as exhilarating and wonderful as she had always dreamed it would be. In Alex's strong arms she felt graceful and poised, in exquisite harmony with herself and the world around her. She was loved, and she was waltzing.

She smiled into Alex's adoring eyes and leaned back in his arms, dancing, and her heart swelled with joy. Alex had not lost his magic.

To her this magnificent man would always be magic.

# Calloway Corners

In September, Harlequin is proud to bring readers four involving, romantic stories about the Calloway sisters, set in Calloway Corners, Louisiana. Written by four of Harlequin's most popular and award-winning authors, you'll be enchanted by these sisters and the men they love!

MARIAH by Sandra Canfield
JO by Tracy Hughes
TESS by Katherine Burton
EDEN by Penny Richards

As an added bonus, you can enter a sweepstakes contest to win a trip to Calloway Corners, and meet all four authors. Watch for details in all Calloway Corners books in September.

# Take 4 bestselling love stories FREE

## Plus get a FREE surprise gift!

## Special Limited-time Offer

**Mail to Harlequin Reader Service®**

3010 Walden Avenue
P.O. Box 1867
Buffalo, N.Y. 14269-1867

**YES!** Please send me 4 free Harlequin American Romance® novels and my free surprise gift. Then send me 4 brand-new novels every month, which I will receive months before they appear in bookstores. Bill me at the low price of $2.71 each plus 25¢ delivery and applicable sales tax, if any.*That's the complete price and—compared to the cover prices of $3.50 each—quite a bargain! I understand that accepting the books and gift places me under no obligation ever to buy any books. I can always return a shipment and cancel at any time. Even if I never buy another book from Harlequin, the 4 free books and the surprise gift are mine to keep forever.

154 BPA AJJF

| Name | (PLEASE PRINT) | |
|------|----------------|---|
| Address | Apt. No. | |
| City | State | Zip |